P9-CFD-572

Small Admissions

Small Admissions

a novel

AMY POEPPEL

EMILY BESTLER BOOKS

ATRIA

NEW YORK LONDON TORONTO SYDNEY NEW DELHI

ATRIA BOOKS
An Imprint of Simon & Schuster, Inc.
1230 Avenue of the Americas
New York, NY 10020

This book is a work of fiction. Any references to historical events, real people, or real places are used fictitiously. Other names, characters, places, and events are products of the author's imagination, and any resemblance to actual events or places or persons, living or dead, is entirely coincidental.

First Emily Bestler Books/Atria Books hardcover edition December 2016

EMILY BESTLER BOOKS / ATRIA BOOKS and colophon are trademarks of Simon & Schuster, Inc.

For information about special discounts for bulk purchases, please contact Simon & Schuster Special Sales at 1-866-506-1949 or business@simonandschuster.com.

The Simon & Schuster Speakers Bureau can bring authors to your live event. For more information, or to book an event, contact the Simon & Schuster Speakers Bureau at 1-866-248-3049 or visit our website at www.simonspeakers.com.

Interior design by Kyoko Watanabe

Manufactured in the United States of America

10 9 8 7 6 5 4

Library of Congress Cataloging-in-Publication Data

Names: Poeppel, Amy, author.
Title: Small admissions / Amy Poeppel.
Description: First Emily Bestler Books/Atria Books hardcover edition. | New York : Emily Bestler Books/Atria, 2016.
Identifiers: LCCN 2016011397 (print) | LCCN 2016021057 (ebook) | ISBN 9781501122521 (hardback) | ISBN 9781501122545 (ebook)
Subjects: LCSH: Young women—Fiction. | School management and organization—New York (State)—New York—Fiction. | Chick lit. | BISAC: FICTION / Contemporary Women. | GSAFD: Love stories.
Classification: LCC PS3616.O345 S63 2016 (print) | LCC PS3616.O345 (ebook) | DDC 813/.6—dc23
LC record available at https://lccn.loc.gov/2016011397

ISBN 978-1-5011-2252-1
ISBN 978-1-5011-2254-5 (ebook)

She wanted to die, and she wanted to live in Paris.

Gustave Flaubert, *Madame Bovary*

Above all, be the heroine of your life, not the victim . . .
It will be a little messy, but embrace the mess.
It will be complicated, but rejoice in the complications.
It will not be anything like what you think it will be like,
but surprises are good for you.

Nora Ephron,
Wellesley commencement, 1996

August

For one whole year, we worried about Kate. We worried to her face and worried behind her back, credited her with being tough, while judging her for being pathetic. Some days we thought she was suicidal; others she seemed homicidal, or as if she had the potential, anyway, not that any of us would blame her. We didn't know how to help. Her sister, Angela, thought she needed therapy, antidepressants, and time to heal. She prescribed hard work and weekend hobbies, like kayaking or photography. Vicki thought she needed to quit wallowing; why not enjoy life as a single woman, celebrate her independence, go out and get laid? The guy who lived below her thought she should turn her music down and leave the apartment from time to time instead of stomping around over his head all day long. The lady at the liquor store suspected she drank too much. I didn't know what to think. We all agreed she needed to get her ass off the couch and get a life. She needed to stop wearing sweatpants and put on a little mascara, for Christ's sake. And would it kill her to go on a date? We were tired of the whole thing. Sure, life had thrown a huge piece of shit in her face, but . . .

Actually, there was no but. Life had thrown an enormous piece of shit in Kate's face.

Whenever the topic of Kate came up, faces got twitchy; eyes got shifty. Our friends would glance at each other and look at me with a mixture of blame and embarrassment, making it clear what they all thought but couldn't say, at least not around me. I could imagine them whispering, after I excused myself to go to the ladies' room:

She must feel like it's her fault.

It *was* her fault.

Well, she certainly is partly to blame.

Apart from him, it was all her fault.

I know! I mean, if only she had . . .

I wonder if she feels responsible?

Yes, bitches. I feel responsible.

To me Kate was something like a figure skater, skilled and balanced one second and then, bam, she's splayed out all over the ice the next. Music still playing, and she can't even get up to finish the damn routine.

But before her fall, it was a different story. Skilled and balanced. I remember Kate sitting cross-legged on her bed in our dorm room, laptop open, wearing glasses and retainers, reading an assignment she'd written out loud to us:

> Day 1. Sundown. I enter a community living structure after the tribe's evening repast. I am in the midst of seven female natives, and while I believe them to be a peaceful people, I approach them cautiously, watching from a safe distance. I see them communicating with each other, using language and gestures, drinking an amber-colored beverage out of red, plastic cups, and listening to music that causes them to jerk their heads in unison. I come closer to observe their rituals and seat myself on a contraption that hosts a variety of food particles in its fibers. When I insert my hand under the cushion, I discover a handful of blackened popcorn kernels, a pair of unwashed male undergarments, and two small copper medallions. The women in the tribe see the items in my hand and begin shrieking, gesticulating, and backing away from me. I fear I have insulted these gentle humanoids by unearthing their relics from the sofa, but they are forgiving. One offers me a large vessel, into which I respectfully lower the clothing and kernels. When I start to put in the copper medallions, the female makes a gift of them to me. I will bring them home to share with my people.

Kate looked up, ready for our critique.

"I don't get it," Vicki said. She was sitting up in her bed with a Town & Country *magazine open across her lap.*

"What?" Kate asked.

"If they're pennies," Vicki asked, "why can't you just say pennies?"

"I like it," I said.

"Thank you, Chloe," Kate answered. She was hunched over, reading through her fictional field notes again.

"I didn't say I don't like it," Vicki said. "I just don't get the point."

"Can you tell I'm from another planet?" Kate asked.

"Totally," I assured her.

"It's inconsistent, if you want me to be honest," Vicki answered. "How would an alien know what popcorn is?"

"You're absolutely right," Kate said, holding down the delete button. "It's so stupid."

"You're a freshman," Vicki told her. "You're supposed to be stupid."

"She didn't say she *was stupid," I corrected. "She didn't mean to say that you're stupid, Kate."*

"It's no good; I'm starting over again," Kate said, closing her laptop and getting ready to go. "I'll work in the Student Center, so I don't keep you up."

"We'll hear you anyway when you come in at two o'clock," Vicki said.

"She'll tiptoe," I suggested.

We had only been roommates for two months, and we had already fallen into our roles. Kate was the bookiest of us. She spent more time in the library and less time in the shower than anyone I'd ever met. Not that she smelled bad or anything. She just couldn't be bothered. She was a scholar in the making, bingeing on nineteenth-century novels whenever she had spare time, the more passion, suspense, and drama, the better.

"You know you're wearing pajamas," Vicki called after her, as Kate walked out of the room.

Vicki was smart and driven in a different way. She was

exceedingly practical, registered for classes only if she found them real-world applicable and down-the-road lucrative. "When would I ever use *that?" she asked when I suggested we all take a history class on serfdom in the Middle Ages. She signed up for stats instead. I had to check a map when I first met her to wrap my head around where she came from: a flyover state that she had no intention of returning to. One time I walked into our dorm room to find Vicki looking through Kate's dresser drawers. Without thinking, I apologized to her.*

And who was I? Among other things, my role in our clique was keeper of the peace. I held us together. For four years I bridged the gap, and it wasn't easy. I was the one who made sure we were always assigned to the same dorm, with rooms on the same hall. I was the one who made plans (Friday-night cocktails and weekend getaways) and posed us in pictures, dressed up or dressed down, with me almost always in the middle. I cleared up misunderstandings and found common ground: in our sophomore year, Kate and Vicki got into a fight about gun control (Vicki's libertarian principles clashing with Kate's progressive sensibilities), and I spent an anxiety-filled week negotiating a truce, apologizing to one on behalf of the other, failing a sociology test in the process.

After we graduated from Wellesley, we decided to move to New York as individuals—still as a trio in spirit, but not as roommates. I figured it was for the best, knowing that our friendships would be far less complicated without the petty problems that stem from too much togetherness. I was relieved to move forward into something simple and more adult.

And then Kate had her disastrous triple toe loop ass-on-ice wipeout and suddenly I found myself reentangled, back in the middle of a big mess.

The spring before Kate graduated from college, she and Angela were summoned. Kate was in New York interviewing for a job, so the sisters took the train together to the house they grew up in, speculating about the reason for the visit. Angela feared it was cancer, while Kate guessed divorce.

"Ha," was all Angela had to say about that, and Kate knew she was right, of course, because they didn't have the kind of parents who did regular, predictable, middle-class-American things like split up.

"One of them published a book?" Kate guessed.

"They wouldn't ask us to come out just for that."

"What if it's a book about our family?"

"We're not that interesting," Angela reminded her.

"A book about their sex life."

"Please, Kate, I just ate."

Amtrak delivered them to the little station in New Jersey, and as they stepped onto the platform and into the sunshine, they saw their mother waving to them, jumping up and down as if Kate and Angela were disembarking from the *QE2*. She was wearing cuffed jeans that Angela suspected belonged to their father, and over them, inexplicably, a handmade, tiered skirt that went to her knees. Her hair was covered with a scarf, knotted at the back, and of course, she had clogs on. Kate also had this habit of throwing an outfit together, but in her case she usually managed to pull it off, even if it wasn't on purpose. She had shown up at Angela's apartment a few days earlier wearing a denim miniskirt, tall rain boots, and a Chilean poncho that Angela remembered well because her mother had used it regularly as a tablecloth in the dining room. Or maybe it *was* a tablecloth, and Kate had cut a hole in it to turn it into a poncho. Either way (and impossibly enough), she had looked cute.

Their mother was now calling to them across the parking lot, "*Tervetuloa! Velkomin!*"

"Can't she ever just speak English?" Angela mumbled. She saw their father sitting in the parked car, clipping his fingernails out the window. "God, who does that?"

"Does what?" Kate asked.

Angela put her bag over her shoulder and checked her phone. "Is it possible," she asked, "that I was swapped with some other baby at the hospital?"

"No," Kate said, looking wounded. "Don't say that."

Older, wiser, Angela felt less of a bond with these spectacled, nerdy academics, and she judged their behavior more as a result. Now that her sister was almost a college graduate, Angela was waiting to see which parts of their parents' demeanor and attitudes Kate would be forced to inherit, given her genes and career choice, and which parts she could freely reject.

They walked down the ramp toward the car together, and Angela pinched Kate on the arm for no particular reason.

"Darling daughters," their mother pronounced and hugged them both. "*Zu Hause* we go. Who's hungry?"

The sisters climbed into the backseat of the old, mustard-yellow Volvo station wagon. They looked at each other while strapping on their seat belts. Kate stuck her tongue out, and Angela elbowed her, glancing around the parking lot, making sure they hadn't been seen by anyone they knew. Their father put his nail clippers in the glove compartment and started the car.

At the house they convened in the cluttered kitchen over a meal that their mother called "Kaltes Abendbrot" or sometimes "Smörgåsbord," depending on the selection, which in either case referred to black bread and things to put on black bread. Sprigs of dill were tucked between tiny shrimp and sliced eggs, not-quite-cooked to hard-boiled, and there was a chunky paté that made Angela wonder, *Chunks of what?* Kate took off her jacket and pushed up her sleeves, saying, "Mmmm, what a spread!" while Angela felt her usual disappointment, wondering what would be wrong with a nice chicken Caesar salad for once.

Angela had longed for normal as a child. She wanted what she saw at other homes, like Mop & Glo floors, Honey Smacks, and *People* magazine. Instead, they lived in a jungle of spider plant vines that draped all over the furniture, artifacts that jumbled up every surface, masks, pots, baskets, and fetishes.

And books. Books everywhere. Piled up high on chairs and on the back of the toilet, in languages that Angela didn't recognize and didn't want to, and on topics ranging from the study of Old Norse and the Viking Age (their mother's field) to family constructs and gender roles among the Yanomami (their father's area). And worst of all, the house had a pan-cultural cuisine odor that was permanently adhered to the brown sculptured shag carpet and the cottage cheese ceiling. In the ninth grade—the last time Angela ever had a friend over—her mother served them hamburgers without buns or ketchup, saying "*Guten Appetit*, ladies! Enjoy your *frikadeller*!"

"What's that?" her friend had asked.

"Balls," her mom said. That story had made the rounds at school. The shame, the shame, Angela recalled. Childhood with Professors Pearson and Watts had been perfectly stable and even loving, but acutely, serially embarrassing.

The four of them together (otherwise known, their parents had taught them, as a clan, or kinship unit, or conjugal family) stood around the butcher-block island to eat, as they had every school night. "Like pigs at the trough," their mother used to say happily.

"Standing promotes digestion," their father reminded them. So did the tiny glasses of digestif they always drank after dinner. Lots of words for that, too: *Obstler* or akvavit. *Kirschwasser* or *Schnapps*. "Corrupting a minor" was what Angela's friend's mother had called it when she notified the police on the evening of the dinner-balls.

Their father leaned against the sink, chewing thoughtfully on a radish, looking out the window. He was scruffy but youthful-looking, a man whose job was his passion.

"Your father is in the middle of writing an important chapter at the moment," their mother loudly whispered, "so we can't penetrate his thoughts today. He just needs to *be*."

"I'm here," he said, "but I'm distracted."

"The girls understand perfectly."

"Not really," Angela said, using her fingernail to scrape something crusty off the tine of her fork. "Kate's distracted today, too. She barely even talked to me on the train."

Kate, hearing her name, looked up suddenly and said, "What did I do?"

"That's my girl," her father said.

"Brainwork. Good for you, Kate," their mother added and winked at her.

"It's not good, actually," Angela answered. "It's textbook antisocial behavior."

"That depends on the textbook," Kate stated.

"Aha!" her dad agreed. "Go on."

"According to the new *DSM*," she said, "someone afflicted with an antisocial personality disorder would have to display a pervasive pattern of ignoring or even stomping on the rights of others. Plus I would have impulsivity issues, which I don't, not to mention tendencies toward aggression and deception. Being quiet on one train trip wouldn't come close to justifying that diagnosis."

"Well argued," her father said.

"What are you talking about?" Angela asked. "I wasn't saying you're clinically sick in the head. I just meant you were rude."

"Now, now," their mother said, pulling a tiny fishbone out of her mouth. "Kate was probably deeply engaged in a conversation with herself; it can be hard to pull out of."

"Sorry, Angela," Kate said. "I didn't mean to ignore you."

"When is the inquisition at NYU?" their father asked.

"The day after tomorrow," Kate told him. "I've been preparing for weeks."

"So you've read most of Professor Greene's papers?" he asked.

"Of course."

"And you're not put off by the dryness of teeth and bones? The lifelessness isn't off-putting?"

"Isn't that from the Bible?" Kate asked. "The valley of dry bones?"

"Ezekiel," their mother said. "Marvelous folklore."

"Why do you want to work in a graveyard anyway?" Angela asked. "I don't get it."

" 'Graveyard'? That's a little morbid," Kate said.

"I rather like it," her mother remarked. "I think it gives the job a gothic, eerie feel. It's certainly more thrilling than 'lab.' Or 'department.' " She lowered her voice as deep as it would go. "Graveyard."

"Graveyard," their father repeated solemnly. " 'Alas, poor Yorick! I knew him, Angela.' "

"*Grave,*" their mother said in a strange accent. "Did you know it's the same word in Basque?"

"I'm sorry I started this," Angela mumbled.

"If we worked with bones in my lab," their mother added, "I would adopt that moniker immediately."

"A graveyard," their father said again. "To me, a graveyard always brings to mind the words of T. S. Eliot," and he began to recite, " 'That corpse you planted last year in your garden, Has it begun to sprout? Will it bloom this year? Or has the sudden frost disturbed its bed?' "

Their mother clapped. "I wonder if Kate will make ancient

femurs sprout into brilliant insights into our past? Will she gather bouquets of blooming tibias?"

"Can we focus, please?" Angela asked.

Kate was smiling. "I'll be insanely happy if I get this job; you can call it whatever you want," she said.

"When you walk in to meet Dr. Greene," her mother said, "stand up tall, give a firm handshake, and proceed to be yourself."

"Who else would she be?" Angela asked.

"How existential," her father said. "Is any of us really anyone?"

"Dr. Greene would like to be someone," her mother said.

"He *is* someone," Kate stated. "Have you read his lab blog? *GangGreene*?"

"That's a wonderful word pairing: 'lab blog.' And what did you learn from the gangrenous lab blog?" she asked.

"That the work they're doing with fossils from the Laetoli site is groundbreaking," Kate said.

"Do you mean innovative?" her father asked. "Or that they literally break the ground as they work, because to me that seems par for the course at an archaeological dig and, therefore, derivative."

"I mean," Kate explained, "the work is pioneering. I'll dig there myself someday, if things go the way I've planned. I just have to land this job first." She was holding a boiled baby potato speared with a toothpick, and one half suddenly broke off and fell on the floor. Angela watched as Kate leaned over and put it in her mouth.

"Do you guys have a cleaning service?" Angela asked. "The whole house looks sort of, I don't know, grubby."

"Such fastidiousness!" her mother exclaimed. "What will you do if you have dinner with the Huli?"

"Who are the Huli?"

"In some places a dirt floor is just called a floor. Be aware of your cultural bias, Angie. You wouldn't tell a fish not to poop where it eats."

Angela stared at her. "I have no idea what you're saying, but this kitchen needs a complete overhaul, starting with all new appliances. Does the ice maker work?" she asked, getting a glass and opening the freezer.

"How's that husband of yours?" her father asked. "Is he a neat freak, too?"

"Doug," she said. "We're not neat freaks. We're just into basic hygiene."

"Never buy anything that says 'antibacterial' on the label," he warned. "Give us this day our daily germs."

"When you girls were babies," her mother added, "we made a point of having you eat right off the floor."

"Jesus God," Angela sighed.

"I don't mean for every meal. Everything in moderation."

"What is that?" Angela suddenly asked, backing away from the refrigerator. "Is that . . . ?"

"He flew against the window a few days ago," her mother explained, "and I want to look him up in the bird book. He's not a tufted titmouse, that much I know."

"You put a dead bird in the freezer?" Angela asked. "Where you keep food? That's so disgusting. It could have a disease."

"Can I see him?" Kate asked.

Angela closed the freezer door hard and turned to face them. "No. I have news, actually," she said.

"As. Do. We!" their mother said, joining Professor Pearson at the sink. "Which is why we asked you to come. We've decided that in two months, after the close of the spring semester," and she paused to allow the excitement to build, " . . . we're going to rent out the house and *go*."

"Go?" Kate said.

"What . . . What does that mean?" Angela asked.

"It means we're taking our work to the field," their mother said.

"What *field*?" Angela asked.

"I think they mean—" Kate started to explain.

"I know what they mean," Angela said. "Where are you going?"

"We have quite an itinerary," their father said proudly.

"We start in Finland!" their mother exclaimed. "Isn't it wonderful? Now, no need to be sentimental," she said, seeing her daughters' faces. "We limited serious, academic travel for almost two decades to rear you little offsprings, and now it's time for us to pack our rucksacks and take to the road before we're too old."

"Sounds awesome," Kate said.

"Rucksacks?" Angela asked.

"Just think," their mother went on, "we've reached the ripe old age where our community could justify senicide. We figure we better make a move before the tribe begins to see us as a burden."

"The whole village might sneak off in the dark of night," their dad added, "leaving us to fend for ourselves in this jungle."

"By jungle you mean this quaint university town?" Angela asked.

"There are quite a few young brutes among the faculty, I assure you," he said.

"You won't leave before June, will you?" Kate interrupted suddenly. "What about my graduation?"

"We'll be there with bells on," their mother said.

"Wouldn't miss it for the world," their father added.

"And after that you're just leaving?" Angela asked. "What about your jobs?"

"We're taking a much-overdue, extended sabbatical," her mother said. "We have the university's blessing and grants to cover the costs, and we've accepted guest professorships in Tampere and Rio, so we'll have home bases. We'll stay away as long as we possibly can."

"Nice," Angela said, deciding to keep her own news to herself. "That's really nice."

"Now, Angie, don't be dramatic," their mother said. "We'll Skype when we can to get updates on our lovely, grown-up girls. And when we've seen all that there is to see in the field, we'll come right back home to die."

"Now who's being dramatic," Angela said.

*

On the train ride back to Manhattan, Angela was the one who didn't talk.

"Are you mad?" Kate asked, like she was trying to figure out how to feel herself. Angela shrugged.

"How long do you think it took to plan this?" Kate went on. "Months? Years?"

"No clue."

"Well, good for them," Kate said. "I think it's cool."

"Of course you do."

"What does that mean?"

"Nothing. I'm going to be rearing offspring without the aid of a multigenerational family structure," Angela said wryly.

"They'll be back."

"Not soon enough. I'm pregnant."

"What?" Kate asked. "When? Why didn't you say anything?"

"It wouldn't have changed their plans."

"But still," Kate said.

"I'll tell them. But my God, they have their heads so far up their asses, I just can't stand it. I hope you don't end up like that, Kate."

"Oh, a baby!" Kate exclaimed. "As soon as I graduate, I'll be with you in New York. I want to help."

"Doug and I'll be fine," she said. "We can handle it."

"But I'll still be there for you."

Angela smiled at her. "That's sweet," she said. "I know you will."

*

Of course, Kate hadn't been there for her. First she'd been too busy and distracted to be useful, or even present, and then she'd been too sad to do anything at all. Ever since Kate's meltdown, Angela had found herself parenting Kate along with her own daughter, Emily, who was about to turn two. It was infuriating, especially now that she had just found out she was pregnant with her second child, and Kate still wasn't showing any signs of improvement, and her parents still weren't making any plans to come home.

It was enough now. Enough. Kate needed a jump start. She needed a job, and it was entirely up to Angela to get her one, no matter how unlikely or even impossible that might be. Gotta start somewhere, and Angela had a lead, a glimmer of hope. The previous Saturday, she'd left Doug with Emily for the afternoon and attended a private school fair, just to get an idea about what the possibilities were once the time came for preschool. It was a noisy, crowded function, held in a school gymnasium, and Angela found the florescent scene dizzying. She started in the front of the room and went straight down the row, from table to table, past Bank Street, Caedmon, Calhoun, Ethical Culture Fieldston, Grace Church, and Graylon Academy, collecting brochures and asking questions. The schools were arranged alphabetically, the only thing orderly about the event, and somewhere in the middle of the room, between Horizons Elementary and the International School, was Hudson Day. While most of the schools had two or three representatives, Angela noticed the man at the Hudson table was all by himself, trying to hand out materials and talk to people, answer questions and collect contact information. He looked frantic. Angela waited patiently until he had time for her.

"We don't offer a nursery school program anymore," he told her over the din. "But when your child's ready for pre-K, feel free to get in touch," and he handed Angela his card. "I'm swamped," he added suddenly. "My assistant director quit out of nowhere."

Angela smiled. "Is that right?" she said. "Are you looking for a replacement?"

She had called Kate right away and made a plan to meet for lunch that Monday to tell her about the job, but so far things weren't getting off to a very good start—Angela was eating alone.

Almost thirty minutes after she'd sat down, she looked up from her salad to see Kate slump into the restaurant, frazzled and breathless. Angela made a face that probably revealed her disgust for her sister's chronic tardiness and complete loss of oomph, not that Kate would have noticed. She had the look of someone who had overslept and taken a fast shower, failing to rinse out her conditioner and using a scrub so frenetically that she'd over-exfoliated her poor face. Her outfit was something a neurotic college student would wear during exam week. What were those? Cargo pants? They'd been slept in, and her white T-shirt had a drippy, brownish stain on the shoulder. They had agreed to meet near Angela's office in the Financial District, and among the suited clientele, Kate looked entirely out of place. And yet, Angela noticed, she still managed to turn the head of a man at the bar who eyed her with a mixture of attraction and puzzlement.

Kate apparently lacked the awareness to know how irritating she was to a full-time working mother whose day had started at six a.m., so she proceeded to tell a detailed story of her "hectic" morning, of missing keys (found in the sink) and missed subways, without ever actually apologizing for being unacceptably late. She seemed completely unprepared when Angela cut her off sharply, saying, "Stop." Hectic morning? Please. Angela had woken up gagging from morning sickness. While she was showering, Emily had poured an entire bottle of body lotion onto the bath mat, no thanks to Doug who was supposed to be watching her. "I didn't know she could open it," he had explained. "But on the bright side, think how soft it will be." At the office she had projects piled up that she absolutely had to finish before the end of the day. She had no interest in whatever manufactured drama Kate had to offer. It had grown so old. She wanted to slap her, to shake her out of this persistent state of dysfunction. Angela felt her hair tighten in its bun. "I have to get back to work. I told you."

"We didn't have to meet today. If it was bad timing."

"Forty-five minutes ago wasn't bad timing."

The waiter came by, cleared Angela's plate, and looked confused.

"Are we leaving?" Kate asked.

"I have five minutes."

Kate turned to look up at the waiter. "Dirty vodka martini. And maybe some rolls?"

"Seriously?" her sister asked. "On a Monday?"

"You can't drink on Monday?"

"It's self-destructive."

"Huh."

"Are you depressed?"

"Just blech."

"Kate—"

"Bastille Day," she said, like that explained everything. "It was a setback."

Angela held up her hand, resisting the urge to clap it over Kate's mouth. "I only have five minutes. I need to tell you about the job."

"Right. The job."

"I met the man who could potentially be your savior," she said and handed Kate the card she'd had out on the table since she'd arrived. "I want you to write to him *today*. His name is Henry, but call him Mr. Bigley. He's the head of admissions at a private school, and he needs someone who can start immediately. I can't promise you anything, but since you're not really the corporate type, I thought a school might be a good fit for you."

"I don't know anything about admissions," Kate said, looking at the card.

"Remind him you heard about the job from me, and let's hope he'll set up an interview. I don't know."

"Write him . . . what, though? Exactly?"

Angela dictated the email while Kate scribbled it down on her cocktail napkin in abbreviations so abbreviated she would find them difficult to decipher when she got home. Out of the corner of her eye, she was watching a waiter getting yelled at by the bartender.

"That poor guy," she said sadly.

"Who?"

"I wonder what he did wrong? Do you think it's work-related or personal?"

"Kate! Pay attention," Angela said and went on to preach the advantages of full-time, gainful employment. Health insurance this and 401(k) that. Important to keep busy, too, for one's mental health. Takes initiative to pull out of a depression; you have to *do* something about it, like see a psychiatrist. And how about weekends? Given any thought to rock climbing classes? Or Tai Chi in the park? Ceramics is very soothing. She ended with her usual "the point being, you just have to get out more and stop moping around."

Kate drank her martini and struggled to stay focused. After the speech was finished, she asked about her niece, and suddenly Angela had more time to spare than she'd let on. She complained about never sleeping and bragged about Emily's smarts. She used the word "advanced" several times. She mentioned moving to the suburbs. Should they or shouldn't they? There were so many things to consider: schools, swing sets, midsize SUVs, and automatic garage doors. Grass. A room for the new baby.

"Baby? What baby?" Kate asked. "Why didn't you tell me?"

"Surprise, I just told you." Angela patted her stomach and got out the ultrasound pictures.

"Wow, *again*?" Kate studied the images while Angela shared more of her many concerns: money, shifting family dynamics, marital happiness, and, of course, space (as always).

"We can't possibly fit a second child in our apartment."

"It's so cute," Kate said. "I think it has Dad's nose."

"Would it upset you? Kate?"

"What?"

"If we left Manhattan? Not now, of course. I just mean someday. I don't frankly see how you would manage. I worry about you."

"I'd be okay."

"You say that but then you lock yourself out of your apartment."

"That only happened twice."

"Are you keeping the cat alive?"

"Stella and I are like this," Kate said, holding two fingers up.

"You'll have to move someplace else pretty soon and frankly I worry about it all the time."

"That's like a year from now."

"Yes, exactly. You need to start projecting forward, Kate, look ahead to the next step."

As they went outside into the horrible heat of the afternoon, Angela gave Kate parting advice, while Kate stood there getting sweaty. "Send him the email as soon as you get home," she said. "Don't wait, okay?"

"I can't believe you're having another baby," Kate said again. "Tell Doug I said congratulations. Have you told Mom and Dad?"

"Not yet, but I will. And, if they call you," she said, "*don't* tell them about the interview."

"Why not?" Kate asked.

"It's not a job that requires a PhD; they'll probably think it's beneath you. But it's not, Kate. Nothing is beneath you."

"That's depressing."

"No—I just mean, this would be a great job for you. It's a real chance to get back on your feet."

"I know. I get it. It's not as if I'm enjoying things the way they are. I'm sick of me."

"This isn't you at all; that's the problem."

"Well, I'm sick of this person."

"Wear something neat and normal to the interview, like nice pants and a blazer, and check your face in the mirror before you go in. Wear makeup, but watch out for that smudgy stuff you always get under your eyes. And for God's sake, don't be late." She sighed. "Seriously, Kate. Try, please. Try to get this job."

College graduations, like weddings and even funerals, create awkward, mismatched combinations of people who should never cross paths. A perfect example was when Vicki's dad, a small-town drugstore manager, was thrust into conversations with Kate's father, an anthropology professor with a ponytail who said something ridiculous about how her dad was like a modern-day medicine man, which couldn't have been further from the truth, unless putting in an order for a shipment of Tylenol could be considered shamanesque. Seemed like a pretty big leap to Vicki.

When her family had walked onto the Wellesley campus, Vicki felt a pang of wretchedness and shame. They so didn't fit in here. Her mother had on the old floral, calf-length skirt, plastic pearls, off-white polyester blouse, and beige pumps she'd been wearing to church every other Sunday, rotating the outfit with her only other dressy rig, a blue dress with a skinny belt made of faux leather and a faux gold buckle. She was the queen of conservatism. Her father, whose voice was just plain too damn loud, kept one hand gripped on Vicki's shoulder as she walked them around the college, as if to prove his right to be there. He made his usual corny little jokes, having no idea how provincial he sounded every time he opened his mouth; Vicki had to suppress the urge to shush him. And her brother, awkward at nineteen years old and 275 pounds, in baggy Champion athletic pants and untied high tops, consistently lagged a few yards behind them, looking pained to be around all of these sophisticated, confident women to whom he could not possibly bring himself to speak.

Vicki was pretty sure she and her brother weren't the only ones suffering through the graduation events, although no one else showed it. Kate's parents were embarrassing, too, even if they belonged on a college campus way more than her own parents did. They walked in and out of school buildings like they owned the place, wearing their weird Woodstock outfits. Much to Vicki's mother's disgust, Kate's father took off his moccasins during the president's picnic and walked around barefoot. They spent more time conversing with professors they met than they did talking to their own daughters. Kate's sister, Angela, didn't look like she even belonged in the family; she was tailored and tidy, a compact little baby bump showing under her J.Crew dress and a handsome, attentive J.Crew husband by her side. She was Vicki's first real, live example of a successful New York City career woman with a condo and a happy personal life. Victoria eyed her with the same admiration and determination that some women might ogle a Birkin bag: *Someday I'm gonna get me that.*

She was off to a good start: Vicki had secured the possibility of a promising career. She had snagged a high-paying, kick-ass job at a New York marketing firm where she would be branding and rebranding businesses, creating hot, sophisticated campaigns that would define her clients' images. The potential for upward mobility was sky-high, and Vicki intended to go straight up.

Kate had something of both her parents and her sister in her; she was professorial but pretty. Appealing in a way that seemed effortless, accidental, which was part of her charm. Slightly disheveled, but able to pull it off just by opening her mouth and letting big words pop out. She could clean up when she needed to. Kate was trying to become some sort of expert on people, but mostly in the abstract. She studied past and present human behavior, examining how people live and why, observing their interactions more than she ever engaged in them. It got on Vicki's nerves because what difference did any of that make? What could you actually *do* with it? Nothing. Kate was smart enough to go into business or finance or corporate law if she wanted to, but she was clearly a snob about professions with such a heavy commercial bent to them, as opposed to those with loftier goals, like the ones that aim to contribute to the collective knowledge of the human race. Kate and Chloe both seemed to turn their noses up at money. *Money? What's wrong with making money?* Vicki wanted to yell at them. She'd never had any in her life and certainly didn't feel bad about wanting to get her hands on some now.

As every year of college passed, Vicki felt that she and Kate had a little less and a little less in common. In fact, all of senior year, Kate had been distant, committing herself entirely to scholarship rather than friendship, submitting a research paper called "Thinning the Hominid Herd" that was getting published in some geek journal that no one would ever read. The week of graduation, while everyone else was celebrating and socializing, Kate was mostly holed up in the library, preparing for her job as an assistant lab manager in the anthropology department at NYU where she would be helping a professor of human origins analyze fossil data he'd collected in Tanzania. Kate was smart, and so her habit of forgetting to brush the hair on the back of her head was something most people could easily overlook. Vicki couldn't.

After the Baccalaureate Concert, there was a supper served in Alumnae Hall. Kate, having skipped the concert, had lost track of time in the library and hadn't shown up yet, but her family didn't seem to mind: The lovely pregnant couple, Angela and Doug, sat together romantically at a corner table like they were vacationing at Sandals, and Kate's parents had a marvelous time engaging the other students, asking them about their majors and recommending further pertinent reading. Vicki walked over to a table where they were now talking to her brother about their upcoming sabbatical; he had somehow managed to steer the conversation to the existence of topless women on Danish beaches (real or mythical?), and they were only too happy to give an impromptu lecture on body, shame, and taboo, a talk without the chalk. The upshot was: what's wrong with showing a little tit in public? Vicki's brother couldn't agree more. Vicki was grateful; it was the first conversation the poor boy had had all week. It occurred to her that she hadn't been very nice to him or her parents since they'd arrived, so she went back to sit with them, to make an effort.

Her father hugged her and pulled her chair closer to him.

"My Big City girl! I feel like I'm in a room full of lady celebrities," he said. "The next Sarah Palin and Rachael Ray everywhere I look."

"They're just people, Dad," Vicki said.

"Smart girls," he said proudly.

"Women."

"What?"

"Women," she said, "not girls."

"What's the difference?" he asked.

"If you ask me," her mom said, "I'm looking at the next Ellen DeGeneres and Michelle Obama, and I don't like it. And I've never seen so many Orientals."

"Asians. You want a glass of wine or something?" Vicki asked.

"Goodness, no," her mom said. "I've had two this week already." She had changed into the blue dress, and Vicki saw that the skinny belt had a hard crease in it from being folded in the suitcase. The gold color was flaking off the buckle. It made Vicki sad.

Chloe, on the other hand, sitting several tables away, was looking perfectly content, tipsy, and relaxed. Like Vicki and Kate, Chloe already had a job lined up in New York; she would be earning less than a living wage as the volunteer coordinator at an organization for the homeless. Chloe's very elegant, stylish aunt had come all the way from France, and she and Chloe's mom were having a tête-à-tête, taking advantage of being together, ignoring everybody else at the table. Chloe was wrapped up in conversation with her cousin Robert. Vicki knew him already, and she watched him closely, waiting for just the right moment to approach. She wondered how in the world those two were related. He was tall and eye-catching, while Chloe was mousey and modest. He was rich and leisurely, while Chloe was perpetually broke and committed to staying broke by choosing a career in social work. She involved herself in causes like picketing for universal health care, fighting for world peace and nuclear disarmament, and raising people out of poverty, while Robert seemed oblivious to anyone or anything outside his beautiful, aristocratic bubble.

"Who's that man with Chloe?" her mother asked. "He looks like a movie star."

"It's her cousin," Vicki said. "I met him in Paris."

"Paris!" her dad said. "Oooolala, kay sirrah sirrah."

Vicki tried not to roll her eyes. It wasn't his fault he'd never been anywhere. "That's not even French, Dad," she told him.

"It's not? Well, what is it, then?"

Italian? Spanish? Vicki realized she didn't know.

Just then Kate arrived, breathless, visibly trying to adjust from the quiet and solitude of the library to the demands of a noisy social gathering. She looked pretty, Vicki noticed. She'd braided her thick hair and put on makeup, and one could almost ignore the fact that she was wearing a backpack. Vicki watched as Chloe jumped up to drunk-hug her and then pointed to where her professor parents were sitting with Vicki's brother, but Kate didn't go to them right away. Instead she made a colossal mistake and simply stood there, looking out over the room, holding on to her backpack straps and bouncing up onto her toes. Chloe hesitated and then introduced her to her handsome cousin who had jetted in from France for the party.

After graduation, Vicki, Chloe, and Kate moved to New York, and for about a year, life went swimmingly for all of them, until Kate fell to pieces. All Vicki could say was, it sure as hell wasn't her fault, but somehow she found herself in the position of having to console Kate all the time, telling her, "There, there, everything will be okay," passing her tissues while she boo-hooed all over the sofa, listening to her go on endlessly about how she had been wronged.

Listening to other people's problems wasn't Vicki's strength; she didn't have the patience for it. So after a year of trying to help Kate rebound from her painful breakup, Vicki was happy to get to talk to her on the phone about something else for a change. An upcoming job interview was exactly the sort of topic Vicki preferred.

"Wear something tasteful," she said, "but don't be afraid to show a little leg."

"So a skirt?" Kate asked. "Like the one I used to wear all the time?"

"The denim one?"

"Yes."

"No."

"I thought maybe I could dress it up."

Vicki closed her eyes, trying to picture it, and smiled. Kate, for all her so-called brilliance, was just plain stupid about matters such as wardrobe dos and don'ts. "Absolutely not. You must have one black skirt in your closet. Do you have a blazer?"

"I hate blazers."

"Wear your black skirt with heels, a blouse, and a cardigan. It's frumpy but classic. Is the skirt short?"

"Probably."

"That's fine, but the heels can't be too high or you'll look whorish. And Kate, sweetie, you can't go in rumpled. You're not in college anymore, and you need to look presentable. Iron everything."

"I don't own an iron."

Vicki didn't say anything.

"I'm so nervous," Kate said. "He's not going to like me."

"Stop it. Everyone likes you." Vicki made her voice go up high to mask her irritation. Insecurities were so unattractive. "You need to be confident. Present yourself with an air of authority. Or fake it, anyway."

"Fake it?"

"Why not?"

"I think people can see right through me."

"Don't be silly."

"I won't mean to, but I'll project incompetence."

Vicki considered feigning a lost cell phone connection. "Kate," she said firmly, "you can't let one bad episode define who you are. If you want the job, march yourself right in there and take the job. Just give yourself a pep talk before you go into the interview. I always look at myself in the mirror and ask: *Who am I? I am a brilliant, capable woman*, or whatever it is I need to be, and watch it happen. It works."

"I'll try."

"Knock 'em dead. Gotta run, sweetie. Meeting." And because she'd spent a week in Italy as a college student, she said, "Ciao," before she hung up.

Kate had never been to Italy but said "Ciao" back, just because.

September

The day I found out that Kate was taking the big, bold step of interviewing for a real job, George came home from work to find me creating a profile on a dating site. I wanted it to be clever, original, full of personality.

"Are you leaving me?" he asked.

"What should her favorite movie be? Something edgy. Unpredictable. Something with a minor cult following."

"Cute pictures," he said, looking over my shoulder.

"But do I use a group picture and have him guess? Or do I just use pictures of me?"

"I'm confused."

"How does this sound?" I asked, and I read with expression: "'Cute, lovable intellectual with a weakness for romance, looking forward to a brand-new chapter in life. I'm in search of a smart and steady companion to turn the pages with me. Plot to be determined, and . . .'"

"What?" George stopped me, shaking his head. "No, not appealing and certainly not sexy."

"BookWorm. You don't think that's a clever handle?"

"Worm? No, it's a turnoff."

"BookTrollop would be better, I suppose?"

"Under the circumstances, I don't think any of this is a good idea."

"If she's ready to look for a job, then she's ready to go on a date, and since I'm the one who screwed up her personal life, I should be the one to fix it."

"To be honest, Chloe, I don't get why you take responsibility for any of this. It wasn't your fault."

"I won't be let off the hook until she gets her life back."

"Who says you're on the hook?"

"No one says it. But it's what everyone's thinking."

Kate was sitting on a park bench—a strange addition for an indoor lobby—waiting for someone to come fetch her. Her stomach made an impolite noise. The woman at the front desk was on the phone and unlikely to hear anything low and gurgly from such a distance, but the large, uniformed security guard sitting silently nearby, very still, eyes glued to the entrance, suddenly raised his eyebrows and glanced at Kate over his left shoulder. She looked away at the clock on the wall and waited, unable to do so calmly. Her skirt was too short, so she could feel her ass on the wood slats, and she tugged to give herself some fabric to sit on. She did tasks, every one of which was fake: looked for something in her bag, pushed random buttons on her cell phone, and blew her nose. She hoped this whole painful exercise would be over with as soon as possible so she could get back to her couch. No way she was going to get this job, so she sat there, trying to ignore the ambitious part of her that was really starting to want it.

Two kids, resembling little Wall Street workers, walked by and Kate wondered if it was "dress like your parents" day, until she realized that they were in uniform and had to wear this formal attire every single day of their lives. Their behavior matched their outfits; they were serious, subdued, and orderly. Tomorrow's investment bankers and corporate lawyers. The girl was carrying a laptop, telling the boy with her, "We have to meet with our group after school."

"Can't," said the boy, checking his phone. "I have an orthodontist appointment at three thirty." He had a mouthful of braces, so Kate figured his story added up.

"Before school tomorrow, then. I'll do the PowerPoint tonight."

"I'll have the graphs ready. Avery's in charge of writing up the final argument."

"Good," she said, clearly satisfied. "Good plan."

They went their separate ways, and Kate turned around to watch them leave, expecting them to shake hands or exchange business cards. Hard to believe a couple of kids could make her feel even more insecure and unprepared than she already did, but that's how it was. *Where's* my *PowerPoint? What's* my *plan? Do I need a final argument?* She turned back around on the bench and was startled to find a tiny woman planted directly in front of her, blocking her from running out the door. It was the director of the school, a breathy, wound-up lady, who put out her hand, introduced herself, and asked only one question phrased as a statement: "I assume you like working with children?"

It was yes or no, but Kate hesitated in spite of the simplicity of it. She honestly didn't know. With no evidence to the contrary, she said, "Yes." After all, she didn't *not* like working with children. The woman stared at her intensely and said, "Wonderful. Call me Janice. Do you have any questions for me?"

"I don't think so," Kate said. "Not yet, anyway."

"Wonderful," Janice repeated. "If there's time, we'll chat again after you meet with Henry. How does that sound?"

"Wonderful?" Kate answered.

"Come with me." She walked Kate down the hall to introduce her to middle-aged, puppy-faced Mr. Bigley. He was in his office with his assistant, Maureen, who looked Kate up and down and asked her if it was hot outside. Why was everyone so old here? Kate wondered. Not a soul under forty. She started to feel outnumbered and anxious. While Janice mumbled things to Mr. Bigley, Maureen tucked one calf behind the other and fiddled with her skinny gold watchband. It pinched her wrist in a painful-looking way, and she was trying to squish her pinky under it as if to get some breathing room.

"How many schools have you been in?" Maureen asked.

Kate misunderstood the question and said, "Four," referring

to her own elementary, middle, and high schools plus college. "Almost five."

"Humph. You get around, don't you?" Maureen said. "For someone so young." Kate suddenly felt slutty. She wished her skirt were longer, her shoes flatter.

"Are you nervous or something?"

"A little," Kate admitted.

"It shows," Maureen said. She stood up and stretched. "School year started, and you know what that means."

Kate hadn't a clue. She nodded and looked at the art on the walls. It was terrible. Disturbing even. A portrait of an ugly, bulgy-eyed girl. A demented still life that looked stupid and out of proportion, like a child could have done it.

"Our student work," said Mr. Bigley, noticing Kate's expression and mistaking it for admiration. "Fabulous, isn't it? We have some real talent in this school."

"We'll leave you two to talk," Janice said. "I'll be in my office," and she walked out with Maureen, closing the door behind them. As Mr. Bigley swiveled his chair to face her, Kate noticed an oversize framed picture of the Colosseum in Rome on his desk. He had a rubber band in his hand that he stretched, wrapped around his fingers, and accidently shot across the room.

"Whooops," he said and settled back in his chair. "So tell me about yourself."

His request was so wide open, so broad in scope, that Kate felt completely untethered. Where to begin? And realizing that the interview was actually starting, she got even more flustered, which caused her to make a string of mistakes.

"I should probably tell you right off the bat—I've never actually had a real job before, so I don't really have many of what you might call *skills*. Well, no, maybe I do have some skills, even if I can't, like, articulate them very well. For example, I'm trying to become a better judge of character, or at least better than I used to be. These days I don't tend to like anyone."

Mr. Bigley looked confused.

"What I mean is, I'm discriminating. *But* I'm not an asshole. I bet that's a good quality for anyone working in admissions. Right?" Her armpits were going damp, and she glanced up to see the bulgy-eyed girl looking dumbstruck. "And in case you're worried—I know that you shouldn't say 'asshole' in front of kids or their parents. So I would never do that. In fact, I remember all the school rules—no swearing, no stealing, no biting. No bullying 'cause some kids take it to heart and"—here she put a finger gun to her head and made a credible shooting sound—"so no using words like 'gay' or 'retard' unless you actually mean gay or retarded and you're being nice about it." *Shut up*, she said to herself. *Please shut up.*

She got a tissue and dabbed her cleavage discreetly. "Whew, it's been a while since I wore something so buttoned up." Mr. Bigley kept his poker face, hands clasped under his chin, and Kate felt an uncontrollable need to fill the silence. "By nature I'm more of a T-shirt kind of girl, but I can tuck in a grown-up blouse when I have to. Of course, in some cultures, women don't wear shirts at all, so I guess in that regard I'm way ahead of the game."

He tilted his head the way a dog does when he's anticipating something, and Kate forged onward.

"You can often glean a thing or two from how people dress. I really didn't know what to wear today. Everyone said, 'Wear a blazer,' but for some reason I feel totally dykey in a blazer. Not that there's anything wrong with being a lesbian, but a blazer is not a good look for me. I swear—given the choice—you'd rather see me naked than in a suit. I don't mean that suits are bad in general. You look good in your suit, for example. But for me? Well, it's like I always say, better a naked lesbian than . . . me . . . in a blazer." What was happening? She shook her head and felt a trickle of sweat run down her back. "Was that out loud?" she asked and fanned herself with a copy of the school newspaper.

"But speaking of apparel," she said suddenly, "clothing can actually be germane to a discussion of pedagogy. What does a uniform say about the culture of a school, for example? What does it tell us about the framework or *fabric*, if you will, of an institution? An intentional limitation of choice shows a value being placed on a willingness to conform, but to what exactly? And does the uniform mold the child or does the child need intrinsically to fit into a certain mold? And in either case, what are the psychological ramifications in an adolescent as he or she develops autonomy? If I were considering this school, as a student I mean, I would seriously ask myself, 'If business attire is required, is this the right place for me? Do I want to get dressed up every day like I'm going to a Michele Bachmann rally?' and personally I think my answer would be 'No,' no offense to Hudson, of course. The kids I saw in the lobby look very professional and hardworking. Law-abiding. Self-motivated. Something tells me that hyperactive free spirits who are lacking in impulse control, having problems with executive function skills, and struggling to reach Piaget's formal operational stage wouldn't do too well at a school like this, am I right?"

A new rubber band had mysteriously materialized in Mr. Bigley's hand, and he was fidgeting with it in a way that signaled either boredom or intense concentration; Kate couldn't tell which. He had a kind face, she noticed, and he was clearly a patient man, given that he hadn't thrown her out of his office yet.

"Is there anything specific you'd like to know?" she asked, hoping to say at least one thing to make a good impression. "Some people, like my sister, Angela, might tell you I'm not very prompt because I'm late *all* the time, but if I worked for you, Mr. Bigley, I'd get here way before the bell rings every morning. I always loved going to school, so I know I'd be happy to be here."

"Call me Henry."

"To be honest, Henry," she said, leaning forward, deciding it was time to go in with her final argument, "I've been in a bit of a funk recently, sort of disconnected. It hasn't been pretty, I admit. And I know I'm inexperienced with the kind of work you do here, but if you just give me a chance, I'll learn whatever you need me to learn, and I'll do whatever you want me to do. Really, I'll bend over every which way to make you happy you hired me. I'll take this job very seriously, I'll work hard, and I won't let you down."

The day after the botched interview, Kate was back to her bad habits, lying on the couch with Stella the cat, watching a talk show, and eating handfuls of Cap'n Crunch, all normal parts of her slothful routine. She self-loathed but couldn't budge. It felt like she was being pressed down into the cushions, like the gravity in the apartment was especially forceful. When she left the apartment—and of course she had to from time to time—she was uneasy and could still feel that heaviness, the weight pushing her down, and the only solution was to get home quickly and lie down; her couch was safe. Her world had become very small, and anytime she ventured beyond her apartment, she felt uncomfortable, self-conscious, like she was trespassing, and people could see it. She often thought of all the things she used to be able to do that were inconceivable in her current state: pull an all-nighter, have a sustained, intelligent conversation, dance, read any novel by any Brontë in a weekend, discuss politics, jog, focus, flirt, fold clean laundry, get dressed before midday, smile.

The phone rang at noon, on the dot. "How'd it go?" Angela asked.

Kate had never been to Angela's office, so every time they talked on the phone, she would make one up in her head. Today's was futuristic, polished marble surfaces with embedded computer screens, floor-to-ceiling windows, and locked safes full of money. Kate didn't know what Angela did all day, but her job had something to do with loans. Not making them, but rather doing something to them, like taking them apart or putting them together. Kate had no idea who wanted this done or why, nor had she ever asked.

"Was it okay?"

Recalling yesterday's interview made Kate feel sick to her stomach. "It went great," she said. "It went really well."

"It did?"

"I don't mean that I got it."

"Did he say you didn't get it?"

"He needs someone with more experience," Kate said.

"Did you tell him you're a fast learner?"

Kate reflected back on her performance. There were at least fifteen minutes that she had blocked out entirely. Self-preservation at work. "I think so."

"Did you tell him what you scored on the GRE?"

"I couldn't work that in."

"But you did sell yourself?"

"I did my best."

"Well, good for you, Kate. I'm proud of you for getting out there and trying. The next interview will be even better."

Kate thought of a "Would You Rather"—Would you rather go on another job interview or shit your pants on a crowded subway? Subway. Easy.

"So what are you doing today?"

"Just busy," Kate said. "Long list."

"Like what?"

"Walking the dogs at three."

"That's hours from now. Did you look into trapeze classes? It would really get your adrenaline going. I'll pay for it."

"I'm afraid of heights."

"Well, kayaking, then."

"Isn't the Hudson polluted?"

"Something, Kate! You need to do something."

"I will. I am." She looked up at her muted TV screen. There was a commercial for a girdle that melted fat off your stomach. A man was wearing it. "I'm doing an exercise thing, actually. Can we talk later?"

"Good for you, Kate! Working out is so important."

"Yeah, health. Eating vegetables. Running." Just the thought made her tired. "I should go—I'm in the middle of a plank series."

"I'll call you later."

Kate dropped the phone and repositioned herself on the sofa. At times like this, she would often imagine Robert showing up unexpectedly. He would greet her, kiss her on both cheeks, and notice that she was dressed in pajama bottoms at noon, ten pounds heavier than the last time he'd seen her. She would invite him in, and before long he would also discover that the bubbly personality he had found so attractive was nowhere to be found. There was no levity at all, just a beaten-down lump of a girl.

But a chance to talk, to hear him explain, was it too much to hope for?

"I'm very ill," she might tell him.

"Eeez eeet serious?" he would ask.

"Well, it's really none of your concern anymore, is it?" she would answer, coughing into a hanky.

He would drop to the floor and apologize to her. Crying maybe? That would be a nice touch. Asking for just a moment of her time, wanting to talk to her.

She was deeply engaged in this imaginary scenario when something completely unimaginable happened in real life: Mr. Bigley—Henry—called her and offered her the job, the job she knew she didn't get. He sounded cheerful, and she could picture him sitting in his swivel chair, fiddling with a rubber band, the framed Colosseum on his desk. When he explained the terms (one week's vacation in winter and one in the spring, four weeks off during the summer, health insurance, and a salary that seemed—*oh my God!*—at least 75 percent too high), she got up off the couch, stood tall in her pajamas, and accepted the position. She tried to make herself sound like a person befitting such an offer, saying things like, "Very exciting. Looking forward to seeing you as well. And thank you. Thank you very much." She went into some kind of automated mode. Within an hour she signed, scanned, and attached the legal contract to a hastily written email and hit send. Starting Monday, she would be employed.

The next step was so obvious, so expected, that Kate marveled at herself for not getting right to it, but Angela—along with everyone else in her life—would have to wait days before hearing the news of the new job because immediately after clicking send, Kate had a full-blown panic attack. *What just happened? Assistant Director of Admissions? The fuck does that even mean?* She started breathing fast and running around the apartment, arms flapping. *What? What a fraud*, she thought. In less than a week she would have to set an alarm and put on clothes—what clothes?—and do *what*? What had Mr. Bigley said she would be doing? Touring strangers around a building she didn't know, and talking to kids and their parents about things like, like what exactly? Like the school? Like the school's philosophy? Like children? And that was another thing—she didn't like children particularly. Didn't know any other than her niece, didn't want to. Didn't know anything about schools in New York City, either, obviously. Or schools anywhere. Or the admissions process. Or administrative anything. She would be expected to answer people's questions, and she wouldn't have the answers because—to get right down to it—she didn't know *anything*.

Kate felt herself go dizzy. *Oh, no no no. There's been a mistake. I can't do it. I can't do it. I can't possibly do it.* Mr. Bigley had called the wrong girl, gotten his files mixed up or something. Why would he hire her? She hadn't lied, had she? She covered her face with her hands and tried to replay the interview in her head, and all she could remember was saying something ridiculous about how schools smelled like bologna sandwiches. And she'd said something about being an energetic person by nature (the last several months notwithstanding) and feeling like the year really begins in September instead of January. She remembered telling him that she wasn't a particularly organized person, but he'd given her a sad-faced smile and said, "Maybe you never needed to be." At the time she thought he was being kind, but now it seemed he had meant it.

There was no joy, no urge to share the news, no impulse to celebrate. Instead, she went into her tiny kitchen and drank a glass of "wine product" she had bought once by accident. ("Just throw in some ice cubes and pineapple chunks," Vicki had suggested recently when she and Chloe had come by to visit her in the tiny sublet. "It's basically sangria.") It was terrible, and who has pineapple? There was nothing else in the apartment other than a bottle of port Chloe had brought her a few months ago, but the port looked headachey and too hoity-toity, and Kate didn't feel deserving of either. She grabbed her wallet and ran to the corner to buy something cheap off the liquor store lady who always had a way of making Kate feel like an alcoholic. There was a sale on vodka. She carried a bottle to the counter and noticed the liquor store lady very subtly shaking her head as she handed Kate her change.

"I got a job," Kate said defensively.

"Congratulations. Early start, then, tomorrow?"

"I start this Monday," Kate explained. "Actually, I may not start at all. I don't think I was supposed to get it. I think they called the wrong person."

"Well, then, I guess you better turn yourself into that person in a big hurry."

"You can do that?" Kate asked.

"You still want this?" she asked, holding out the paper bag.

"Why wouldn't I? It won't make me any less qualified than I already am."

She shrugged. "Your life."

Kate got back to her building and stomped up the stairs. She poured vodka and orange juice in a coffee mug, sat on the couch, and tried not to cry, hoping the booze would dull the panic and fuzzy her mind. By four in the afternoon, Kate was drunk and had forgotten all about the dogs. She ate random snacks she had in the apartment—olives and stale crackers—and spent the next few hours talking to herself and to Stella while she ransacked her closet to prove that she had no suitable work clothing. She turned her music up and modeled ridiculous outfits. Denim miniskirt and a Nordic turtleneck sweater. Nike shorts with a sequin tank top. "So lovely to be working with you, Mr. Bigley," she said to the mirror on her closet door, wearing nothing but a bikini top and pants that she couldn't get buttoned. "I mean, *Henry*," and she gave a dramatic curtsy, bowing her head upside down. The room got spinny. She focused in on her face in the mirror, and said loudly, as Vicki had suggested, "Who am I?" She waited to see what the mirror would tell her. *You are an impostor,* it said. *A failure. A fraud.*

She sat down hard on the floor and closed her eyes, trying to think of a way out. Instead she could only see the image of a dark hallway with a locked door at the far end, and she felt some familiar, overwhelming need to either drop dead or take off running. And then—phew!—it suddenly came to her. She thought of a solution, an escape plan. It was simple, really: she would just call Mr. Bigley and explain that he'd made a mistake. *Poof!* No job. She would keep things just as they were. Dog walking, couch time, and credit card debt. With that decision made, she felt tremendous relief and got up off the floor to find Mr. Bigley's business card. She said his name: "Bigly. Bigely. Biggally?" Phone in her hand and unmanageable pumps on her feet, she tried to drunk-dial his number but lost her balance and threw up olives all over the floor. Stella hid under the bed.

The next morning she woke up with a crushing headache and a vomity feeling that lasted the entire day. She couldn't move. The dogs around town peed on their carpets, Stella went hungry, and the kitchen floor went unwashed. Kate stayed in bed, trying to sleep it off with a pillow over her head.

It was dark, she realized. She was starving and felt a desperate need for anything with melted cheese on it. She opened one eye, looked around at the mess she'd made, and saw Stella staring her down from the top of the bookshelf. She looked disgusted.

"Okay, yes, this is a new low," Kate acknowledged, rolling over and going back under the covers. "You should have known me back in college. I wasn't like this. I was well adjusted. I had plans."

She closed her eyes and imagined Stella crossing her little arms and saying something smug and judgmental: "You fell apart over a guy? What is the matter with you?"

"It was more complicated than that," Kate argued. "You wouldn't understand."

"Maybe not," Stella would likely say, "but your behavior is extremely unhealthy, not to mention unattractive."

Defending oneself to a cat isn't all that healthy or attractive, either, Kate thought.

A door slammed somewhere in the stairwell. Kate came up for air, wrestled with whatever was pinching her side, and found she was still wearing her bikini top. She reached down under the covers toward the foot of the bed and took off her shoes. Yes, this was definitely a new low. She threw the pumps on the floor and tried to recall the exact moment when her life took *so* sharp a turn that she landed here, in this bed, in this condition. Just like the day she found her lost keys in the sink, she wondered if she should retrace her steps, minute by minute, starting sometime around college graduation. That would be a torturous exercise, about as much fun as taking a bubble bath with Stella, and it wouldn't solve anything anyway. And besides, it would require precision, intuition, and grit, qualities she had once thought she had in abundance but that were apparently lacking, according to He-Who-Must-Not-Be-Named.

She thought of Mr. Bigley, spinning cheerfully in his swivel chair to face her, looking at her expectantly, hiding any kind of disappointment, listening carefully.

Something kicked in—she turned on the lights, got out of bed, and went to brush her teeth. She took a shower and shaved her legs. On hands and knees she cleaned the floor with anti-bacterial Mr. Clean and paper towels. She fed Stella and washed her water bowl. Things got separated into categories: trash and recycling, clean clothes and dirty laundry. Sitting on the couch in clean pajamas with her wet hair combed and her fingernails trimmed, she ate a toasted cheese sandwich, took Tylenol PM with a big glass of water, and then put herself to bed. As she was falling asleep, a little fantasy played out in her head: She was walking quickly to work, wearing high heels and a pretty dress. She had an edgy haircut and a cool workbag thrown over her shoulder; suddenly she heard a voice.

"Kate? Eeez it you?"

"Robert? What a surprise."

"I've beeen hoping to see you. How are you, Kate? You look so beauteeful."

"Why, thank you—I'm sorry I can't stay to talk."

"Perhaps later?"

"No, I've got trapeze class after work. Good to see you, though."

"No, Kate, stop. Please, Kate."

She fell asleep before she could find out what she would do next.

She woke up calm and rested and tried to see things in a grown-up, positive light: she had been offered a real job, a kind of interesting job. Shaping the lives of children maybe? No more borrowing money from Angela. No more scraping rent together from her dog walking gigs. She was a terrible dog walker anyway. She lacked that pack-leader mentality, preferring to let the dogs work out the route on their own. She never had a clue where they were going, veering around the sidewalk, getting tangled up in their leashes, and crossing streets against the lights. At the dog run, she always had a hard time identifying which dogs she'd brought with her, and on more than one occasion she had been caught leaving with someone else's pet. It was perilous and confusing (getting the right dog back to the right apartment), and it occurred to her that she wouldn't miss the job or the dogs.

By this time she had seventeen texts and eight voice messages, mostly from Angela. But rather than call her back, she thought about what the liquor store lady had said—"You better turn yourself into that person"—and she wondered if maybe she could.

With one day already lost due to her hangover, there were only four days remaining for a transformation. She went into her serious, hyper-productive mode and got to work. She looked up the Hudson Day School website and read the principal's welcome letter. Under the Admissions tab she went to the "Meet the Staff" page and found pictures of Henry, who was smiling, Maureen, who wasn't, and a young man named Nathan with a goatee. She studied the procedures for applying and noted the numerous dates and strict deadlines. There were offers for open houses and group tours beginning in the early fall and an invitation to download an introductory video that outlined the academic program.

The Internet was full of information about the New York City private school scene and the admissions world, and Kate did research all morning, jotting things down whenever she felt something was particularly noteworthy. After spending hours at her computer, she flossed her teeth, went out for a walk, and read the *New York Times*. The next day she spent the whole morning learning about Hudson's history (*founded in 1888 with twelve boys and a philanthropist named Ebenezer*) and philosophy (*guiding principles: mutual respect, integrity, community, and especially scholarship*). She did push-ups, sit-ups, and planks, showered, and went out to spend money she hadn't earned yet on appropriate work clothes. She got her hair trimmed and her brows waxed.

Back at her apartment building, she picked up her mail and headed up the stairs, trying to think of what else she needed to do to transform herself into whomever Mr. Bigley thought he'd hired.

4C opened his door as soon as her foot hit the landing. She dreaded these encounters since all he ever said to her was that she was loud and heavy on her feet. He made her feel oafish and clunky. "How am I supposed to get around my apartment without walking?" she would ask.

"Softly." He came across as humorless and irritable, like a seventy-year-old man in a thirty-year-old's body. "Maybe you could buy a few thick rugs or take your shoes off."

"I'll tiptoe," she would answer.

And here he was again. "I'm sorry to complain," he said, leaning out into the hall. It was his usual opening line. "I couldn't sleep the other night. There was quite a ruckus upstairs."

"I got a little deep in the vodka."

"Threw a party?"

"No, just me."

"I thought I heard talking."

Kate shrugged.

"Were you doing some type of exercise perhaps?" he asked. "Like bowling?"

"Funny," she said dryly.

"There was definitely furniture being moved around."

"I got a job," Kate said, holding up her shopping bags.

"So you'll be out of the building more of the time, I suspect."

"Maybe. I don't know. I don't think they meant to give the job to me. I think they called the wrong girl."

"Why would you think that?"

"I have no qualifications."

"Did they hire you to be a doctor?"

"No."

"Are chemicals involved? Use of deadly force, that sort of thing?"

"Of course not."

"Then fake it," her neighbor said. "That's all anyone does anyway. Dress the part, sound the part. They'll figure you are the part."

"Eventually they'll find out I'm a fraud," she said.

"By then you'll know what you're doing. As long as it's not an ER. Or guarding a nuclear facility."

"It's a school. I've spent the last couple of days studying up, trying to get informed."

"Yeah? I'm sure you'll be fine. Don't even worry about it."

"Thank you," Kate said, and she felt relieved. "You're right, you know. It's not an ER."

"No one will die," he said, "no matter how incompetent you are."

Jonathan, she remembered, recalling his name from seeing it on mail that mistakenly ended up in her box.

"I'm Kate," she told him.

"Yeah. I know," he said, looking hurt. "We've been neighbors for, like, a year." He shook his head and closed his door.

Kate went back into her apartment and looked through her mail. There was a postcard from her mother with a picture of a shriveled-up corpse:

> Dearest *figlia*,
>
> I am consumed with thoughts of Ötzi! So much speculation about this mummified copper smelter, from his fertility to the grainy contents of his stomach, when probably all the poor man wants is a bit of privacy. He has 3 floors of the museum in Südtirol, so he is spending his afterlife in pure luxury. Nevertheless, it reminds me that I wish to be cremated and sprinkled on an azalea.
>
> Your father and I think of you as being on a sabbatical of your own, taking the time you need to contemplate your past and discover your future. How thrilling!
>
> *Baci e abbracci* from your loving *madre.*

Kate put the postcard in a shoebox where she collected all the mail she got from her parents. In bare feet, she put clean sheets on her bed, scooped the cat box, and swept the floor.

Who knew that good old Mr. Bigley would be the one to raise Kate off the couch after such a long stretch?

To: Chloe, Vicki
From: Angela
Subject: Kate??????????????

Hi ladies,

I don't want to freak you out, but Kate is missing. She isn't answering phone or texts. I'm worried sick. It's not like her to be out of touch with me and, as we all know, she is still struggling with personal issues. I went to her apartment today, and she wasn't there. Have you heard from her? I can't understand why she isn't calling me back—I left her a million messages. This is not like her. Unless you know where she is, I'm calling the police.

Angela

To: mbranson@prestigeschoolplacement.com
From: Nancy Smith
Subject: Your services

Hello Mel,

Thank you for taking the time to speak with me yesterday. Sam and I are looking forward to working with you to find the next step for Gus. His current school, Horizons Elementary, has always seemed flaky to me, a lot of "self-discovery" and finger painting for $40,000 a year, but as far as I can tell, Gus has liked it. I was disappointed to learn that Horizons' role in placing their students is limited to sending grades and writing recommendations, so I have no doubt we will be in dire need of your services. I assume you'll put together a list of choices for us? Or am I supposed to research all of these places? Because, to be honest, I would rather defer to your expertise. As for me, my one request would be that we only consider schools that go all the way through 12th grade so that we don't have to apply again 3 years from now.

I have sent in our check to secure your services for the application season. In terms of the kind of assistance you offer, will you be helping us with the essay portions of the written applications? I got online as you suggested and found this all to be rather overwhelming. Some of the questions for the parents are odd—"What would you like the committee to know about your child's learning style?" I really have no idea. Can you advise? And "What are your child's strengths and weaknesses?" I'm not sure exactly what they're looking for with that.

Finally, Sam made a mistake on his schedule, and it turns out he's away on business on the day we chose. Do you need him to be present when we meet? He travels a lot. I am happy to reschedule or we can keep the meeting if I can come on my own.

All the best,
Nancy

To: Chloe, Vicki

From: kpearson@hudsonday.org

Subject: guess what . . .

Sorry I was M.I.A. last week, but note the new email address?? Yes, I actually got the job and survived my first whole day. Can you even believe it? I'm going through cat and couch withdrawal, and I'm scared to death I can't do this. I'll fill you in on the details later but wanted to let you know that I'm back in the world, hoping I don't burn up on reentry. We'll see how it goes.

I am writing from my very own little office. (I have no window, but I'm not complaining.) I'm getting a magnetic name tag and business cards next week—this shit is real! I work with a lady who hates me, but I think she hates everyone. She rolled her eyes at me so hard today I thought she was going to hurt herself.

Remember all that time I spent getting ready for my job at NYU? Studying all things anthropological from brain phylogeny in primates to the evolutionary history of cercopithecoids? Well, obviously none of that is going to help me around here, and this time I'm going to have to learn everything all on the fly. Good luck with that, right? I'll be lucky if I last the week.

Off to Angela's. She's super pissed off at me.

All ok with you?

Xoxo K

Angela was working herself up into a full fury, cooking an angry dinner and planning out the fight she was going to have. *Inconsiderate. Thoughtless. Worrying everyone to death. What were you thinking? Not how we do things in this family.* Since the brief moment of relief she'd felt when Kate had finally contacted her, Angela found she was becoming more and more outraged at her sister's behavior. *After all I've done for you . . .*

Doug got home from work before Kate arrived for dinner and right away could smell the rage above the carbonara.

"For starters," she said as he came in, "could you clean up all the toys and crap over there? We can't even sit down. I don't think it's so much to ask—"

"Okeydokey," he answered, briefcase still in hand, picking up Duplos and newspapers off the couch. With that done, he couldn't identify what other crap she was referring to. He went to the kitchen and patted Emily on the head. She smiled back at him, kicked her legs, and threw a fistful of cottage cheese on the floor.

"Kate owes me an explanation," Angela was saying as she ripped lettuce into small, bruised scraps. "I want to be able to sit down and question her."

"She doesn't actually owe you anything."

"I had a very bad time because of her. I mean, my God, I called our parents." With a whisk and violence she emulsed oil and vinegar until they behaved. She was still in her work clothes, high heels, and serious slacks, and she yelled—"Oh, for fuck's sake!"—as one drop of dressing dared to land on her silk blouse.

"Can I get you a drink? Bottle of glue? Something to calm you down?" Doug asked.

Angela put her hands on her hips and stared at him.

"I forgot," he said. "This is going to suck. If things get too ugly—I'm just saying—I'm clearing out before all the crying gets started." Emily started singing something loud and out of tune, while she drummed a wooden spoon on the high chair tray. He felt a longing for his office, quiet and orderly.

"Oh, come on," Angela said, unbuttoning her blouse. "No one's going to cry." She disappeared into the bedroom, and he heard the rattling of hangers.

"Someone's going to cry unless you stop being so pissed off. She didn't do anything wrong." Doug took off his blazer and tie and threw them on the couch, an act of rebellion against Angela and her rotten mood.

"Well, I wouldn't say *that*," Angela yelled from the bedroom. "I wouldn't say she didn't do *anything*—"

"She's an adult. You need to let go a little. She doesn't have to tell you every single thing—"

"Don't make me out to be unreasonable. I never said 'every single thing.' " She came out of the bedroom, tucking in a clean shirt and checking herself in the mirror by the front door. "She can't expect me not to worry given that she barely leaves her apartment for months, and then suddenly she goes missing—but I'm not supposed to worry?"

"Why aren't you in jeans?"

"They're too tight, thanks for asking."

"Pajamas, then. I don't like where this is going. I see what you're doing—it's a superiority thing. She's going to show up here, wearing dirty sweatpants." Doug headed into the bedroom. "I'm going to have to balance things out and wear nothing but underwear."

The downstairs buzzer rang.

"That's a surprise," Angela said to Emily. "Auntie Kate is actually on time?"

"Smile so you don't scare her," Doug called out from the bedroom, "and try to keep in mind that she's an adult."

Angela opened the door and waited while Kate walked up

four flights of stairs. It was a nice apartment, a great Tribeca address, but everyone arrived at her door put out and panting. Angela checked her hair and made a face that she hoped looked aged from worry. She would extract the truth and a big apology if it took all night.

Kate reached the fourth floor, only mildly winded and overly chipper. Everything, absolutely everything, was different. First, Kate wasn't in sweatpants at all. She was wearing clothes that Angela had never seen before, a pencil skirt, a cool slinky belt, mid-heel peep-toes with blue nails peeping. *What is this?* thought Angela. Her hair was different as well, and she was entirely too put together. Second, as if this weren't strange enough, Kate was holding out a bottle of nonalcoholic champagne with a starchy ribbon tied around the neck.

"A peace offering!" she said sweetly. "Sorry you worried. Mmmm, smells so good in here." She walked past Angela into the kitchen, putting her new bag on the counter, and went to say hello to her niece.

Doug walked in barefoot wearing shorts and a ripped T-shirt.

"Hey, I hear you're knocked up!" Kate said to him.

"I heard that, too," Doug answered. "It's quite a shock."

"It's not a shock," Angela corrected.

"Look at you!" he said. "So elegant."

Angela was looking Kate up and down, even turning over the back of her shirt collar to see the label. "That's some makeover," she agreed.

"Thanks. I'm starved," Kate said, taking a bite of salad right out of the big wood bowl with her fingers.

"That's not surprising, is it?" Angela asked. "Given where you *say* you were all that time."

"You're probably right," Kate answered.

"Did you get diarrhea?" Doug asked.

"Oh, please," Angela gagged. "Do we have to—?"

"No, it was great," Kate replied. "I just ate and drank all the stuff they gave me, antioxidants or whatever. Soup made of cabbage and fennel and I don't know what. A lot of beets. And that's pretty much it."

"Huh," Doug shrugged, sitting at the counter and opening Kate's bottle of fake champagne. "I thought those juice diets gave you explosive diarrhea. Guy I know went on one of those power cleanse things for, like, a week and got the shits so bad he ended up dehydrated at the hospital. They had to give him IV fluids."

"You're disgusting," Angela said flatly.

"What?" Doug asked. "I'm interested."

"It was fine," Kate said. "I told you I was on a health kick. It's a lovely spa."

"A spa?" Angela asked, eyebrows raised.

"Yes."

"Was it rehab?"

"No."

"Because you do drink a lot."

"Thanks. No, it wasn't rehab."

"Well, you look great," Doug said. "Doesn't she look great?"

"I don't understand this. Why didn't you tell me you were going?" Angela asked.

"No cell phone service. And it was a last-minute thing; I just jumped on the train. Spontaneously. I'm sincerely sorry I upset you."

"I think it's weird," Angela said. "Completely out of character. Not to mention outrageously inconsiderate. And thoughtless, and not how we do things in this family. You have no idea how worried I was. And your friends were hysterical. We didn't sleep."

"I slept," Doug said.

"Mom was extremely upset."

"I talked to her yesterday," Kate said. "She seemed fine to me."

"She was worried."

"Well, it was one of those things," Kate explained.

"See," Angela said, taking Emily out of the high chair, "I don't even know what that means. 'One of those things'? Plus how could you possibly pay for it? Also, since when do you go to spas? And third, I thought we were focusing on getting you a job, not taking a vacation."

"I got a job. I started today."

Angela made a whole series of faces and sounds, from baffled to irritated to ecstatic, while Doug went over to give Kate a high five. "That's awesome," he said. "Good for you."

"What? How? Why didn't you tell me?" Angela asked.

"Surprise!" Kate smiled. "I just told you."

At 10:55 a.m., Nancy's driver opened the back door of the black Escalade and, as a courtesy, offered his hand to help her out. She didn't take it; she was young and fit, and she could sure as hell step out of an SUV on her own. And gracefully, too, regardless of the height of her heels. She could imagine being eighty someday and accepting the steady arm of her driver. New York was full of elegant elderly women, and Nancy would be the especially glamorous kind, wearing a Eugenia Kim fedora from Bergdorf's and a Burberry cape. She would be single, since Sam would surely be dead and buried by then. Even though they were about the same age, she would outlive him by a decade. Single at eighty, dignified and well-preserved, sporting Sam's mother's diamond brooch; Sam's mother would be dead as well, after all.

"Eleven forty-five?" her driver asked.

"Two o'clock on Fifty-Third near Fifth," she corrected, "in front of the Modern. No, make it one forty-five and circle if you have to." She looked at her phone, rolled her eyes, and walked under the green awning to the door of the building.

The lobby of Dr. Richards's Midtown office was more upscale than the office itself. The lobby was sleek, mirrored, and marbled, while the office was dark and shabby. In two appointments, Nancy, a woman who believed in remodeling everything from her Upper East Side town house to her ass, had redecorated it in her mind in several different styles. The carpet needed to be replaced, the furniture reupholstered. Dr. Richards didn't seem bothered by the mothy drapes or the hideous, worn armchairs. Dr. Richards didn't seem to have feelings at all. She took the idea of being a neutral presence to the extreme.

"Sam texted," Nancy said. "Can we start without him?" She threw her phone in her bag and sank into the sofa. She tried to position herself on one side but found herself tipping toward the crack between the two seat cushions. The couch was too soft. It reminded her of the kind she'd slept on in college, only with fancier fabric. In college the couches were twill or corduroy and stained with beer, close mimics of the male students who sat on them. Nancy moved her bag to the floor: Sam would arrive eventually, and he would need a place to sit. He would come in distracted, not even pretending like he gave a flying fuck about being there, and they would fold in on each other on this stupid couch in spite of their urge to hug opposite arms. Nancy wondered if this was part of Dr. Richards's therapy: physically force people on each other.

Dr. Richards looked at her, making her defensive of her husband in spite of hating him. "He's very busy," she explained. "We're both very busy. It's so hard to make the time work." She looked around the room at the faded museum posters and marveled at their tackiness. Dr. Richards could certainly afford signed prints. "I'm more flexible, obviously, but Sam works all the time."

"How have things been since our last session?" Dr. Richards asked without moving any muscle other than the ones required to make her mouth form words. "Did you and Sam get a chance to spend any time together?"

"Sam was out of town for the past two weeks, and when he finally got back, I tried to get him to talk to me about this whole admissions thing for Gus, at least do some of the unemotional tasks, like start *one* application, the Dalton one, maybe, since it's in our neighborhood. But we both got completely overwhelmed, and next thing you know we're screaming at each other. Have you ever looked at these applications? They go on and on, asking all of these questions that no parent knows the answers to, like 'How does your child handle setbacks?' How should I know? I can't even think of a setback, much less try to figure out how Gus would handle one. Should I get a divorce just to have something to write about?" She chuckled self-righteously and tried to sit up straighter, but the couch closed in on her on all sides, making her spine roll into a ball. "I could kick myself for not enrolling him in a K-through-twelve school from the very beginning. I don't know what I was thinking. This whole admissions process is a nightmare; I'm getting incredibly anxious about it. It's not like Gus is some kind of genius, and it's not like I know how any of this works, nor do I care. I just want it to be done."

"Will you and Sam be able to take this on together? A joint mission?" Dr. Richards asked.

"No. I realized that's not really how we do things. We hired a consultant."

"So you and Sam came together to make that decision. Does that seem like progress?"

Nancy sighed in a manner sounding like boredom when in fact she was pissed. "Not really. Because the only thing we decided together is that we can't get it done together. We can't do anything together. Which is strange because we do so well together on our own."

Sam came in loudly and unapologetically, phone in one hand, briefcase in the other. "I'm late," was all he said as he sat down next to his wife on the couch, finishing up an email on his BlackBerry. Sam's energy was exhausting. No matter what time of day, he was moving at full speed, making it known that he was coming from somewhere and was on his way to somewhere else, never at rest. Nancy tried to pat his leg like she was happy to see him but it landed aggressively, more like she was smacking him.

"Isn't that right, Sam?"

"What's that?" he asked.

"We do well together, on our own."

"What?"

"We're not good at joint projects. We're good together as long as we don't have to *do* anything together. Like collaborate or make decisions or I-scratch-your-back type stuff."

"Sure, I guess," Sam answered.

"Like we both work out every day, but we would never work out together," Nancy explained.

"I'm out of town a lot."

"But when you're in town, we still don't work out together."

"Do you see yourselves as a team?" the doctor asked.

"Yes," said Nancy, "but not the kind of team that involves passing or cooperation. More like a track team, but not a relay. Too much room for blame. Nothing with batons. Two separate races," she said, slicing her parallel hands vertically through the air to illustrate. "Different heats."

"So you feel you're in a race? Are you racing against Sam?"

"No, certainly not. We're both trying to beat everyone else, but when we try to join forces, we end up arguing."

"Sam, do you see your marriage as a team?" Dr. Richards asked. "Or as a race of some kind?"

"I see us more in a pool," Sam said, typing in his phone. "Like water polo in a pool. Very vicious. A lot of defense and cheap shots. Or water polo in an ocean. Alligator-infested. Something you could drown in."

"Our marriage?"

"Especially when you add in the complication of having a kid. He's like a Labrador. You think it will be fun; you're swimming along and then suddenly he's trying to save himself by drowning you." He hit send on his BlackBerry, put his phone in his shirt pocket, and looked up for the first time. "Not a Labrador. What's bigger? Bigger than a Labrador and clumsy as fuck. A Newfoundland."

"Gus is drowning you? Gus is *drowning* you?" Nancy asked.

"No, of course not. The two of you are drowning me together."

"So I'm a Newfoundland now, too? Fuck you, Sam."

"Let me ask you," Dr. Richards interrupted, "just to know if it's a point of contention, do you plan to have more children?"

"No," they said at the same time.

"It's the only thing we don't fight about," Nancy said. "One kid is more than enough."

"I didn't know Gus would take up so much space," Sam said. "He doesn't blend. When he starts talking? I can't get interested. I hate being ignored, but at the same time, I want to be left alone."

"You're selfish," Nancy said flatly.

"I know. I never hid that from you."

Nancy shrugged. "I used to see it as attractively masculine. And anyway, in my opinion, you're drowning yourself."

"How can I drown myself?"

"By tying concrete blocks to your ankles."

"Is Gus the concrete block?"

"No. You are."

"How can *I* be the concrete block?"

Dr. Richards tried to redirect. "Why don't we shift gears . . ."

"Why are you bringing Gus into this?" Nancy asked. "I was saying something positive. I was saying something nice. I was explaining that I think we're a good team as long as we don't have to interact in any way." She could feel the gravitational pull; both she and Sam were tilting toward the center of the couch, shoulders almost touching.

"I thought we were *here* about Gus," Sam said.

"Well, yes. I mean no. It's about *us*. Gus can't apply to school on his own, can he? We have to do it with him. But we don't seem to be able to work together like a normal couple."

"Like the kitchen renovation," Sam said.

"A catastrophe."

Sam turned to Dr. Richards. "She said, 'I want your input,'

and I thought maybe I cared. But it was obvious she didn't really want me involved, and I hated hearing her argue about stupid things like . . . like tiles. She wanted a low-hanging pot rack, like she *wants* me to smash my head on things. And then I said fuck it. Who cares? Like I care about appliances? Like I'm ever going to load that dishwasher? It's a fucking kitchen. We eat out every night anyway."

"Do you like the new kitchen, Sam?" Dr. Richards asked.

"It's fine."

"Then you must have resolved your differences somehow," she suggested, "if the end result is one you both like."

"It had nothing to do with us," Sam said.

"We moved to a rental and had a designer make all the decisions," Nancy explained. "We let someone else handle it. She called us one day and said, 'You can come home now. It's finished.' It cost a fortune and was worth every penny."

"It's always better to pay someone. Hire an expert. We're not experts."

"Which is why we hired Mel Branson. People say he's the best school-placement counselor in the city; he performs miracles. My hope is that Gus will be like the kitchen," Nancy said. "We'll let Mel handle the details."

"It's only day care," Sam said. "You're making too much out of this."

"It's not day care, for Christ's sake. It's middle school. You don't know what you're talking about."

"We'll be fine."

"What are you going to do about the interviews?" Dr. Richards asked.

"We'll be fine," Sam repeated.

"Will we?" Nancy asked.

"Are you kidding? What do you think I do all day? Do you know how many people I bullshit? How many people I manipulate into doing whatever I want? What do you think a lobbyist is paid to do?"

"Yes, of course," Nancy said, rolling her eyes. "You're a very powerful man."

"Don't mock me."

"You think this is going to be so easy?" Nancy asked him. "You have no clue how hard it is to get a kid into private school in New York. Do you even have the slightest idea of the ends people go to?"

"I don't know anything about it."

"Getting into private school in Manhattan is like getting into Harvard."

"I got into Harvard."

"Like getting into Harvard *now*. Not in 1990."

"We got Gus in once before; we can do it again," Sam said.

"This isn't kindergarten. The process is different, the expectations, the applications, the testing. And frankly I worry about the interview. I think we should practice."

"Just keep Gus from wearing those damn pink socks, and let me do the talking." Sam's phone made a series of noises. "I have a meeting in D.C. and there is literally a helicopter waiting. It's been a pleasure," he said, and because he was fit and energetic, he popped up off the couch. "We hired the guy, so all we have to do now is go to a couple of schools and talk about our kid. Piece of cake."

"We have to appear stable," Nancy said, after he'd turned his back. "Like we get along."

"We get along fine."

"And we'll have to convince everyone that Gus is a normal kid and a joy for us to be with."

"If you ask me," Sam said, "we need acting lessons more than we need counseling."

"That's rude. And unfair," Nancy answered.

"Get Dr. Richards here to give you a prescription before you leave. Something to take the edge off," he said, opening the door. "It'll be fine," he called over his shoulder as the door shut behind him.

"He's very busy," Nancy said. "It's a wonder he was able to come at all."

Hudson Day was a city school, meaning it had no campus, no green space, no carpool lane. Certainly no pool. Rather it had nine floors, cramped classrooms, a gym in the basement, and a rooftop play yard that was caged in all directions to keep basketballs and children from falling down to the sidewalk below. The building was on the Upper West Side, one block from Central Park, where the PE teachers would set up cones, and the students would play games in matching royal blue and white sports uniforms.

Hudson offered arts classes, but it wasn't known for being artsy. It had sports teams, but it wasn't considered sporty. Hudson was academic. Rigorous. Traditional. The students wore their uniforms, and they sat in rows. They were motivated self-starters who thrived in the school's competitive atmosphere. Hudson taught them to buckle down and manage their stress. There was a well-stocked library. The science department was cutting edge. The Wi-Fi was fast and reliable. The teachers were known for their high level of expertise in their subject areas. The chair of the English department was a published poet, his works appearing in the *New Yorker* from time to time. Hudson graduates went to Ivies.

Kate was beginning to see what set one New York City private school apart from another. She thought about what parents might look for when choosing where to send their kids all day, every day. She got to know the character and reputation of schools like Horace Mann, Trinity, Dalton, and Trevor, and she knew what set Hudson apart. She understood Hudson's mission, philosophy, methods, and she learned the lingo used to talk about it all.

But Kate knew that there was theory and then there was practice. Nothing about this place resembled the simple, homey public school she had attended, so Kate viewed Hudson Day as an unknown culture that required her exploration. She took time in her first two weeks to walk the tidy hallways and stairwells. She observed the teachers in their classrooms, noted order and discipline. She listened in on students' conversations and looked over their shoulders to see what they were reading and writing. A few times she went in the cafeteria and invited herself to sit down at a table full of sixth-graders, which made them all go suddenly and completely quiet.

"Who are you?" one of the kids asked her.

"Kate," she said. "I'm new."

"Are you a twelfth-grader?" he asked. "You're too big to sit at the sixth-grade table."

"I work here," Kate explained.

"You're a teacher?" a girl asked.

"I do admissions. You know, for new kids who want to come here. I'm trying to learn about the school," she said.

They all started talking at once:

"We're never allowed to call you by your first name."

"Monday is pasta day."

"Your shirt isn't tucked in."

"It's against dress code to look sloppy."

"Latin's the dumbest class in the school."

"Not as dumb as you are."

"Shut up, Scott."

"Saying 'shut up' breaks the Mutual Respect rule."

"You can't say 'stupid,' either."

"We're only supposed to get thirty minutes of Latin homework every night but it's always more."

"You have pretty hair. It's so soft."

"You're not allowed to touch other people."

"You're not allowed to touch other people's *things*. Hair isn't a thing."

"The Latin teacher is mean."

"Ms. Butler is not mean. She just doesn't like you 'cause you never know the answer."

"She doesn't like anyone."

"Ms. Banter is the nicest teacher in the school."

"We're reading *Whipping Boy*."

"She lets us start on homework in class."

"Scott's in Study Session. That's what you get when you're three assignments behind."

"I'm caught up now, so shut up."

"Mutual Respect? Hello?"

"I never get Study Session."

"Can I try on your bracelet?"

"Jackie got sent home today because she stood up when we were supposed to be sitting down and then she was sassy about it."

"Jackie's late to Morning Meeting every day."

"My advisor says timeliness is next to cleanliness."

"The Latin teacher is the only one who yells."

"Ms. Banter never yells, but if you don't put the right heading on your homework, she takes off five points."

Kate got the real scoop on teacher expectations and advisor personalities. As she got to know the students, they revealed the nature of morning meetings, the stigma of study sessions, and the inflexibility of homework headings. They exposed the real culture of Hudson, the good parts and the bad. So during her first week of work, when all she was trying to do was keep Mr. Bigley from realizing what a tremendous mistake he'd made in hiring her, she inadvertently impressed him by showing she had a grasp, superficial though it might have been, of everything the school stood for. She had costumed herself in Banana Republic and found she looked the part of whoever it was she was supposed to be. Now it seemed she sounded the part as well, and Mr. Bigley started complimenting her all the time.

"Really nice work today," he told her during her second week.

Kate looked behind her.

"No, Kate, *you*. You're doing a great job."

Kate braced herself for criticism. "But . . . ?"

"But what?" he asked.

"No, I thought you were going to add a disclaimer. 'Good job, *but* . . .' "

"No," he said, "no 'but.' "

The praise seemed unwarranted, so she decided to work even harder to deserve it.

Whenever she had a question, which was about a dozen times a day, she would reluctantly go to Maureen's office next door. "Sorry to bother you again, but what exactly is an ISEE?"

Maureen sighed and took off her reading glasses. "Independent School Entrance Exam. Stanines range from one to nine, one being the kid is dumb as a brick. We don't see ones here. We want seven and above, but we'll stoop to six if we like someone."

"So nine is good," Kate said, taking notes.

"Some kids get nines in all four categories."

"There are categories?"

"Look it up. And there's a timed essay, too."

"Do the kids get stressed out about it?"

"Some take prep classes for more than a year before, if they can afford it."

"And the ones who can't?"

"No one said life is fair."

"Does it really cost $44,000 a year to go here, or is that a typo on the website?"

Maureen smiled at Kate, standing there with her little notebook of questions, and said, "So just to be clear, you don't know anything at all about admissions, is that right?"

"I don't know anything about anything."

Maureen shook her head.

"But I'll learn fast," Kate said. "I'm usually a fast learner."

"Have you ever interviewed anyone before?"

"No."

"Are you a good judge of character?"

"Not particularly. I don't tend to like people."

"Well, at least we have that in common. Are you a fast reader?"

"I think so."

"And you're what, like, seventeen?"

"Twenty-five."

"Look, Nellie, let me fill you in on a few things."

"It's Kate, actually."

"One, in January we don't sleep, and two, it's the parents you have to wise up to, not the kids. New York parents, most of them, anyway, are crazy."

"I don't need to sleep," Kate said. She was trying to write things down, but the information was coming in a way that seemed to lack order, in spite of the numbered points.

"Three, don't fall in love."

"Huh?"

"Don't fall in love with applicants. Just because you love them doesn't mean we can take them and just because we take them doesn't mean they'll come."

"I don't think I'm likely to care all that much."

"That would be an asset if it's true, but we'll have to wait and see."

Kate stopped scribbling and looked up at her. "I'm going to get fired."

"He doesn't have time to fire you now," Maureen said. "There's too much to do. If you're going to get fired, it won't be until spring. I'm guessing late April."

"Maybe I'll know what I'm doing by then."

"Hmph. Maybe, maybe not. Just don't end up like the last guy."

"The one with the goatee? Why? What happened to him?"

"Want my advice? Do your work, but don't get caught up in it."

"I don't understand."

"And stop being so damn nervous all the time. You make me uncomfortable."

"Sorry."

"Make to-do lists every day. And don't get sick. You don't have time to take a day off, even for the flu. And if you get the flu, don't breathe anywhere near me."

Kate started making lists and taking vitamins. She found typos on the website and one ungrammatical construction in the school facts brochure. She took a family from Hong Kong on a slightly awkward tour of the building and got lost only once. They were smiling the whole time, so Kate was pretty confident that they liked what she showed them. She sent polite, well-written emails, and people responded in turn.

At the end of her second week, she was sitting in her office when Mr. Bigley came in and placed some marked-up papers on her desk. "Excellent work," he said, putting his hands in the pockets of his high-waisted khakis.

"It was only a comma or two."

"Attention to detail. Very well done."

"Thank you, Mr. Bigley."

"Call me Henry," he said. "Nice flowers."

"Aren't they pretty? My friend sent them."

"Maureen thought maybe a boyfriend . . . ?"

"Oh, no. I don't have one, long story." She was tempted to tell it but decided it was best not to. Instead she handed him the card that read *Best of luck on your new job! Love you, Chloe.*

"I don't think you need luck. You're doing great."

"Thank you. I'm a little nervous, to be honest."

"No need. You're doing a terrific job. How do you feel about interviewing?"

"I'm not good at answering questions, you might have figured that out."

"Ha! No, I mean giving interviews. I assume we should talk about that before things start up."

"Yes, of course."

"You'll meet with the child and then with the parents," he said, sitting down. "Mostly students applying to sixth."

"So they would be . . . fourteen or something?"

From Maureen's office they heard a loud "Ha."

"You're funny, Kate," Henry said. "Think of the interview as a conversation. Keep it relaxed. Get to know them by making them comfortable."

"So just talk to them?"

"Find out if they have good work habits. Do they take notes and do their homework? Are they avid readers? Are they intellectually curious and self-directed? There's no need to question them about their grades; it puts them on the spot, and we see all of their school reports anyway. And never ask them where else they're applying to school. ISC rules."

Kate grabbed her notebook, opened to a blank page, and scribbled *WTF is ISC?*

"But you do need to know if they're passionate about anything," he continued. "In what ways would they participate in student life?"

Figure out—Are they good students? What are they into?

"The parents are a different story. They'll have a lot of

questions. Answer them and otherwise let them do the talking. You're not actually interviewing them. You're trying to determine if Hudson is the right fit for the student."

Fit, Let them talk. "Got it."

"And here's a really important thing: never, ever make promises. Don't give the parents or students the idea that anything's decided, one way or the other."

No promises. "Right, that makes sense."

"We make decisions as a committee, and we consider all the parts of the application."

A committee of three?

"This is stressful for the parents, so they'd love to get assurances while they're here—but we can't give them that until we send out official notifications."

"When is that again?"

"February. And those decisions are final. We never discuss the reasons for our decisions, that's a rule."

Decisions final. No explanations.

"It's not always easy saying no, especially once you get to know the kids, and some of the parents take rejection really hard. But try not to let it get to you."

"Get to me how?"

"Don't get too emotionally involved. Take Maureen, for example. She makes fun of the applicants."

"She what?"

"Even I do from time to time. Not to their faces, of course," he said.

"Isn't that, I don't know, wrong?"

"Maureen takes her job very seriously, even though it might not always look that way."

"I heard that," Maureen yelled from her office.

"We should have dinner some evening," he said. "We'll be working together every day. It would be good to have a chance to discuss our strategies for this season, and I'd be interested to hear ideas you have for making things run smoothly."

Strategies???? Think up something not stupid. "I'd love to," she told him.

"Keep it up, trouper," he said and walked out whistling.

October

Soon after Kate got dumped, I met George. I swear I didn't mean to. It just happened. And it wasn't right, given the shit show that was Kate's life at the time. Given what I did, or didn't do. It was totally unacceptable that she was alone and I was in love. Guilt was my normal state of being, and one way I handled it was by keeping George a secret. It made sense to me: I wanted to see Kate in a happier state before I told my friends about him.

I got seven possible guys for her with my phony online profile. I narrowed them down to three and read their messages out loud.

"What are you after?" George asked. He was packing for a work trip, folding his shorts and counting his socks. He would be gone for a month, organizing food relief in Haiti. It was the first time we'd been apart since we'd met.

"Someone steady, and above all kind and smart. And interesting. Someone we would want to have a beer with." I read the messages again. "They don't sound like dicks to me," I said. "Should I see them?"

"Would it help to see them?"

"Do you mind if I see them?"

"Why would I mind if you see them?" he asked.

"What will I say?"

"I don't know. 'I'm here to interview you for my friend'?"

"Can I say that?"

"It's weird."

"Or I pretend to be her."

"Frankly I think you should stop worrying about all this. It's not your problem."

"Of course it is."

"You spend all day worrying about other people, and then you come home and you keep at it with your friends. You have no reason to feel guilty."

"Angela thinks . . ."

"Why do you care what Angela thinks? Go do something nice this afternoon, something for yourself for once. Go to a movie."

"Without you?"

"Why not?"

"It won't be fun."

When George wasn't looking, I hid a jar of Nutella and a note in his suitcase. He flew to Haiti, and I went alone to see a deeply depressing film about life in Germany after World War II. It felt punitive in a way I figured I deserved.

After the movie I met Vicki for a drink at a trendy bar she suggested. It was crowded, loud, and full of guys who were hitting on her. I went to the bathroom as soon as I arrived and came back to find her surrounded. She shooed the men away to clear my barstool.

"You went to a movie alone?" she asked.

"I had no idea so many women got raped in the aftermath of the war," I said, having delivered a lengthy summary of the film. "Such brutality, not to mention the starvation, homelessness, and disease." Katy Perry was blaring over our heads. "The inhumanity of war is appalling."

"You're seriously killing my buzz, sweetie. I'll take you out to a real movie sometime, something a little less enlightening and a little more Hollywood, preferably with Channing Tatum."

"Who?"

Vicki shook her head. "Where have you been?"

"Not at the movies, I guess."

"So what are you doing these days? I don't see you enough."

She was right, of course. We hadn't seen much of each other now that I was spending all my free time with George. "I started running," I lied. "I try not to miss a day."

"Treadmill?"

"No, just out."

"That's great. You know what you should do?" she said. "You should run a half marathon."

"Impossible."

"Not at all," she told me. "If you set up a training schedule for yourself, you could absolutely work your way up to it. All you need is a one-mile-at-a-time kind of mind-set. You could totally make that goal, if it's something you want to do."

She had said the same thing to me before in a million different ways, and it was one of the things I liked most about her. Freshman year, I considered taking Russian for a brief spell, and she was my biggest supporter. While everyone else was saying, "Oooh, Russian? Sounds really hard," Vicki was telling me, "Of course you can learn Russian, Chloe! Just get into a one-word-at-a-time mentality." Or last year when I casually mentioned that someday I hoped to write a book, she said, "You should totally do that. Why not now? You just have to get into a one-page-at-a-time frame of mind, you know? Go for it." As someone who leaned toward self-doubt and cynicism, I relished her can-do attitude and hoped it would rub off on me. She loved a challenge and believed in all that American Dream perseverance crap, which unfortunately meant she also had the accompanying lack of sympathy for anyone who stumbled and flailed.

"Have you talked to Kate?" I asked.

"Not since she started working."

"We should do something nice for her, don't you think? Like cook her dinner maybe. I hope she's not feeling neglected."

"Oh, please," Vicki said. "Seriously? I think she's gotten enough attention to last her a lifetime."

The next day, I bought Kate a plastic pumpkin filled with Halloween candy. I thought maybe kids would be nice to a lady with candy in her office.

She took the call, expecting to hear from a prospective client, and was quite pleased with the tone of her own voice. She'd been working on sounding more throaty and less nasal in an effort to come across as professional but amiable. Mature but young. Smart but sexy.

"Victoria Taylor, good afternoon." Nice. Better than Vicki. More sophisticated. Classy.

"Hello, Vicki. Eeet's me," was all the caller said. Vicki was stunned. She recognized Robert's voice immediately, the cartoonish accent, but she didn't appreciate his presumption.

"I'm sorry, who is this?" she asked.

"Eeet's Robert. You know." Why was his phone voice so sexy without even trying? "Can you meet me for dinner?" he asked. "Don't say no."

"You're in New York?" she asked, trying to stay cool.

"Not yet, but I'm coming. There's a new hotel that has caught my mother's attention. Five stars in a renovated turn-of-ze-century building. I agreed to evaluate eeet."

"And you call that a job?"

"Why should work be a torture?"

"It shouldn't," Vicki agreed. "But your jobs always sound more like vacations."

"I need to see you."

"I don't know," she said. "That doesn't seem like a good idea."

"Please, Vicki. Eeet's important."

"It's Victoria." She drummed her pencil on her knee and swiveled in her chair. What would be the harm really? Maybe he could explain himself, make amends. Besides, she could always cancel.

"I don't see the point," she said, "but I'll think about it."

He sighed long and sad. "Come on. A nice dinner with me at any restaurant you like. What do you say?"

"Have you talked to Chloe?" she asked.

"She won't speak to me, my own cousin. I simply can't understand eeet."

"Seriously? You can't?"

"I'm not so bad, Vicki."

"Victoria," she corrected him again. "Let me know when you arrive. Maybe a quick drink if I can find the time."

"And are you well?"

"I'm fabulous, actually. Better than ever. I've been promoted."

"How eeez Kate?"

Kate, Kate, Kate. God, it was tedious. "None of your business," Vicki answered. "And what do you care?"

Kate escorted a young boy to the doorway of her office and pointed to the two empty chairs sitting across from her desk. He stopped, blocking her from entering. "Sit anywhere you like," she said. The boy looked at the two chairs, turned, and decided to sit in the swivel chair at her desk instead. That seemed presumptuous. She thought about saying something, like "Not *that* chair" in a polite way, but it might hurt his feelings to ask him to move, so she took her clipboard and sat in the chair intended for him.

"Hi," she said.

"Hi."

"Doing okay?"

"I guess."

"Dillon, right? What kind of a name is Dillon?"

"It's a boy's name."

"It could be a girl's name, too."

"No it couldn't."

"Why couldn't it?"

"Because I'm a boy."

What kind of logic was that? Kate looked at her clipboard where she had placed a copy of Henry's Interview Guide Sheet. She noted the first heading, "Academic Preparedness," and next to it she scribbled, *Sucks at reasoning*. "So how's it going?" she asked.

"You said that already. Does this chair spin all the way around?"

"Yes. I think so. I don't know."

He started turning in circles. "My dad's chair spins all the way around. My dad's desk has a drawer that locks."

"That's useful. I wish I had one of those."

"Why?"

"I don't know. That way you can keep things safe. Or secret."

"Like what?"

"I don't know. Like money, I suppose."

The boy frowned at her. "I'm not supposed to talk about money," he said.

"No, of course not. Well, papers maybe. Like a letter. Like a secret love letter," she said, trying to be cute, trying to get him to warm up.

"Who wrote you a love letter?"

"No one. I only meant if someone did, I could lock it in a drawer."

"That's not what my dad has locked in his drawer."

"How do you know what he has locked in his drawer?" Kate asked.

"I don't," he answered.

"Well, then."

"You don't know, either."

"Obviously." Kate looked down at the list of suggested questions and started with the first one: "So," she cleared her throat and read, " 'What do you like about your current school? And what would you most like to change?' "

"Ummmm," he said and swiveled a little to the left, a little to the right, and once all the way around. "I like my friends and my PE teacher," he said, "and I like PE and lunch and recess on the days we have recess but sometimes we don't get to have recess when the class is too noisy and we have to stay lined up until everyone's quiet and then no one is, and then we don't get to go outside at all. I hate math, but I'm not supposed to tell you that."

"That's okay. I hate math, too. But in general you would say . . . you like school," she said, summing up by putting words in his mouth. She looked at her blank form and wondered what to write down and what to ignore. *Has friends, likes P.E. & lunch, hates math. No recess = bad.*

She skipped over the next question—"What academic challenges do you face and how do you overcome them?"—because he'd already fessed up to the math thing. Why beat a dead horse?

Moving on: "What extracurricular activities do you engage in outside of school and how much time to do you commit to these activities?"

"What?"

"Like, what do you like to do on the weekend?"

"You mean like soccer?" Dillon asked. He was moving around in the chair, getting tangled up in his own legs.

"Yeah. I guess so."

"Soccer."

"Okay. Would you say you play it . . . a lot?"

"I don't know. Sometimes."

Soccer sometimes.

"Anything else you like to do?"

"Yes, but I'm not supposed to say video games." He had taken her stapler and was slamming his fist on it repeatedly. He spotted the tape dispenser and started pulling off long strips and doing what almost looked like origami. He was folding pieces of tape into shapes and then taping those together into bigger and bigger chunks.

She read the next question, which was under the heading "Social/Emotional Development": "What methods do you use to resolve conflicts with your peers?"

"Huh?"

"I don't know. I guess, like, do you fight with your friends?"

"Sometimes."

"Call 'em names?"

"Yeah."

"Hit people?"

"Sometimes. My mom says don't hit, but my dad says it's fine. I never hit first because then you get in trouble."

"Okay." *Name-calling. Hits people only with good reason.* "I'd hit, too, if someone hurt me."

"You're not supposed to hit people. You're a grown-up."

"But still."

"Who'd you hit?" he asked. He had taped his fingers together like a boxer, and he was punching his wrapped fist into the palm of his other hand.

"My ex-boyfriend. Well, I didn't hit him, really. I threw something at him. But believe me, he deserved it."

"Did you leave a mark?"

"I hope so."

"It's better not to leave a mark," he said seriously. "You get in more trouble when you leave a mark."

"That's true. But," she assured him, "sometimes you want to leave a mark."

"Why?"

"Because you're really mad."

"Did he hit you first?" Dillon asked.

"No, not exactly. But metaphorically he did. You know what I mean?"

"No."

Seriously? *Doesn't understand metaphor.*

"My mom says you have to control your temper, and that shows you're getting more grown up."

"Well," Kate said, a little miffed, "I don't think your mom knows my ex-boyfriend. Ex-*fiancé* almost. Unofficially, anyway."

"Next time you want to hit someone, try counting," he told her, busily pulling the tape off his hand and rolling it into a ball.

"Why? I thought you said you hated math."

"I don't know. That's what the school counselor says."

Sees shrink at school? She checked her watch and then looked back at the paper. There was only one question left, and she still had twenty more minutes to spend with the kid. More chitchat? About what? " 'Ask the candidate'—that's you," she said, " 'Is there anything that you would like to ask me?' "

"Yeah—what did he do?"

"Who?"

"The one you threw something at."

"No, I think they mean something about the school. Anything you want to ask me about the school?"

"No," he said, "except do you have recess?"

"No, but we have a gym in the basement and Central Park's right across the street."

"Can I have a piece of candy?"

"Sure."

He reached into the plastic pumpkin and took a fistful of Starbursts.

"Any other questions?" she asked him.

"Did you get in trouble for leaving a mark?" he asked.

"Why would I get in trouble?"

"You could go to jail."

"Look, I'm not going to jail. He . . . Let's just say he tricked me."

"Like a joke?"

"No, not like a joke. Like a really mean trick."

"I don't think my dad would say it's okay to hit because of a trick."

"What if the trick ruined your whole life?"

"You're not supposed to take tricks that seriously. They're *tricks*."

"Are we done here?"

"I don't know," he said. "I've never done this before."

"Me neither."

At the bottom of the page, it said, "Based on the interview, would this student be a good fit for Hudson?" Kate drew a big, loopy question mark, wondering if she would ever get the hang of this.

*

Dillon's parents, Silvia and Kenneth Blake, took their seats in her office, and Kate got ready to make her way through the list of suggested parent questions she had in front of her, but they didn't notice her or her clipboard. Silvia Blake was busy parking her briefcase and handbag and taking a sip from her Smartwater bottle. She was young and put-together, and she said enthusiastically, "I can't wait to talk about Dillon." Her husband, Kenneth, handsome, gray-haired, and formidable, was looking around the room as if he'd been sent to a broom closet, like the walls were too close to him on all sides, and he sat uncomfortably in his chair. He looked down at it, and Kate kept expecting him to say, "Back in my day, we had real chairs." They were both suited-up, looking like they'd stepped right out of a Brooks Brothers catalogue, except they were the real thing. Authentic and both slightly plus-size.

"Great," Kate said, just to get things started. "Let's do that."

Mr. Blake began with, "I'll give you some background about myself. I'm CEO of Universacom. You've heard of us. We're huge. Here's my card."

"And I'm a lawyer with Stein, Blake, Stern, and Stein," his wife added. "Here's my card. We're not huge. We're more of a boutique firm."

Kate gripped her pencil and nodded. They steamrolled right over her.

"We live in the neighborhood," he said. "Bought our condo a few years back. It's prewar. A beauty."

"So close to Hudson," Silvia added, "which would be absolutely perfect for us. I can walk Dillon right over on my way to the office. I'm one of those working women who loves mommy time."

"She certainly does. My wife," Mr. Blake said proudly, placing his hand on her back, "is an outstanding, highly respected attorney, and yet she always makes time for Dillon. She's a terrific mother."

"Ohhh," Silvia said modestly.

"Now, I've been at this parenting racket for ages. I have a son in his last year of college and then there's my daughter, Bailey, from my second marriage who lives with her mother, and she's in high school now. My wife, my ex-wife, that is, Bailey's mother, and I had a heck of a time deciding where to send her, but the all-girls thing works great for her, not that that helps Dillon any. She acts in plays and participates in Model UN, and I don't even know what else. She's a very accomplished young lady, if I may say so. And my older son—"

"I went here," Silvia interrupted suddenly. "But maybe you knew that already."

"I should hope she knows that," Kenneth said. "Legacy is everything."

"We only filled out the preliminary application so far, and I don't remember if that was on it. But I did go here," Silvia said again.

"Silvia thinks that Dillon would do well here, and I'm sure she's right about that."

"He's been so happy in elementary school," Silvia said.

"Best public school in the city," he bragged.

"It's a bit too focused on testing and performance if you ask me, but it has a very nice playground, lots of professional, well-to-do families there. It's a happy place."

"And now we need a top-notch next step for him." He pointed at Kate, and clicked. "That's where you come in."

"We went to Columbia for our advanced degrees," Silvia said.

"A few years apart, of course," he laughed. "Business"—pointing his thumb at himself—"and law"—aiming it at his wife.

"I hear you have very strong college placement. Is that true?"

"Of course they do." He patted his wife on the thigh. "That's why we pay the big bucks."

Kate was busy scribbling on her paper. *Half-sis, half-bro. Mom is 3rd or 4th wife(?)—Alum-attorney, Dad is OLD and ceo uni-something. College placement. Mr. and Mrs. Big Bucks.*

"You look very young," Mr. Blake was saying. "Is there someone else we'll be meeting with? Someone in charge?"

"We're used to going straight to the top."

"Why waste time?" he asked. "I hate wasting time."

"Who has the time?" she said. They looked at each other and laughed.

"Dillon," Kenneth remarked, "and I appreciate this, Dillon keeps me young, and he's a good example to me, to both of us, because Silvia and I work hard—I look at Dillon, and I'm reminded every day that you have to find time to play, and that's what Dillon does, always makes time for the monkey bars; I respect that."

Kate wrote *playtime* and drew a dog face on her paper.

"I know I'm totally biased, but Dillon really is special," his mother said. "So imaginative and spirited. Kids love him, and he's developing a strong social platform. He has friends here already, so you won't have to worry about him socially."

"We know loads of Hudson families. Socially and through work. I play golf, of course."

"Dillon plays golf," she said.

"And we attend charity events with them as well. We're already plugged into the Hudson parent body."

"We're very involved in charity," she added. "Very sensitive to those in need."

Kate made a serious face and nodded, writing *Oh please* in a bubble coming from the dog's mouth. The dog looked a bit like Mr. Bigley.

"We're generous people," she went on, "with our time and, well, *otherwise*. *Very* generous."

"Gotta give back," Kenneth agreed.

"I love Hudson, especially the uniform," Silvia said. "I can't wait to see Dillon in that little blazer with the crest on the pocket."

"Did he tell you he plays soccer?" Kenneth asked.

"He's an amazing soccer player. Very fast. He just loves to *run*, and he has such stamina."

"He's a natural. His coach says he's never seen anything like it. He's by far the best in his league."

Best in Show, she wrote above the dog.

"And he reads," Silvia said, "sometimes just for fun. I'm sure he told you. He's voracious; we have spent thousands on books because he rushes through them so quickly. He's voracious," she said again.

Reads. Duh.

"Also, he was the best in the talent show last year," she went on.

"He didn't win a prize or anything, but believe me," Kenneth said, "he won."

"He did," Silvia agreed. "It was obvious, and everyone said so."

"Damnedest thing, but did you know they say they don't give out prizes anymore these days? They're too afraid of hurting kids' feelings."

"They did give one girl a gift certificate at the end, but that had nothing to do with the talent show. If they gave out prizes, Dillon would have won first place."

Kate drew a squiggly circle around *Best in Show* and wrote *not quite* above it.

Mrs. Blake sighed and said quietly to Kate, "The girl played this long, boring thing on her violin, almost put me to sleep. But the school wanted to do something nice for her because her father *died* the week before, and everyone felt sorry for her."

"It's not like it was unexpected," Mr. Blake said, shrugging. "He had cancer."

"She did this whole dramatic thing, 'I'd like to dedicate this to my dad,' and everyone started crying."

"I mean, is it a talent show or a memorial service?" Mr. Blake asked.

"It was deadly. And then Dillon, poor baby, Dillon has to come out and face this teary-eyed audience. Everyone passing tissues around."

"But he comes out . . ." He paused here for a moment and made Kate wait. She couldn't decide if she should be writing or not, so she held the pencil tip to the page, sort of in anticipation. "And he stands there for a second, and . . . kaboom! He brought the whole show back to life."

"It was a very difficult thing to do," Mrs. Blake explained. "To get the audience back to the point of the thing—talent. He was spectacular."

"Bruce Springsteen couldn't have done it better."

"Harry Styles! No one!"

"Well, I don't know who that is," Mr. Blake said, "but Silvia has the show on her telephone if you want to see it."

"Oh, can I show you? Is there time?"

"She'll make time," Kenneth said.

Kate used her feet to walk her swivel chair three steps over to their side of the room, and they all leaned over the iPhone while Silvia played the clip. There was Dillon, wearing dark glasses, holding an electric guitar. Kate leaned in closer. The guitar didn't have any strings.

"I can email this to you later," Silvia said. "Dillon's part, I mean. I didn't film any of the rest."

Dillon came to life, moving across the stage. He pumped his fist in the air a few times and shouted something that Kate couldn't quite make out.

"He looks like Justin Bieber, don't you think?" Silvia whispered. "I think he looks just like Justin Bieber."

Dillon air-strummed his guitar violently while "Walk This Way" played over a loudspeaker. He shouted the words along with Steven Tyler. "He has a beautiful singing voice," Silvia added quietly. "I get goose bumps whenever I hear him sing."

Kate nodded, watching Silvia's face as she studied her son's performance; she was entranced.

"Isn't he wonderful?" she asked.

The clip went on until finally there was a smattering of applause. Kate walked her chair back to its spot. Mr. Blake checked the time on his thick, shiny watch, saying, "Look, let's get right to the point: you want Dillon. He's the whole package, and we'd like to move this process along as quickly as possible. Sign things. Contracts, all that. I'd be happy to leave a check now if that would put anyone at ease, maybe throw in a little extra. We've made up our minds that this is the place we want."

"We'd like it settled," Mrs. Blake explained. "I went to Hudson, Dillon should go to Hudson. It's where we want him to go."

"Oh," Kate said, startled at the sound of her own voice. "I'm sorry. There's a process, you see. There's a, ummm . . . a committee. And we all review the files and talk. And we discuss. And then there's a date, one specific date in February, I can't remember exactly when, but that's when we tell everyone at the same time."

They frowned at her.

"It's the rules," she explained. "I'm only one person. I can't decide anything on my own."

"I see," Mrs. Blake said, picking up her purse and putting on her dark glasses. "That's disappointing to hear."

Kenneth Blake sat forward in his chair. "I took an hour off work. Certainly you can give us an indication?"

"Well, there's the whole file to consider," Kate said. "And I'm part of a committee."

"Yes, yes, you read the file and all that. But what are his *chances*? I assume his chances are very good, am I right?" He looked at her as if seeing her for the first time and narrowed in on her name tag. "Is there someone else we can talk to? Isn't there a *head* of admissions? Who runs the department?"

Kate realized that these people had never had to wait for anything before, and they always got what they wanted. She felt herself weaken.

"Did he mess up his interview?" Mr. Blake asked.

"No! Not at all," Kate assured him. "He was very comfortable."

"So what do you need to know?" he asked. "You haven't asked us anything. You were with him what? Twenty minutes? I'm sure in that time he showed you what a strong candidate he is. And given what we've told you, I think you could be a little more encouraging of our son's application."

Kate squirmed. "No, I am," she said. "I'm sure it will turn out fine. I mean, I can't tell you for sure . . ." She looked at the scribbles on her clipboard: the dog was wearing a top hat. "But he plays soccer. He, well, he reads. And the talent show was, wow."

"So you're saying you can see him here?" he asked.

"I'm saying . . . I don't not see him here," Kate said, wondering what it even meant.

"Excellent!" said Mr. Blake.

"Fabulous!" said Mrs. Blake. "That is such a relief."

"I'm glad that's out of the way."

"But there's a process—" Kate interjected, trying to sound authoritative. "There's the whole rest of the file . . ."

"It's okay, I get it," said Mr. Blake, and he winked at her. "You go ahead with your 'process.' As long as we have an understanding, then we're all set."

"I figured you'd see Dillon the way I do," Mrs. Blake said. "You'll be so happy having him here."

Oh God oh God oh God.

*

After they left, Kate typed up her comments as Henry had asked her to do. Her notes were of little help, so she tried to remember everything that seemed relevant and to relay it as accurately as she could:

> Dillon is a lively, sporty kid who enjoys some aspects of his current school, although not so much the academic ones. He loves to run around and play (big fan of recess/PE) and manages subjects like math with far less enthusiasm. His inability to sit still for five seconds makes me wonder if he has the temperament to make it through a fifty-minute Latin class. That said, he performed in his school's talent show and showed a great deal of confidence in front of a crowd. He is a fan of Aerosmith, along with other rock bands, one could assume. We had a conversation about what is and is not acceptable behavior when dealing with friends and other people.
>
> His rather forceful parents say they are generous and give back. Mother (Silvia) is an *** ALUM *** and a doting mom. Dad (Kenneth) is ancient. They say Dillon reads books and plays soccer very well. He is "the whole package," whatever that means.
>
> This is a spunky kid, but he didn't strike me as particularly Hudsony. The structure would possibly be very hard for him. But then again, maybe structure is exactly what a boy like this needs. I hope the school reports will shed some light on this when we get them. If his teachers think he's great, then I think this is possibly a yes. If it turns out they don't, then probably not.

*

A week later, she received a handwritten note in the mail:

Dear Ms. Pearson,

Thank you for talking to me at your scool. I liked meeting you and taking to you at your scool I wuld really like to go to Husdon next year.

Sinceseerley,
Dillon B.

She read it again and put it in Dillon's file.

Westchester County. A four-bedroom house, three-and-a-half bath, basement rec room, and a fenced backyard. Train station close by, a forty-minute ride to Manhattan. Good public schools, a nice neighborhood. Trees. And what was that? A bay window in the kitchen? Nice. There were reports of cars getting broken into at night, but why leave your car outside when you have a garage? This was Angela's idea of porn: surfing the Internet for pretty suburban houses. She always spent part of her lunch break trying to imagine herself as a homeowner, a person who carried big garbage cans out to the curb at the crack of dawn. A person who complained about things like lawn care and leaky roofs and drank a beer in her own backyard.

At some point they would move because they couldn't afford to raise two children in the city, not with tuitions over $42,000 per year and rising. Times two. Their city neighborhood had an excellent public school that could certainly do the trick through fifth grade, but then what? After the innocence of elementary school came those risky, pubescent, scary years of middle school, and Angela had heard stories of gateway drugs, sex in stairwells, and bullying. To counter those images, she conjured visions of suburbia, with all its clean air and simplicity.

Since moving was an inevitability, Doug felt it was better to shove off now and get settled in a house. Give them all some space and a chance to do wholesome things like ride bikes and splash around in a plastic baby pool. Doug was ready to go; Angela wasn't, and this had become a source of conflict. Like him, she longed for a house, for a real kitchen, for an upstairs and a bathtub that didn't have toys in it. But the reality was—she needed to stay near Kate, who clearly wasn't able to manage life on her own. She was employed, yes, but who knew how long this job would last? Kate had displayed epically bad judgment, she was financially irresponsible, and she was lonely, so she relied on Angela for guidance, money, and company.

It was hard to erase the memory of Kate after Paris and impossible to minimize the amount of stress her breakdown had on Angela. When she was a new mom, Angela wasn't exactly laid-back, but she had her reasons. Emily was a colicky baby from the start, and by the time she was six months she was prone to catch every virus living in Manhattan. She had recurrent ear infections, periodic asthma, and a chronic, crusty case of pinkeye. It was a long, crappy first winter.

But when summer finally came, Angela had hoped that warmer weather would bring better health. She was mistaken. In the first week of June, on the big day that Kate was taking her transatlantic flight bound for her new life in France, Emily spiked a fever of 104 degrees. Angela and Doug rushed her to the emergency room where a young doctor babbled words like "bacterial meningitis," "brain damage," and "lumbar puncture," terrifying the young parents. To handle the fear, Angela asked the doctor dozens of intelligent questions while Doug froze up and couldn't think up anything to say other than "But she's going to be okay, right?"

Somewhere in the height of this crisis, as Angela sat in the little triage area in the middle of the night, holding her fretful daughter and listening to the beeping of a hundred different medical devices from all around the room, Kate called from Paris, stunned and weepy.

"I don't understand what happened," she kept repeating over and over.

Doug, without even being asked, went out to the waiting room with his phone and bought Kate a one-way ticket back to New York.

Several hours later the test results came back normal; Emily broke out in a rash and was diagnosed with roseola, yet another virus to add to the list in her baby book. Angela took a brief moment to enjoy the relief before she left Doug at the hospital and got in a cab. She picked up Vicki, and they went to JFK together, waiting until Kate came out of customs, wearing the same clothes she'd put on the day before, and bawling.

They brought her to Angela's apartment and settled her in on the sofa with the remote control and a sleeping pill.

"I can't just leave her here," Angela whispered.

"It's fine, go," Vicki told her. "She's just going to pass out anyway."

"Can you stay with her?" Angela asked. "I'll send Doug back in a few hours."

"I guess so," she said, "but I'll have to cancel my date."

"That would be great, thanks."

"He bought tickets to a show, but whatever."

The next day they came home from the hospital. Strung out and weary, Angela and Doug didn't know what to do next. Their baby was fragile, they were emotionally exhausted and sleep-deprived, and their apartment, like most in Manhattan, was small and cramped, squelching any hospitable impulses. With Kate planted on the couch, the living room became off-limits when she was sleeping or crying, which was all the time. Her bulky suitcases, containing literally everything she owned, were stacked up by the door, and her clothes were in tall, tippy piles on the coffee table. They were all sharing the one and only bathroom. The babysitter arrived the following morning as Angela and Doug were going back to work, saw the mess, and whispered, "If your sister is here all day, where are Emily and I supposed to be?" Angela didn't like thinking of Kate as an imposition, but oh my God, she really was.

By the time she had her bimonthly Skype date with her mother a week later, Angela was completely desperate.

"Darling girl!" her mother said. "How are things in the land of the free and the home of the brave?" She was tanned, and her gray hair had gone wild. "We're having a ball."

"Where are you?" Angela asked. "I need you to come home now."

"What's wrong, love? Come closer to the screen; you look haggard."

Angela began with an accounting of her daughter's terrible illness and recovery—the sickening height of her temperature and the equally vast breadth of Angela's worry.

"You didn't breastfeed her long enough," her mother said. "Did you read the article I sent you about the mothers in Bangladesh?"

"Please don't blame me."

"Any reflection on one's mothering always leads to blame and guilt."

"Good, then let me update you on Kate's life."

Angela gave her all the details, including a description of the heaps of snotty tissues on the floor and the very audible sobbing at all hours of the day and night.

"She's heartbroken, totally lost, and I really have no idea how to help her," Angela said. "I don't know what to do."

Her mother listened to the whole sad story and inserted occasional truisms and platitudes that Angela found completely useless: Live and learn, and Life's a bitch. Twist of fate, and Get back on that horse. She threw in quotations: *Love does not alter when it alteration finds . . . That which does not kill us . . . When one door closes . . .*

"Sure, Mom, and *I get knocked down, but I get up again.* So what?"

"I was just reading this book," her mother said suddenly, jumping up so that her head vanished and only her torso appeared on-screen, "about methods of redefining one's self after trauma. The author applies her theories to amputee veterans coming home from war-torn nations. It's very apropos. Hang on," she said, tipping her head sideways to the computer camera, "I'll go find it."

"Please, Mom," Angela called out. "Sit down. I don't need an abstract analysis."

Her mother came back in view, saying, "I don't know how else to help."

"I want some kind of concrete solution, so just tell me what to do."

Her mom thought for a moment and presented one suggestion, an idea that Angela found appalling and appealing at the same time: she proposed that Kate stay for a spell in the New Jersey house, until she was back on her feet. Sure, there were three visiting anthropologists in residence, but not to worry, there was plenty of room. They would be happy to have Kate "crash" with them for few weeks or months even. She would call them and arrange it right away.

Angela agreed, and that weekend she and Doug got a Zipcar to drive Kate through the Holland Tunnel to the house.

"It's like dropping a puppy off at the pound," Doug whispered as they carried her suitcases up to the front door.

He was right. Leaving Kate at the dingy little house, which now hosted a rice cooker and three Japanese postdocs, was the most depressing event Angela had ever taken part in. The tenants welcomed Kate, asking her, please, to take her shoes off at the door. Why? To keep the carpet clean? What a joke. That wall-to-wall hideousness had never experienced more cleaning than a "go over" with an ancient Hoover that had no suction. Taking your shoes off only meant getting your socks dirty.

Kate was pretty much catatonic at that point, and Angela couldn't even tell if the sight of the neglected, outmoded house was making her feel comforted or flat-out suicidal. Either way, she settled in, and for the whole summer Kate lolled around in the company of the world's most productive academic researchers, surrounded by hundreds of books and journals, constant reminders of the life she'd abandoned.

After Kate had been there for two weeks, Angela went to visit and found her unclogging the downstairs powder room toilet, wearing her mother's house shoes and a graduation robe, belted with a bungee. Her hair smelled like the carpet, and it was clear she hadn't left the house since she'd been dropped off.

"Let's get you showered," Angela said.

"Why?"

"Because I want you to go out and take a walk with me. Get some fresh air."

"I don't want to," Kate said. "I'm too tired."

"Come on, let's try to get going here."

"I can't."

Angela took Kate back to their father's study, which was serving as her younger sister's bedroom for the time being, and saw that Kate was still living out of her suitcases. "You haven't unpacked?"

"I didn't know I was supposed to."

Kate found a T-shirt and a pair of unwashed sweatpants on the floor and put them on, while Angela started gathering dirty laundry into a pile. "Can you at least go wash your face and brush your teeth?" Angela asked. "It'll make you feel better."

"I can't find my toothbrush. It's gone."

The sleeper sofa was opened up, but there were no sheets on the mattress. "What happened to the bedding?"

"How should I know?" Kate said.

"Well, you sleep here, don't you?"

Kate looked around the room, and from under the bed she pulled out a ball of sheets that were linty and disgusting.

"How in the world did that happen?" Angela asked.

"You're asking so many questions."

"Have you been to the store yet? Are you eating?"

"Stop," Kate said and stuck her fingers in her ears.

Angela was distressed. She sat down at her dad's desk to make a list of solutions to the problems that were presenting themselves everywhere she looked. The desk was cluttered with books, papers, and empty beer bottles, and Angela tried to straighten it up, feeling a need to create one clean surface. She unearthed Kate's laptop under the debris and found a postcard with a photograph of the Little Mermaid perched on a rock, looking forlorn. She turned it over and read:

Dearest daughter,

Is this København card too fitting? I'm at a loss. Your situation brings to mind that of Phineas Gage, does it not? Iron rod right through the frontal lobe, blood everywhere, impossible to remedy. And what happens next? He becomes a new person—belligerent and carousing maybe—much to the surprise of those who knew him. So why not go a little wild? Become an unlikely and surprising version of your very own self?

Meanwhile, behave badly if you feel the need. In Tom Stoppard's The Real Thing, Henry says of heartache, "I believe in mess, tears, pain, self-abasement, loss of self-respect, nakedness." I wish you recovery, Kate, in whatever form it takes.

Your father

The fuck? Even in English these people made no sense. And whatever it meant, Angela thought it sounded like lousy advice.

She found a working pen and used the back of an empty envelope to write:

Toothbrush, toothpaste, shampoo, HAIR BRUSH
Food
Cleaning supplies
Weekly laundry service for sheets and towels
Find psychiatrist (meds?)

She hoped that Kate was simply in a transition and only needed time to pull herself together, but as the weeks went by there were no signs of improvement, in spite of Angela's efforts. She invited Kate into the city for the Fourth of July, but Kate wouldn't come. She asked her to come along with them on an outing to Coney Island, but Kate refused. She wouldn't make plans or talk about her future.

Finally in August, Angela went to visit again one weekend and noticed that Kate seemed a tiny bit better, in that, for starters, she wasn't in bed. She was sitting in the living room in the dark, wearing the same sweatpants she'd put on when Angela had forced her to get dressed weeks earlier; fortunately, the sweatpants appeared to have been washed at least once since then, and Kate's hair looked as if it might possibly be clean as well. Moreover, she had made herself a sandwich, and she had her computer open in her lap.

"Gosh, you look so industrious!" Angela said, turning on a lamp and sitting across from her. "What are you working on?"

"I'm answering an email from Sherman, a guy I worked with at NYU. He asked me how things are going."

"That's wonderful! I didn't know you were in touch with anyone from the lab."

"Just Sherman."

"So," Angela asked, "how *are* things going?"

"Everything's fine."

"Is that what you told him?"

"Yeah. 'Hey, Sherman, Nice to hear from you. Paris is awesome. I'm sitting at a café that has become my usual morning hangout. From my flat, it's a lovely, sunny walk across the bridge to get here, and I am in a spot where I can choose which museum I want to visit, depending on my mood. I never knew it was possible to be this happy. How are things there? I can't say I miss New York because life in Paris is divine.'" She continued typing.

"Oh God, Kate."

"I still have to tell him about the excursion I'm taking this weekend to visit Mom and Dad in Helsinki. I may make a stop in Berlin."

Angela shook her head. "Kate, this house isn't good for you."

"Why?"

"We have to get you out of here. Immediately. What was I thinking?" Angela went back to the comfort of list making. "I need to find you a new place," she said, "and it needs to be much closer to me; it's crucial actually."

"I'm fine."

"And I think you need to start meeting with a counselor on a regular basis. And you need friends around you and activities . . . sports or crafts or something that will give your days some structure."

"You just described day camp."

"We'll make you a schedule, maybe yoga three times a week. Maybe, I don't know, maybe a creative writing class at the 92nd Street Y. But this?" she said, gesturing to indicate everything around her. "This situation here? No, this is not working." She got up and pulled open the ugly, pea-green curtains. Kate turned her face away from the onslaught of sunlight. "Wait, I'm so confused. What time is it?"

"Two o'clock."

"In the *afternoon*?"

That visit was the final straw. Angela went on a mission to find some kind, any kind, of cheap, furnished sublet close to her, or at least in Lower Manhattan, and she quickly succeeded—an East Village studio with a cat. The tenant was away getting his master's in library science at Chapel Hill, and he would be gone for at least another year, possibly more. Angela grabbed the place sight unseen. It was a tiny apartment with decent furniture and a "half kitchen," which meant it had a sink, a toaster oven, and a mini fridge. It would do for the time being. Angela paid first, last, and deposit and helped Kate move in. The dog walking jobs came next, also thanks to Angela, who kept an eye on TaskRabbit, looking for something reasonable to keep Kate occupied and to bring in a few dollars here and there. Dog walking meant getting outside, taking responsibility for someone other than herself, and being cheered by a herd of lively animals. Bit by bit, Angela was piecing Kate's life back together.

Once Kate moved into the sublet, she became slightly more functional. But then she plateaued. Angela thought it was obvious that she needed to see a psychiatrist to work through what had happened, discover why she'd let herself be so manipulated, and begin to set appropriate goals for her future, but she wouldn't go. She said flat out that she didn't want to talk about any of that. Instead she settled into her new role as a subpar dog walker as if that were it for her. She never showed a glimmer of ambition; she was low and lazy, unreliable and lethargic, and she showed no sign of coming out of her funk.

Landing the admissions job was a major step forward, to be sure, and Angela was frankly amazed that Kate was getting herself up and out the door to work every morning. And at the same time she was worried. Would she keep it up? Could she be trusted to use this job as a springboard into the life of an independent, stable adult and a return to something even more intellectually demanding? Or would she wake up one day and decide to quit out of the blue, to take off with some new guy to Barcelona or Marrakesh? Angela was not optimistic and wanted to stay close by to ward off whatever rash decision Kate made next.

As she clicked along through Westchester County real estate pictures, Angela had a fantasy: she would be walking through one of these homes looking for Doug, calling out for him, and the house would be too large for him to hear her, her voice getting lost in a maze of hallways, vestibules, and maybe even a butler's pantry. Fantasies aside, she accepted that moving would have to wait a few years. She loved Kate too much to resent her for it, but she hoped the day would come when her little sister would grow up and stand on her own two feet, so that Angela could focus more of her attention on her daughter. And on her husband. Doug liked a little attention, too.

November

"So, tell me," I said coolly to my coffee date, "what made you decide to become a veterinarian, as opposed to being, say . . . I don't know . . . a pediatrician?"

"Are you asking why didn't I go to medical school?"

"Am I? Really I just mean—why animals?"

"Large animals," he said.

"Oh?"

"I work with large animals. Horses mostly. But llamas are in fashion these days. I'm becoming rather the llama specialist."

"Is that right?" I asked. "I read an article in the Times *about llamas. Apparently they're a lot like dogs."*

"Not really."

"Oh."

"I'm building quite a name for myself among llama and sheep breeders in New York."

"I didn't know people could breed llamas and sheep in the city."

"Not the city. I spend a lot of my time upstate, making house calls at farms anywhere from Millerton to Saratoga."

"Is that right?"

"I'm finding I don't like city life anymore. By the way, I don't like children, either, so being a pediatrician really wasn't an option for me anyway."

"Ah, I see."

"Veterinary school wasn't exactly a walk in the park, you know."

"I'm sure it wasn't."

"Do you like the country?" he asked.

"I don't know," I answered, trying to imagine what Kate would say.

"I'd like to move there. Live on a farm. Raise llamas. Live a quiet life."

"And no children on the farm?" I asked.

"Just llamas. Some pygmy goats maybe. Alpacas if things go the way I'd like."

"I've really enjoyed talking to you."

"You're leaving?" he asked.

"Well, the thing is, I don't think she's ready to rule out kids in favor of goats."

"Good one. Wait, who?"

"What?"

"You said 'she'—'she doesn't like goats.'"

"I never said she doesn't like *goats, and by 'she' I meant me. I sometimes talk about myself in the third person, so I can see things happen from the outside. Develop a more impersonal opinion."*

"You should talk to someone about that. I'm no people doctor, but that's weird."

"Best of luck with your llamas." I put on my coat and left the coffee shop, crossing Bachelor #1 off my list.

Victoria justified her mad-hot outfit by pretending she was doing it for Kate. *See what you lost?* her tight leather skirt was saying. *You were once part of my group, but we've cast you out.*

They were meeting on Sullivan Street in SoHo, at a chic little bar that had just opened. Victoria prided herself on being up-to-date on all things Manhattan, and it reflected well on her that she even knew this restaurant existed, a place too cool to have a sign. You just had to *know*.

As she sat at the bar, some boy-hopeful came over. "Are you waiting for someone?" he said. "Or can I buy you a drink?"

"Yes and no," she said, turning her back on him.

When the bartender came with the wine list, she went Californian, as a little fuck-you to France. These minor hostilities made her feel better about what she was doing, although what was she doing after all? Meeting a friend's out-of-town cousin for a drink? So what? She'd known him longer than Kate, and it's not like the Kate-Robert thing was some kind of match made in heaven anyway. It was a mistake. It was obvious, at least to Vicki, that they were completely ill-suited for each other, and Kate certainly should have picked up on that. It made no sense that she got so carried away.

Vicki had avoided seeing them when they were dating; why subject herself to it? She and Chloe went out to dinner with them one time a few months before the breakup, and Kate wasn't herself at all. While Vicki had always been critical of Kate for putting too much emphasis on work and not enough on play, now she'd gone and wildly overcorrected, swinging the balance completely off in the other direction. She didn't talk at all about the details of the research she was doing at NYU. Instead she told stories about a smelly postdoc she worked with who twice a day would prop his bare feet up on the edge of a trash can in the middle of the lab and coat his toes with powdery antifungal foot spray. And she joked about another scientist named Sherman who spoke with a formal, Shakespearean flair and who ate homemade couscous out of Tupperware containers for lunch every day and always offered to share it with her. She was giggly and dumb, like she'd checked her brain along with her coat on her way into the restaurant, actually making a joke about missing an important submission deadline for a proceedings paper, angering the professor in charge of the project. At one point, she told them, she skipped an entire week of work when Robert was visiting. "Whatever," Kate said with a smile when Vicki expressed concern about her burning bridges in academia. "I don't even care. I'm so over it."

"What about graduate school?" Chloe asked.

"Oh. I got in," she said, sounding like she'd been inconvenienced.

"What? Why didn't you say anything?" Chloe asked.

"I don't know," she said, shrugging. "I'm having second thoughts about it."

"What does that mean?" Vicki asked. "Second thoughts?"

"I'm not sure I want to go anymore."

"Of course you do," Chloe said.

Robert took that moment to pull off his sweater, raising his arms up over his head and showing his abs. He looked up with his perfectly disheveled hair and said with his beautiful accent, "Why should she be confined? Kate eeez young and clever, and she can do whatever she likes, no? She shouldn't be chained to somezing like a . . . like a dog."

"But I thought you wanted this," Vicki reminded Kate. "You always said you wanted to study"—she waved her hand in circles trying to come up with the correct discipline—"evolutionary sociology—"

"Biological anthropology," Kate corrected.

"—since freshman year."

"But I don't know anymore," Kate said. "It's really boring. Sherman, the couscous guy? His whole life is spent determining the food selection of early hominins. Who even cares?"

"Well," Vicki said, trying to make sense of this enormous change, "if you're so bored with anthropology, then what *are* you interested in?"

"Who knows?" Kate said. "Maybe nothing," and she laughed.

Nothing? Hearing Kate talk stupid was a shock. It was as if she had been taken over by someone else, by a vapid girl lacking goals and seriousness of purpose. While it was true that Kate could be an insufferable know-it-all, Vicki counted on her to be someone who knew at least some-of-it-all. Ever since college, Vicki was sold on the idea of surrounding herself with bright, interesting, successful people. Like fabulous accessories. And the older she got, the higher her expectations of her peer group became.

"What eeez so terrible with changing direction of what she wants to do with her life?" Robert had asked over Vicki and Chloe's heated protests. "Life eeez too short to be wasted. She should follow her heart."

"But seriously, if you don't go to grad school, what will you do instead?" Chloe asked.

"Follow my heart, I guess," Kate responded happily. "See where it takes me."

"Exactly," Robert said, rubbing her back. "I don't see ze problem."

After the breakup Kate acted as though Robert had proposed to her or something, but Vicki knew better. She knew that Robert was one of those men who talked mushy and romantic but didn't really mean it. He was a bit shallow, she remembered. Shallow and more than a little in love with himself. A man like that doesn't monoga-mate easily.

But she was very curious, sitting there, her legs crossed in black boots up to the knee, neckline plunging: what did he want from her? Surely he could do the bidding of his family business without bothering to see her. In fact, he had probably been to New York countless times in the past year, visiting a spa his mother was planning to imitate in Paris or checking on the progress of some commercial building his father had recently purchased. Why call her this time?

And then she saw him walking in, his eyes scanning the bar to find her. For fuck's sake, it was no wonder Kate had fallen so hard for him. What a face. A bit more rugged now than the last time she had seen him, and it suited him. All jawbone and stubble. His look didn't just happen; it took thought and grooming. Not that his appeal would work on her anymore, but you can't blame a girl for liking what she sees. And my God, she liked it.

He spotted her and walked swiftly across the room, unwrapping a black cashmere scarf from around his neck. Just like when she first met him in Paris that summer in college, he was angular and dashing, wearing shoes no American man would be caught dead in. Girls noticed him as he walked by, elbowed each other and pointed. Victoria sat still on her barstool and held her breath, watching him own the room as he walked through it. He came up to her, squeezed her by the shoulders, and kissed her on both cheeks. Flinging off his coat, he sat down close to her, knees on either side of hers, and opened his mouth to say *"Ça va?"* when without any warning, she grabbed his face and French-kissed him all over the bar.

"Eww. Kate's boss asked her to go out to dinner," Angela told Doug. It was only nine o'clock, but they were in bed, whispering to keep from waking Emily. "How disgusting is that?"

"Disgusting?"

"You know what I mean. *Inappropriate*. Plus he was wearing a wedding band. He didn't strike me as a sleazebag when I met him."

"So what makes you think he wants to sleep with her now?"

"I'll bet you anything that's why he hired her—he's attracted to her."

Doug shrugged. "Maybe she's doing a good job."

"I don't want her to screw this up like always and get fired."

" 'Like always'?"

"Like before. I can't trust her. A stable person doesn't do what she did."

"Seems like you've defined her as unstable based on that one episode."

She gasped. "You can't simplify it like that. 'One episode.' "

"Shh."

"You can't."

"Just support her."

"That's so unfair. Seriously? After all the time I've spent nursing her back to life. I'm killing myself to support her. I've lent her money, got her a job; I call her almost every day. I think I've been more than supportive."

"Well, now you need to let go a little. Let her move on, make mistakes even. She's a big girl. I think she can handle her own boss."

"You want her back on our couch? If she'd seen a psychiatrist like I asked her to, I might have more confidence in her recovery, but she never worked through any of what happened. If she falls apart again, it'll all land on us, and I just don't want to deal with it. So shoot me for caring so much about her."

"You just said two totally different things."

"What?" she asked.

"Stop worrying about her."

"I will, just as soon as I get her back to where she was before Robert came into her life and wrecked it."

"I thought you didn't want her to end up being an academic like your parents."

"Well, maybe I was wrong about that. I don't know."

"Huh," Doug said, "that's interesting."

Angela turned away from him and checked her phone.

"Now you're mad?" Doug asked.

"My back hurts. I'm more comfortable lying on my side," she said. "And it's not your fault that you aren't someone's big sister and can't understand what my role is."

"I think maybe you don't understand what your role is," Doug mumbled.

"That's odd," Angela said, sitting back up with her phone. "I got an email from Vicki."

"Who's she?"

"You know, Vicki. Kate's friend. The beautiful one?"

"They're all pretty. They blend together."

"Vicki's the glamorous one. I don't understand what this means: 'Angela, can we meet for a drink this week?' "

"How can you not understand what that means?"

"Does she mean with Kate? Why would she want to have a drink with just me?"

"For fun?"

"I wonder if something's wrong. Maybe she knows something about the boss," she said and gasped suddenly.

"How would Vicki know Kate's boss?"

Angela looked at him. "You do this on purpose."

"What?"

"I'm saying maybe Vicki's concerned, too."

"Who's Vicki?"

"Oh my God. College friend. The one who went with me to pick Kate up after Paris. Chloe felt too guilty to go with us."

"What a complete and total asshole."

"I know! Chloe is such a bitch."

"I was talking about Robert."

Kate sat in her chair, looking at the girl across from her. For a child, she sure was intimidating, and Kate realized that this student's outfit was one Kate would kill to wear herself: short suede skirt, tights, riding boots, and a sweater that looked very expensive. New York City kids were ridiculous. This girl sat right on the edge of her chair with her hands gripping the armrests. Ready to go.

"I like your boots," Kate said.

"Thank you. I got them when I turned ten."

"Nice. When I turned ten, I got a yo-yo."

The girl didn't say anything. She looked at Kate like she felt sorry for her. Kate looked at the file that was open on her lap. Annie Allsworth. Likes horseback riding. Skis in Switzerland. What a little bitch. *Miss All-That*, Kate wrote on her paper.

"So, Annie, how's school?"

"I love school. I look forward to it every single day."

"Any classes that you particularly like?"

"I like math and science the most this year," she said. "Some students don't like math, but if you think about it, we use math all the time. And science is so exciting. I like to learn how things work and what properties substances have."

Lines so rehearsed, Kate could practically see them written on the page. She scribbled, *Big bullshitter?* "What do you mean?"

"We finished a unit on water this week. We did experiments involving evaporation, freezing, even water displacement. It was very easy. And interesting."

Not. "Do you read books?"

"I love reading."

"Like what?"

Annie looked up at the ceiling. "Fantasy mostly. Like the Carcassonne Castle series."

"Never heard of it."

"I read all twelve of them. They take place in France."

"Really?" Kate said, mildly impressed since she hadn't managed to finish *Madame Bovary*, which she'd started two years ago and stopped reading for obvious reasons. "Are they long?"

"Not really. They're like," and Annie used her fingers to show the thickness of the books. She'd recently gotten a manicure. "They're very exciting books that transport you to a different place and time in your imagination."

Rote answers, very overprepared. Yuck.

"I love reading about France," she went on.

"France, hmm?" *Fucking France*, Kate wrote.

"We have a house there, so we go there a lot."

"Do you."

"Yes. Every summer."

"Hm. They teach French here, just so you know."

"I wouldn't take French since I speak it fluently already. I'd like to learn Mandarin."

"We don't have that."

"What do you have?"

"French, Spanish, and Latin."

"Spanish, then. I love to travel. Have you been to France?"

"Not exactly," Kate said.

"You should go."

"I don't think so. India maybe. Or Darfur. But not France."

"What's wrong with France?"

"Nothing."

"France is my very favorite place in the whole world," she explained. "My parents like the Mediterranean coast, but I'm all about Paris. The cafés, the shops, the museums."

"Seriously? How old are you?"

"My parents say I'm mature for my age." She adjusted her headband, which held her hair tightly off of her face. It wasn't a good look for her because she had a big, protruding forehead that Kate found slightly grotesque. She wanted to recommend heavy bangs to cover it up, but oh well.

"I've always been immature for mine," Kate said, "and I'm supposed to be living in Paris, if you must know."

"Then why aren't you?"

"I don't want to burden you."

"Okay."

"But since you asked, I got dumped. I gave up my apartment, turned down a spot in a graduate program at CUNY, got a passport, and next thing I know he's saying maybe we better 'slow things down.'"

"Who?"

"My boyfriend. 'Slow things down'! Can you imagine? How am I supposed to slow things down when my friends have thrown a good-bye party for me, and I'm standing there with all of my suitcases in Charles de Gaulle, for Christ's sake? Slow things down? *Slow things down?*" Kate shook her head. "What does that even mean?"

"I don't know."

"Of course you don't. Because there's no slowing things down at that point. There's only going ahead as planned or coming to a complete halt, and he didn't want to go with the plan. Let me tell you something, Annie, you feel pretty foolish for taking an expensive Berlitz class and giving up a lease in Manhattan along with all prospects for what was supposed to have been a serious and fulfilling career in academia to move to Paris to start a new life with a guy who ends the entire thing out of nowhere in the middle of an airport terminal and refuses to give you a reasonable explanation. Am I right?"

"I guess."

Kate took a big breath. "So anyway," she said and exhaled in an effort to get back on track. "What classes do you like this year?"

"You asked me that already."

"Oh yeah, water and all that." Kate looked up to see Annie smiling, just enough to notice. "What's funny?"

"Nothing."

"Hmm. 'What do you like most about your current school?'" Kate read. "'And what would you most like to change?'"

"I like my teachers and friends the most. I like being challenged in my classes and working in groups. And if I could change anything? . . . I'd like the boys to be less rowdy, and I guess I'd like to be able to leave school for lunch. There are a lot of good restaurants in the area. I want to be able to step out for sushi."

"Aren't you too young for that?"

"Some schools allow it."

"We don't."

"Well, I can always go to Starbucks with my friends after school gets out."

"What else do you do when you're not in school?"

"I ride horses and paint."

"Simultaneously?"

Annie raised her eyebrows up her colossal forehead and spoke slowly. "I go to my stable in the Hamptons every weekend. I take an art class at the Met on Wednesday afternoons. Painting is my favorite way to express my creativity."

"That's great. Really. And I assume you have loads of friends. Get along with everyone?"

"Yes, I'm very popular, and I love my friends."

"Is that right?"

"I can be myself with them. I like girls who make me laugh and who listen to me."

Vomit, Kate wrote. She was getting bored. "And is there anything you would like to ask me?" she asked.

"Why didn't you just move to Paris anyway?"

"About the *school.* Is there anything you would like to ask about the school?"

"How many arts classes—"

"But since you asked, I obviously couldn't stay there since I had nowhere to live. I had no job, no friends there. What was I supposed to do?"

"I don't know. Stay at a nice hotel and go shopping for some new clothes? Why couldn't you move there on your own? That's what I would have done."

"It's a little more complicated than that. You wouldn't understand."

"Maybe, but it's not France's fault that your boyfriend broke up with you."

That afternoon, Kate wrote up her thoughts on the interview:

> Annie Allsworth is a know-it-all, Neanderthal-headed brat. She is incapable of thinking outside her own experience; zero ability to put herself in the shoes of others, which I know would make her a lousy community member at this school. I hated this girl and think she is probably a bad friend. Clearly a mean girl. And a fake. I don't want her to come here, as I will likely shoot myself if I ever have to see her again. No way. No fucking way.

Kate read the paragraph over, and then held down the delete key. Why was it so pleasurable to direct her irritable mood at horrible Annie Allsworth? And why was she feeling so grumpy anyway?

"You think too much," Robert used to say to her when they were first dating. "Must you always be so cerebral? You know, eeet's not at all sexy." And "I like you best, *chérie*, when you're not feeling ze need to express every thought running through your pedantic mind. I was never before involved with a woman so . . . so ruminative." And finally, "When you laugh more and talk less, you are quite nice to be with."

She attempted to be more airy and impulsive and found he liked her much better that way. This change in personality flew in the face of her upbringing, of her nature really. "Cogitation is digestion for the brain," her father always said. "It's an essential bodily function for someone like you, Kate." But Robert had tried his damnedest to put a stop to that. Why had she been so willing to comply?

She looked at her blank screen, carefully considering the interview she'd had that morning, and tried again:

> Annie is a bright girl who can probably memorize facts and please her teachers quite easily. My guess is that her grades will be close to perfect. However, in terms of true intellectual ability, she is, I believe, stunted by an inability to go a step further with those facts and apply her knowledge to making real discoveries and insights. Furthermore, she has never experienced hardship of any kind, so while I do not doubt that she has the smarts, skills, and motivation to do the work here, I worry that her lack of empathy might stand in the way of her making serious connections with students and teachers. I also think it will hurt her ability to make thoughtful observations in her academic work, about characters in literature, for example. This is a girl who would tell Oliver Twist to stop asking for so much food all the time and just order something in from Seamless. Annie did not come across as genuine, even when discussing her interest in reading and riding horses. Everything about her felt staged. Since I never got to see the real Annie, I can only go by what she presented to me.
>
> Her mother, Tess, put on the exact same display; she bragged incessantly and seemed incredibly phony. It is hard for me to see Annie as a good fit here, and, based on her "performance" during the interview, I cannot recommend her for admission.

Albert the security guard knocked on her door and leaned in, handing her a box of macaroons from a fancy store on Lexington Avenue. "They're from that same girl who brought you the Halloween candy."

"She's so sweet," Kate said. "Here, have one. Have two."

"I guess you'll be working late a lot now," Albert said, taking a macaroon and a seat. "Entering the dark time."

"That's what Maureen keeps saying."

"You know she covered your ass yesterday," Albert told her.

"What?"

"You forgot about a family she scheduled, and Maureen came running out to the lobby before Henry knew about it and rescheduled them for some other day."

"Where was I?"

"I don't know. Lunch?"

"Oh shit."

She went to Maureen's office and put the box of macaroons on her desk with a sticky note that said, "Sorry I screwed up yesterday, it won't happen again."

Later Maureen put the note back on Kate's desk, flipped upside down, where she wrote, "It probably will, but don't worry about it."

Thanksgiving was a time to enjoy the company of family (or "loved ones," as some people called them), and Nancy didn't. She liked her daily routine, and along came Thanksgiving to throw everything out of whack. Sam and Gus were under foot and making themselves at home in rooms that were normally her own private spaces. Her cleaning lady took the afternoon off. And worst of all, her gym was closed. Nothing was as it should be, and she found herself incapable of pretending she was having a good time.

When Sam's mother arrived at the town house, Nancy was supposed to act like she was happy to see her, but she simply couldn't do it. Sam's mother was an impeccably dressed, stone-cold bitch, and she never missed an opportunity to impose. She came every Thanksgiving for what she called a long weekend when it was in fact five days. She planted herself on a Swan chair in the living room and commented on things she saw around her: "Your cleaning lady comes every day now? I couldn't bear having help around the house that much, but that's just me." "With the way you and Sam spend money, you might want to think about getting a job." "I suppose poor Gus knows he'll never have a brother or sister?" "My word, Nancy, you catered the entire Thanksgiving dinner? Why spend all that money on a new kitchen when you don't even cook?"

When she was newly married, Nancy would do all kinds of stealthy maneuvers to get prepared foods refitted into her own Le Creuset cast-iron baking dishes and hide the foil pans. But with age came confidence, and now she owned her way of doing things, proudly announcing the time that the caterer and waitstaff would be arriving. "Hope everyone's hungry," Nancy said, "because this meal is costing us an arm and a leg."

And speaking of arms and legs, Nancy made a pledge to be disciplined this Thanksgiving so that she didn't undo all the hard work she was putting in with her nutritionist and trainer; her body had never looked better. It wouldn't be easy given all the temptations in the house: wine, potatoes, and warm bread with butter. And then there were the desserts the nanny was whipping up just to keep Gus occupied throughout the day. At least someone was using the new kitchen.

"Gus's been in there all day," Sam said, looking disgusted. He had changed into exercise clothes.

"So?"

"Can't that lady do something else with him?" He got down on the floor and did a set of push-ups, grunting and counting under his breath.

"Use a mat, Sam. You're sweating all over the carpet."

"Why is she even here?" he asked.

"Your mother?"

"No, the babysitter."

"She's the nanny."

"What's the difference?"

"She *lives* here. And it's not like you don't know her name."

"Olga. Whatever. Why is she here?"

"Where exactly would you like her to go?" Nancy asked.

"I assumed she took time off every so often."

"Not today. I'm not going to entertain him. Are you?"

"For once can't he do something normal," Sam asked, "like sit on the couch and watch football? She's got him wearing a goddamn apron."

"What do you care?"

"He's weird. They're in there having a whole discussion about gnomes, for Christ's sake. I'm buying him an Xbox for Christmas with every violent game I can find. Jump-start his testosterone."

The day went from bad to worse. Nancy was expecting fourteen for dinner, and for reasons she couldn't fathom, Sam had randomly invited some politician and his young wife without telling her.

"The table seats eighteen. What's the big deal?" he asked. A question that didn't even deserve a response.

The caterer broke the turkey platter, and they had to find an alternative, which meant digging around in cabinets since Nancy had no idea where things like that could be located. While she was rummaging around, Sam showered, primped, and got an early start boozing it up. Nancy had chosen a spicy, whiskey-based martini as the evening's signature fall cocktail; Sam tasted it, made a face, and then started messing around with the caterer's recipe. By the time the guests arrived, he was in full jackass mode, acting the part of merry host, son, husband, and father. He played bartender, in spite of the fact that they'd hired a professional, gave toasts, and slapped all the men repeatedly on their backs. He got flirty with the ladies.

"Son!" he yelled loudly. "How about you and me go toss a ball around after dinner?"

Gus, sitting on the couch with a book, looked up at him like he didn't know who he was.

They somehow got through the meal and through the day. As Nancy went upstairs to settle into bed that night, with a glass of wine on her nightstand, the terrible truth hit her: it was only Thursday. She had three more days of family togetherness to endure.

Just having Sam around at all was difficult and wore on Nancy's nerves. He was out of town so much of the time, and Nancy liked her schedule without him. Wake up, let in the housekeeper, drink coffee, say good morning to the nanny, watch her morning show, go to the gym for an hour and a half, shower, take a ride with the driver to a self-improvement appointment (hair, nails, waxing, laser, psychiatrist, dermatologist, reflexologist, spray tan, fake lashes, massage, or facial, depending on the need of the day), lunch with a friend, do an errand or two, come home, open the wine, and get ready for bed or a night out on the town. It was a lovely life really. Then Sam would come back, smelling like airplanes, cologne, and Sam, and Nancy would find everything—from his comb on the bathroom counter to his sweaty exercise shorts on the closet floor—an intrusion.

There was one reason only that Nancy needed Sam around this weekend: to go over Gus's applications and discuss their upcoming school visits. There was no room for error during the interview. Mel, the placement specialist, had said they needed to present themselves as a united front, as a solid, loving, supportive family, and Nancy wasn't even sure what that might look like.

Friday morning, after an hour on the treadmill, she saw she'd missed a call from a woman she barely knew. They'd met at a yoga class, and it struck Nancy as odd that she would call her on Thanksgiving Day. A little too personal. "Hi, Nancy, it's Angela. We met at yoga, remember? Happy Thanksgiving! You mentioned that you're looking for schools for your son, Gus. I've still got a few years before all that starts for us, but I thought I'd let you know that my sister, Kate, works in the admissions department at Hudson. In case you're looking there for Gus, let me know. I can call Kate and give her a heads-up. Maybe we can grab a coffee next week. Call me."

Hallelujah! A connection! A connection just landed—boom—in her lap. Now *that* was something to be grateful for.

Dear Admissions Committee,

Thank you for my tour and interview at Hudson Day School. I appreciate the time Ms. Pearson took to speak with me. Our conversation was interesting, and I learned so much about her (and Hudson) during my visit. I believe that your school would provide me with challenging educational and extracurricular opportunities.

I have many goals for my future, and Hudson Day could help me reach my aspirations.

Yours truly,
Annie Allsworth

Angela sat on the uptown 1 train, anxious about her evening with Vicki. First there was the obvious issue—they only knew each other through Kate, so it felt awkward to be meeting without her. But also, they had so little in common. Vicki had the single, hip, money-to-spare thing down. Every time Angela saw her, she was manicured, pedicured, and put together in a way that was very "this season." Angela, on the other hand, was currently at that awkward stage of pregnancy: big enough to look fat, but not big enough to be obviously pregnant. And even when she wasn't in maternity wear, she dressed from a closet full of timeless, proper, often expensive work clothes, so when it came to dressing down for the weekend or for a night out, she was lost. What did people wear to look casual-sophisticated-cool? She couldn't pinpoint why exactly, but she knew her jeans were dated. She had the same haircut from ten years ago and didn't know what was wrong with it, but something was. For years, she'd gone for a look that she thought was classic but was now reading as frumpy, and while she could see it, she didn't know how to fix it. She liked the idea of changing her style, of shaking things up, but who has the time and money to keep up with these things? Apparently Vicki.

The nerves also came from being out of practice; as embarrassing as it was to admit, Angela didn't go out at night anymore. Her friends had stopped asking. Few of them had children, and they never seemed to fully appreciate the limitations in Angela's schedule. They would suggest meeting for happy hour, which in Angela's world meant dinnertime. Angela was making an effort to cultivate some new friendships with women who had children, with women who would understand how hard it is to juggle work, yoga, and family. With women who would know what being a mother was all about.

But Vicki? What would she and Vicki have to talk about?

Doug was looking forward to a father-daughter evening; he was always so steady, balancing out Angela's tendency to jump at things, to wind up. "She feels warm to me. Does she feel warm to you? Did you feel her head?" Angela asked.

"Just go, have a nice time," he'd said, half covering his eyes, pretending not to see Emily hiding in plain sight across the room. When she jumped out from behind the floor lamp, she knocked it over. "Whoopsy-daisy," he said and went to stand it back up again. "Take a banana with you," he suggested, as Angela was leaving, "just so you don't get too hungry."

"I can't put a banana in my clutch."

"A sandwich, then."

"What? No. It's not like I have to eat all the time."

Doug made a face that Angela understood immediately. "Don't make me feel like more of a cow than I already am," she said in a huff.

Vicki had suggested meeting at her place, so Angela got off at the Christopher Street stop in the West Village, a grittier, younger, and louder version of her own neighborhood. She walked west past pretty little restaurants, all of which were packed full, and past stately brownstones, some of which had single buzzers next to their massive front doors. She found Vicki's building and double-checked the address with the one Vicki had texted. Above the door the street number was written clearly, along with a garish sign for the ground-floor store, "Village Vibrator." *Well*, Angela thought, *how convenient*.

Vicki greeted her warmly. Such a hostess. She took Angela's coat, smiled at her stomach, and offered Perrier. She was a woman who owned her space, who handled things in a practical way. Angela remembered Vicki's calm in the cab on the way to JFK to pick Kate up.

"How could he? How could he?!" Angela had shrieked.

"We don't know what happened yet. Let's just wait to talk to her."

"But what a fucking asshole! Who does that? Who does something so cruel?"

"Let's just take care of Kate," she had said, patting Angela's hand. "Robert isn't the problem. We don't have to fix him, but poor Kate must be so humiliated," and she turned and looked out the window, deep in thought. Angela had admired her ability to eliminate Robert from the equation, to put the attention on the real problem, on her broken, miserable little sister.

Vicki's apartment was small but supercool. Immaculately clean and minimalistic. No clutter. One wall was bright orange. A pristine, white bike leaned against it and above hung a supersize clock that looked like it came from Grand Central. Angela pictured the wall covered in marker and dirty handprints. The bike was a hazard; it could tip over and crush someone. And the clock, which didn't actually tell time, looked weighty, like any minute it would pull itself and the plaster wall crashing down onto the head of a child below. The place was dangerous. And quiet. It was strange to Angela that they were all alone in the apartment, that there was no one else to keep track of. She kept turning her head, looking for someone to come in and need something. *Help me find my keys. Read to me. I'm hungry. Shoes, Mommy. No, the blue ones.* But here it was peaceful. The bright orange wall was clean and the mirrored cocktail table was neatly arranged with big, beautiful, breakable objects. There were bright, patterned pillows on the couches, whimsical, groovy, and too pretty to lean on. Angela had seen those very pillows in the window of Jonathan Adler and knew they cost over $100 each, and now, glancing around Vicki's living room, she counted six of them. One had a big blue "V" woven onto it, and Angela wondered if Vicki had bought that for herself or if someone had splurged to give her a personalized gift. Either way, the "V" pillow set a tone of serious self-involvement that she envied.

In contrast to this bright, swanky space, Angela's apartment suddenly seemed impossibly boring. She pictured her Pottery Barn living room with its beige twill couch and clunky wood coffee table, playpen crammed in the corner and stuffed animals all over the floor. She had liked it all until now.

Vicki slowly poured two ridiculously long-stemmed glasses up to the brim, one with wine for herself, and one with sparkling water for Angela. Everything she did was graceful and deliberate. Angela sat on a tall barstool that had no back to it, the kind a child would fall off of and crack her head on the floor. It was difficult for Angela not to see catastrophes everywhere. Those wineglasses wouldn't last five minutes in her house.

"Thanks for coming over," Vicki said, holding up her glass.

"No, Vicki, thanks for inviting me," Angela answered, taking a sip and wondering why exactly she was there. And would there be food?

"I prefer Victoria actually."

"Oh, I thought—"

"My college friends can't seem to make the transition. But with everyone else, I just prefer to forgo the nickname."

"Victoria, of course." Angela decided to save time and get right to their common denominator. "Kate has a fabulous job. You heard about it, right?" Angela asked.

"It's great news. Finally."

"I'm so glad it worked out," Angela said. "When I connected her to her new boss, I had no idea if he'd offer her something or not. It's not like she has any kind of a résumé. I was so worried that I was setting her up to fail."

"You got her the job?"

"Well, I wouldn't say that," Angela said, feigning modesty. "All I did was make the connection, and she took it from there. Of course, I gave her advice on interviewing with him. On what to say and wear. Other than that, it was all her."

"I didn't realize. Well, here's to you, then," Victoria toasted. "Nicely done."

"Oh, it was nothing really. I mean, I feel responsible for her, naturally. In any case I'm just so happy she's off that couch. Did she ever mention her boss to you? Say anything about him?"

"No, but I've barely talked to her since she took the job."

"He asked her out to dinner, and I told her not to go."

"Why? You think he's hitting on her?"

"It occurred to me."

"I'll let you know if she says anything, but I wouldn't worry about it," Vicki said. "I'm sure you've got enough on your mind." She was busy preparing things on the counter that Angela couldn't see. "How are you feeling anyway? You're due soon, right?"

"Not exactly. I have a few more months."

"And how's your little girl? Emily?"

"She's great, thanks." Angela thought for a second. "Really, thank you."

"What for?"

"Asking."

"Well, what could matter more?"

Angela swung her legs back and forth, feeling her feet swell as they dangled off the barstool. "Yes, but it's just that most people I know who don't have kids never think to ask. No offense."

"I want a family."

"Really? I mean, you do?"

"I want what you have—a husband, companionship. You're very fortunate."

"How sweet," Angela said.

"Well, it's true."

"I can't imagine you would want anything to change. I mean"—she flung her arms out—"look at this."

"It's great, but I'm ready for a real relationship. I want someone who puts me first. Kate's lucky she has you keeping an eye on her."

"I annoy her. And it's not fair really. Kate doesn't appreciate everything I do for her," she confided. "And Doug says I'm overprotective."

"She should be thanking you. I'll tell her that next time I see her. I don't have anyone looking out for me. Obviously being single has its upsides—I'm totally selfish, I never have to check in with anyone or answer questions about where I've been. Nobody's business. I date a guy until one of us isn't into it anymore and then move on. I spend my money my way, and I have the whole closet to myself."

"You must get asked out constantly," Angela said. "I mean, look at you."

"Sure," Victoria said. "But those are just guys." She refilled Angela's water and held up a board of raw vegetables and dips, bruschetta, and toasted, salty walnuts.

"Pretty!" Angela said, enjoying being taken care of more than she could have anticipated.

"For me," Victoria said, "the part I can't wrap my head around—and I hope you won't be offended that I'm saying this—but where was Kate's show of strength? Her pride even? How could she fall apart like that? It was excessive, don't you think?"

Angela had tolerated Kate's emotional collapse for so long, had endured her whining without ever shaking her like she'd wanted to, she could hardly contain herself when she heard those words spoken out loud. "Yes!" she admitted. "Yes! I agree completely. I mean, I understand heartbreak and the difficulty of adjusting to a new plan, but seriously, it was too much."

"It seemed like she was wallowing."

"She was. She wallowed, she wallowed more than she should have."

"Thank God that's over."

Angela, watching Victoria carry the crudités and her wine over to the coffee table, asked suddenly, "Can you explain her friendship with Chloe? She obviously isn't good for Kate. I can't understand why Kate doesn't see that."

"Believe me, Chloe's a really good person, very down-to-earth; she just didn't know how to handle such a tricky situation."

"I don't know," Angela said. She tried to see Chloe as incompetent rather than cruel and supposed it was a possibility she could at least consider. She hopped down from her barstool to follow Victoria and the food to the sitting area, knocking her bubbly water over with her elbow. The tall glass rolled a bit toward her, fell, and smashed on the floor.

There was a flurry of activity. Angela dropped down on the floor to try to pick up the bigger broken pieces, while Vicki got out a dustpan and broom, paper towel and a trash can.

"God, Vicki. Victoria! I'm so sorry."

"Forget it. It's nothing." They got every tiny shard off the floor, and Victoria went back to the kitchen to get a new glass for Angela, choosing to give her a short and stocky lowball this time. Angela took it and tried not to be offended. Feeling like a fat, clumsy toddler, she went and sat down on the couch, carefully moving one of the glassy, sequined pillows off to the side. "Can I do anything to help?" she asked. She looked down and noticed that the rug under her feet was pure white, and she quickly checked the bottoms of her shoes. "Your apartment is, well, it's like a spa in here. You have beautiful taste."

Victoria looked around as though she, too, admired the taste of the person who lived there. "I adore contemporary," she said and sat down. "Where were we?"

"Kate?"

"I hope she meets a new man at work," Victoria said. "A teacher maybe."

"No!" Angela said abruptly. "She needs to focus on her job."

"But it would be good for her to start dating again. And I don't think she'd repeat the same mistakes."

"I'm not so sure. She doesn't know what she wants. I never thought she'd fall for someone like Robert."

"Well, he's very handsome and *charmant*, I suppose. Gorgeous really, let's be honest."

"But he's got no depth, from what I could tell. I doubt he ever reads anything. I'm no scholar, but I certainly have respect for intellectual work. Kate was too smart for him."

Victoria looked skeptical. "I don't know about that, but I thought she was too smart to change so much for someone else. She wasn't herself with him."

"That's because he's such a manipulative person. He managed to talk her out of her biggest interest, brainwashed her into giving up school. He's malicious."

"I think that's going too far. I give them both more credit than that."

"What do you mean?"

"She wasn't happy with her work at NYU. If she had really liked anthropology, she would have stuck with it, but she didn't want to go to grad school. She said so."

"No, no, no, no," Angela said, realizing that Vicki didn't understand the situation at all. "She loved her research. All that complex stuff she was doing? Looking at bones and whatever? She was perfectly happy with it until she met him. He talked her into *thinking* she didn't like it."

"Well, we'll have to agree to disagree," Victoria said, passing the platter. "I saw him, Robert. I thought I should tell you."

"What? Why?" Angela asked. She breathed in too quickly, inhaled a breadcrumb, and started coughing.

"He was in town, and he asked to see me."

"But why?" Angela choked.

"You okay?"

Angela took a sip of water and nodded her head.

"I've known Robert for a long time," Victoria said coolly, "longer than Kate has, and I wanted to hear what he had to say."

"Well, my God. What did he say?"

"He's sorry."

"Ppffft."

"No, really. He is, Angela. He was very contrite."

"I hope so. I hope he feels terrible."

"He does. He wishes he'd handled it differently."

"If he wants her back," Angela said, "he can forget it."

"He doesn't want that."

"What, then?"

"He's sorry, and he wants to make peace."

"Who cares what he wants?"

"Well," Vicki said, "I thought you should know."

"Sorry? Seriously? He should be sick with guilt every minute of the day. My God, if it weren't for him, she'd be halfway through a PhD program by now."

Victoria handed her an endive leaf filled with herb cheese. "She made her own choices, though, right? You can't put all the blame on him."

"Why can't I?"

"He didn't force her to turn down her spot in grad school. That was Kate's decision."

"That's not the point," Angela said, getting muddled about what exactly Victoria was saying. "What do you mean?"

"Robert knows he did things that were very wrong, and he wants to apologize to her, to make amends, to move on."

"Oh, I'm sure he's moved on just fine. He's probably got some hot girl in France, and he's busy messing with her head as we speak."

"He doesn't have a girl in France. Don't you think it might help her move forward to hear him say he's sorry?"

"What? No. No, and I don't think he should get the pleasure of apologizing. So that she'll say, 'Oh, it's fine, don't worry'?"

"But she *is* fine now, right? She has a job, she's back on her feet. Maybe seeing him would be good, a healing part of all this."

"He crushed her," Angela said dramatically. "He broke her heart."

"But did he really? Or did he just mess up her plans?"

"What do you mean?"

"I'm only wondering," Victoria said, "could it be that she liked the *idea* of him, the *idea* of moving to Paris, more than she actually liked *him*? And could it be that she was more humiliated and disappointed than actually heartbroken?"

"I don't know. It all happened too fast," she conceded. "Way too fast, I told her that. I said to slow down."

"She should have listened to you. I'm not trying to be mean," Victoria said, "but she took a big risk, and it didn't pan out. Now she needs to get over it. It can't be good for her to harbor all this hatred for him. I read that holding on to anger causes cancer. And there's also Chloe to consider. Her relationship with Robert is ruined."

"It is?"

"Chloe hasn't spoken to Robert since he broke up with Kate. She won't take his calls, won't answer his emails. It can't go on like this forever. She's going to have to see him eventually, and it would be best if she could get past this. If Kate forgives him, then she'll feel like she can, too."

"I didn't know she stopped talking to him." Angela took another bite of bruschetta. "This is delicious," she said with her mouth full, her hand trying to catch the crumbs that fell. She realized that Vicki wasn't eating anything at all. "So Chloe just cut him off?"

"Completely. And it's not easy for her. Regardless of what Robert did or didn't do, he and Chloe are way too close to throw their whole history together away. Can I be honest, Angela? It's time for Kate to grow up. She should face Robert, and then we'll all know that she's over him, and you can expend less energy on her and put your attention where it belongs, on your husband and your little girl. And Chloe can have a normal relationship with her cousin again. Everything back to normal. Wouldn't that give you some sense of relief?"

Angela found it gratifying to be acknowledged so fully; her sacrifices had been noted by someone. "When would this be?"

"I don't know exactly, but I was wondering if it might be better if it happened sort of by accident, without some elaborate plan."

"Like an ambush?"

"Why make it a thing? He could run into her somewhere. Keep it quick and casual. Just a coincidental encounter."

"So," Angela found herself saying, "she won't get worried in advance, anticipating it?"

"I'm not trying to be devious. I'm only trying to help. I think this is the best way. Here, have some more crudités."

Later that night Angela walked down Bleecker Street, looking for a cab. At the corner of Seventh Avenue, she stopped and took a moment to feel the baby move. An ambulance and a fire truck were working their way downtown through traffic, sirens blaring, horns honking, and she pulled her padded down coat across her stomach to muffle the offensive sound, wondering if New York City babies could be born with hearing damage. It was awful to feel like you couldn't protect someone so vulnerable, someone you were supposed to be taking care of.

Wait, she thought, running through the conversation she'd just had with Victoria. *What did we decide?*

The applicant folder checklist: the preliminary application, the student supplement, prior year's official transcript, current grades, the parent statement, ISEE scores and essay, two teacher recommendations (math and English), additional recommendations (optional), a graded writing sample, and the interview. Every day the mail came, either snail or e-, and papers needed to be filed and checked off, both on the folder and in the electronic tracker. It was best to read the files once they were complete, but Kate would often take a peek at things as they arrived, especially with the kids who stood out for one reason or another.

Annie Allsworth

Student Supplement: Essay Question #2: Consider a problem, setback, or disappointment you have faced. How did you overcome it, and what did you learn from the experience?

A problem that I once faced in my life was when Hurricane Sandy ravaged the East Coast, leaving wreckage and misery in its wake. Hurricane Sandy was a devastating storm for people living in New York and New Jersey, as many victims lost power, their homes, and sometimes even their lives. We have a home in the Hamptons, and sadly I suffered the devastation firsthand. This experience really made me remember what is important to me.

When our caretaker called us in the city to tell us that our Hamptons house had been hit, I started crying and crying and could not stop. How could this happen to me? And why? How could I lose a place that means so much to me and my family? We have made so many wonderful memories at my weekend house, and I am attached to it in a way that is hard to explain to anyone who is not in my family. I am even more attached to it than I am to my summer house in France. Fortunately the damage was not as bad as I feared. A tree fell on one small part of our home, crushing the guest suite and the sunroom. The pictures of it made me upset, and I was even sad about the pretty tree that lost its life from the harsh gusts of wind.

But then things went from bad to worse. We got another call, this time from the police, saying that the house had been robbed. Greedy thieves took advantage of our tragedy and broke into the house through the opening in the wall where the tree fell. They took the family silver, the computer in the playroom, and an expensive set of my dad's golf clubs. When I heard this, I was so angry. How could people be so evil and take things that do not belong to them? I couldn't believe that people would invade our house, and my first thought was, "I never want to go back there ever again." But then I realized that if I never went back to my weekend house that would mean that the robbers had won. How could I let them win? If my dream is to spend time in the home I love, then that is what I should do.

As my mother always says, "Everything happens for a reason," and I think she is so right about that. Because of the storm, we had to fix the house, and guess what—now our house is even better than it was before! And because of the burglars, the insurance company replaced all the items that were stolen, and we got a brand-new computer with a huge screen. I learned many valuable lessons from my experience of Hurricane Sandy: I learned that good things can come out of a bad situation. I also learned that I should never let the actions of bad people destroy my life plans or make me change what I want to do. I have learned that it is important to be strong, to know what I want and who I am, and to always remember what matters the most to me.

Sitting at her desk that afternoon, Kate resisted the strong urge she felt to light the piece of paper on fire. She wasn't egotistical enough to think that this revolting essay was some kind of masked message being directed at her specifically, but she was disgusted by its preachy, judgmental quality and didn't appreciate getting life lessons from a spoiled brat.

Kate had already learned plenty of lessons from the shit storm she had lived through. It took a while because she hadn't wanted to examine her own role in the fiasco; it was easier to be a victim and put all the blame on Robert, leave herself out of it. But recently when she looked back, she was starting to see things differently. She had begun asking herself sticky questions about her own behavior, acknowledging things she did that now seemed suspect and worth contemplation, and she came to realize that neither France nor Robert had ever been the problem. The problem was that she'd given in to a romantic delusion. She'd created and become committed to a new image of herself. She imagined walking down a cobblestone street, pushing a bicycle with a wicker basket on the handlebars, a basket that held a bottle of French wine and a bouquet of wildflowers. She was a breezy, sociable girl who didn't carry a lumpy backpack full of textbooks that weighed her down. She wore cute A-line skirts and sandals that she bought on vacation in Italy or Spain because that's the thing about living in Europe—you can fly anywhere in an hour. She had money, somehow, and she answered the phone in French. She hosted dinner parties and walked lightly on her feet. Kate had been hijacked by a fictional version of herself: a girl who didn't take it all so seriously, a girl who was experiencing life instead of studying it, a girl who ran away. The scariest part of all was that she bought this bullshit fantasy so completely, that when the possibility of it was taken away, she had no idea who she was anymore.

She put Annie's essay in the folder and sat back in her chair, looking around her office, hearing Maureen's and Henry's voices as they talked to each other next door. Things were good here, where she'd ended up. She had struggled for sure, but she was overcoming it. She felt like she was seeing things clearly and realistically, like she recognized herself again. Perhaps hers was a case in which something good actually *had* come out of a bad situation.

Recently she had searched through the shoebox that contained all the mail her parents had sent her to find a postcard she'd received soon after she moved into her sublet. It was a picture of a nineteenth-century fashion plate, showing a fancy woman cinched into a painfully tight corset. On the reverse side her mother had written the words:

> Hello Poppet! Instruments of torture on display at the Vic & Al in London. How is it that one person winds up caged in a crinoline while another ambles about in a loose leather loincloth? I wonder how it feels to be fastened into rigid whalebone undergarments. As Margaret Atwood said, "You fit into me / like a hook into an eye / a fish hook / an open eye." I wear my elastic-waist skirt with pride today! Celebrate being yourself. Toodle-oo!—Mum

Kate was being herself, and it felt right. Not that her life was perfect or easy. She was working long hours and didn't get home until late in the evenings, dragging her computer and a bag of groceries with her. Sadly, she had heard from her crotchety downstairs neighbor that Stella, her ward and companion, had been missing her.

"She has an incredibly powerful yowl for such a small animal," he'd said. "It *is* a cat, isn't it?"

"I'm sorry. I can't help it that I'm not home to entertain her."

"No, it's okay. I just wanted to suggest that I check in on her when I get home from work. On the nights that you're working late."

"What do you mean?" she'd asked.

"I could keep her quiet."

"Wouldn't that mean I'd have to give you a key?"

"Umm, I guess."

"Jonathan, right?"

"You still don't know my name?"

"Is it Jonathan?"

"Yes."

"Then I do know your name. But I don't know you well enough to give you a key to my apartment."

"Sure. Okay."

"You understand."

"Hey, it was just a thought. Trying to calm down the creature with the nuclear, ear-splitting meow. Sounded like she could use a friend."

After that Kate felt guilty about Stella being lonely. And guilty about Chloe, whom she was also neglecting. Chloe always managed to make sure Kate knew she was thinking of her, and Kate never reciprocated, something she hoped to remedy someday soon. No guilt about Angela because she demanded contact, usually in the form of her noon phone calls. And Vicki? Not so much guilt about her, either. Vicki was becoming one of those friends who says, "Oh, I've been meaning to call you, meaning to write you, meaning to see you," but she never did. But with Chloe it was truly a matter of finding the time when there simply wasn't any, which was too bad because she was deserving of a lot more attention than Kate gave her.

Kate picked up the phone to call her, just as Henry came to her door.

"Ready to go?"

"Sure," she said, putting the phone back down. "Is Maureen coming?"

"She said—what did she say?—she'd rather be waterboarded with cat pee than spend an evening having dinner with us."

"Nice," Kate said, closing her laptop and getting her coat.

"We can cover a lot of ground tonight," he said. "Test results, financial aid distribution, and file-reading procedures."

"And I'm missing all the fun," Maureen called from her office.

"You can still come," Henry said back.

"Going home," she said. "My feet feel like baked potatoes."

"It's just you and me, then," Henry said, making a gallant gesture with his arm to allow Kate to walk out ahead of him. "This is good. We should make this a regular thing."

To: Kate Pearson
From: Sherman Gregson
Re: Hello there and news about the Ass. Cult. Anth. Conf.

Salutations from your NYU compadre! How are you? I hear thou farest well. Please allow me to share from whence that happy information came to my possession: I went to the ACAC in Berlin last week, which was thrilling. The department had nary a farthing for my expenses, so I paid for the pilgrimage out of mine own pocket, but I assure you, it was well worth it. The best part of all: I had the opportunity to attend your father's electrifying keynote speech on the history-slash-*Grund* of the exclusion of females in yopo snuff practices among the Yanomami. He was extraordinary!—and you should have seen the response he got from the *muy* multinational audience. A god hath spoken.

And here cometh my confession, Kate: I took the liberty of telling your illustrious parents that I know you so that I could get a moment of their time—I truly hope you won't take offense at that. I was starstruck and desperate to connect with them, and it worked—your parents not only met me; they actually took me out to dine in a restaurant, with a menu and courses and *wine*, AND—hold on to your headgear—they offered to read my latest paper: "Stable Isotopes, Unstable Diets," an SEM micrograph analysis of dental microwear, tooth enamel surface complexity, and masticatory robustness supporting a mixed diet (C3 and C4) in early hominins. I am dizzy with excitement.

But I am worried that you'll now think me a major Machiavellian a-hole. Prithee, be honest—was this in poor taste, Kate? Anyway, I'm writing to thank you for the connection, and I hope you don't mind that I "used" you thus.

Drs. Watts and Pearson tell me you're back in ye olde Mannahatta. I had assumed you were still living the gay life in Paris. I sure would love to hear from you, to find out what you're up to, how you're doing. Maybe meet for coffee? I think about you often—so much of what happened in the lab with our supportive, sympathetic mentor Dr. Greene (*note sarcasm! haha, speaking of a-holes*) seemed wrong to me, and I guess I'll always feel frustrated that things went the way they did. I'm not meaning to bring up something that's unpleasant for you, but I always wonder if maybe there was more I could have done. Not that you needed *my* help. I just don't understand what happened. You're one of the smartest people I've ever met. And entertaining, too. I'll never forget the laughs we used to have, talking about anything and everything—like that time we imbibed a pint of ale, and you explained to me that some people keep a list of aspirational sex partners, in the event that an improbable opportunity should arise (no pun intended, upon my word!). Is John Oliver still your #1? I have invested a lot of time fine-tuning my list and will reveal to you my current roster: Mindy Kaling has taken the honoured top spot, replacing physicist Lisa Randall, who moves into the number 2 position, followed by numero 3 (you said I could take liberties with time), the lovely Jean Simmons in the role of Ophelia (1948). Sticking with your suggestion that I name only people who are truly out of my (nay, *any* mortal's) league, I removed that lab technician I told you about because although she hasn't shown any interest in me specifically, she has slept with over half the people in the department, which makes me think she isn't what you defined as "aspirational."

Dost thou remember Lakshmi? She sends greetings. We were both asserting recently that the lab (or "graveyard" as you often called it) was much more fun when you were toiling there alongside us. The biggest change since you took your leave of us is that Prof. Greene is away on sabbatical promoting his new book. He is hoping to reach a more general audience in order to generate interest in the work we do. In the meantime, I'm finishing up my dissertation and entering the job market, which will be a bit tricky without the guidance of said mentor, not that he ever gives me the time of day, but alas. If everything goes really well, I could land a sweet, tenure-track position at the Univ of KS, aka KU. Have you ever been to Lawrence? Do you think I'd be happy there?

I'd love to hear from you. You were always so nice, and I, for one, appreciated it because, in case you didn't pick up on this, I don't always have great success when conversing with the ladies. I've missed your friendship. And I hope you never underestimate yourself because I think the world of you.

Thine evermore, whilst this machine is to him,
Sherman

December

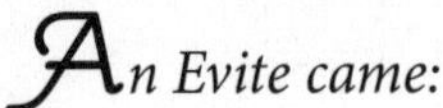

An Evite came:

Please come to an Open House Holiday Cookie Exchange With The Upton-Pearsons

December 8

2:00 until 6:00

Bring the kids and a dozen cookies along with the recipe.

Merry, Merry!

Angela, Doug, and Emily

I happen to be very good at baking cookies, and I'm the only person I know who likes to hang out with children at a party. It crossed my mind that this might be a perfect moment to come clean with everyone about my new roommate. I liked the idea of a coming-out party for George, but I couldn't for the life of me understand why Angela had invited me. And then I realized that the invitation had been forwarded from Vicki.

I texted her: What's the deal? I wasn't invited, was I?

Hours later she texted me back: Just come anyway! It's casual, and I'm sure Angela won't mind.

"We're not going," I told George, climbing into bed with him. He was wearing a wool hat and long underwear. Our heat didn't work at all, so I got as close as I could.

"Why not? I thought I could finally meet your friends."

"Angela's not my friend. You can meet Kate some other time. And Vicki, too, although you may fall in love with her."

"Why will I fall in love with Vicki?"

"Everyone does. But she's going by Victoria now, so don't call her Vicki or you may put her off."

"You call her Vicki."

"I'm not trying to sleep with her."

"Neither am I."

"I don't get why Vicki would try to get me to go to someone else's party. It's weird, don't you think?"

"I don't know her, so it's hard to say. Are you going to tell Kate about the veterinarian you broke up with?" George asked.

"The veterinarian's a better fit for me actually. I could get used to an old farmhouse. A barn? Rescue llamas? Acres?"

"If there's a llama in need of rescue, you would be the one to take him in."

"You think?"

"Knowing you," he said, "you'd be outdoors feeding all the wildlife, and making them get along with each other so they can share a trough."

"I wouldn't want conflict on my acres."

"And you would make them all presents for their birthdays."

"Obviously."

"Are you running off with the veterinarian?" George asked. "Or can I come to the farm with you?"

"You're definitely coming with me," I told him.

The next morning I baked four dozen chocolate chip oatmeal cookies. Who needs a stupid party anyway?

Applicant: Claudia Gutierrez
Date: December 14
Interviewed by Kate

Claudia is a funny, bright, sensitive, wonderful girl applying to 7th—She is terrific! I liked her right away. She was entirely present in her conversation with me—clearly knows what she wants in a school, has numerous interests (a science girl, biology in particular) and great curiosity. The time flew—we talked about school, friends, and life in general. She's a very mature, motivated young lady, and she thinks she wants to be a doctor when she grows up.

This sweet girl was bullied last year, but she has an amazing upbeat, optimistic attitude. The bully did NOT get the best of her. We could all learn something from Claudia. She said, "There will always be a few mean kids out there, and one thing I learned is how important it is to make friends with the nice ones." So true! Claudia struck me as such a perceptive young woman that I presented her with a hypothetical scenario, just to get her take on it.

Let's say—hypothetically—a girl was invited to her sister's holiday cookie party. She shows up about halfway through the party and finds out there was an incident earlier that got ugly. Doug, a member of the family, is on the couch with an ice pack on his nose and a bag of frozen peas on his balls. Her sister is eating cookies and raving, and the party guests look at the girl like she's got explosives strapped on her back.

"What's going on?" the girl asks.

Her sister tells her that a friend, whom we'll call "Vicki," showed up at the party with the biggest bully of all time, a boy who once did something really mean to the girl.

"He was here? With Vicki?" the girl asks. "Why? And what happened to Doug?"

"Doug threw him out," the girl's sister explains. "He didn't want him here."

The questions I posed: What would make someone bring a known bully to a party? Is Vicki a friend or not? WWCD?

Claudia is thoughtful and says, "Don't jump to any conclusions. It's like when you read a novel, and you need to find out a character's motivations." So true, and nice metaphor, by the way! This girl is only eleven, and she knows how to handle cookie party drama better than I do. Her message was: "I would be direct and confront my friend. Ask her why she brought the bully to the party, why the bully wanted to come, and why they were together in the first place. Rather than speculate, just ask her."

Claudia talked about how she learned that some friends aren't good for you. She said that a person who treats another person badly isn't a person that that person should want in the person's life. (She said it better than that.) She also said, "That guy Doug? He's one of the good guys."

Claudia and I had such an interesting conversation, talking about the people in her life, the friends she can count on and the ones who are cruel or just plain stupid. Claudia has her head on straight.

I met with Claudia's mother who is a real-life superwoman. She works two jobs and is raising Claudia all on her own since her husband died (cancer, something Claudia didn't talk about). She wants her daughter to go to a school that will challenge her, and she noted that Claudia, like Hudson itself, is neat and orderly. She keeps her room spotless and her backpack organized. She color-codes everything and loves nothing more than making flash cards. She and Claudia both like the idea of a school with a uniform because it would help mask glaring socioeconomic differences that are so obvious among kids when they are free to choose their own clothes.

All in all this was a wonderful interview with a smart, sweet, and conscientious girl. Did I mention she plays violin? Her troubles contributed heavily to the minor academic struggles she had there (mostly As but a few Bs). But believe me—Claudia would be a superstar here, academically and in every other way. She will need financial support (like the whole thing), and we should give it to her. I love this girl! Yes! Yes!

To: Angela
From: Nancy
Subject: Apologies

I'm so sorry we couldn't make it to your holiday party. What a lovely invitation. We were all set to go when poor Gus started complaining about a sore throat. He's fine by the way, but I didn't want to risk spreading a bug, especially during the holidays.

Would really love to meet your sister who works at Hudson. When would be good? How about early January? Coffee or lunch would work best for me.

Nancy

To: Kate
From: Victoria
Subject: Misunderstanding

I'm glad you asked me about the situation at Angela's party because I've been meaning to get in touch with you anyway. The whole thing was absurd because Doug totally overreacted, and I can't understand why. Given his insane reaction, it was better that you weren't there when we showed up, unless you could have calmed him down.

I was only trying to help. Since you're doing so well, I thought it would be good for you to see Robert. He wants to apologize to you so that we can all be friends. It's awkward for us, you know. I've known Robert since college, and suddenly I'm supposed to never speak to him again? And what about Chloe? She and Robert are family—what's she supposed to do? Cut him off permanently? It's important to her that we can at least all be in a room together.

I was *of course* planning to tell you that Robert had been in touch with me. I told Angela first because I wanted to make sure it was a good idea for you to see him, and she agreed that it was. I assumed you wouldn't mind hearing what he has to say. Just a chance to apologize—is that really too much to ask? Angela and I thought it seemed reasonable, but her crazy husband completely flipped out and started a barbaric fistfight right in front of everyone. It was embarrassing and unnecessary.

So tell me honestly: are you over Robert or what? I assumed after all this time that you've finally moved on. Was I wrong?

Ciao,
Victoria

To: Kate

From: Angela

Subject: Christmas at my place, you're coming, right?

I don't know what she told you, but I had absolutely NO idea Victoria was going to bring that asshole to my party. All she told me was that she thought at some point Robert should apologize to you in person so that you can really feel like that entire nightmare is behind you. How she translated that to bringing him to my apartment, I really can't begin to understand.

Your choice of friends has me baffled. These girls do not seem to have your best interest at heart. And what's the deal with the date you brought with you—*Sherman?!*—and why was he wearing a "tuxedo" sweatshirt? The guy is short on style, I guess. I didn't get a chance to talk to him, but Doug said he was very nice and insanely smart. But be careful, Kate. Go slow. Sloooooow.

And another thing—why would you go out to dinner with your BOSS? I thought we went over this already. I mean, Kate, you must, you absolutely must set appropriate boundaries with him. Seriously, that's just common sense. You're new to the whole workplace dos and don'ts, but I'm not. Dinner for two is a big don't. How do you think his wife would feel about it?

Mom sent us marzipan and a Christmas card with a drawing of that sadistic Knecht Ruprecht and the bundle of switches he uses for hitting naughty children. A god-awful invention if you ask me (the switches, not the marzipan).

The card says (verbatim):

Happy Christmas, my dearest girls. As we enter the New Year, keep in mind that finding a grub can define success.

Southward Ho!

All our love,
Mami and Papi

P.S. The children in Finland read late but brilliantly.

Translate, please, because as usual, I don't get it. Grubs?? What?

On another note—I have a friend Nancy whose son Gus is applying to Hudson, and she asked if she could meet you. I know you're new there, but anything you can tell her about admissions, she'd appreciate.

Angela

To: Nancy

From: Sam

Subject: what is your problem

---

how can you be this pissed off. i'm in singapore for christ sake. i was supposed to come back for a fucking cookie party? are you out of your fucking mind? mountain out of mole hill. ask dr. richards. he'll tell you you're being crazy.

S

To: Sam

From: Nancy

Subject: Fuck off

Dr. Richards is a she. How can you not know this? Gus needs to get into a school, and this would have been a perfect way to make a personal connection. Whatever. I'll handle everything on my own like I always do since you're NEVER here and clearly don't give a damn about me or Gus. You should be honest if you're cheating on me. I do not want a disease.

Gus might be a big pain in the ass but guess what's a bigger pain in the ass? Homeschooling.

—me

PARENT STATEMENT for Gus Smith
From: Nancy and Sam Smith

Gus is our delightful ray of sunshine, and we believe that Hudson Day offers an environment that is wonderfully suited to his happy disposition and perfectly in line with his learning style. He just loves to go to school every day. Gus has had a fabulous elementary school experience, and we are excited to watch him venture off to the next steps: middle school and beyond! As an only child, Gus is a wonderful and caring family member, and we continue to be impressed by his leadership and example.

Gus, while special to us, is in many ways a typical young boy and spends his time on all the activities other boys his age enjoy: sports, friends, homework, and play. He is quite an artist! We noted that even at an early age he had a real "eye." When he was younger he would color and color until every single bit of white paper was covered in crayon. As he got older he developed a gift for rendering objects, whether in colored pencil or acrylic paint. He is truly quite remarkable! His picture "Still Life with Watermelon" is hanging on the wall of our kitchen. His ability to create works of art is one he will surely wish to develop in the art studios of Hudson Day, and it is our wish to see his paintings gracing your lovely halls.

Sam and I support Gus in every way we can; it is a constant joy to be his loving parents.

We are happy to share any further insights about Gus, and we look forward to hearing from you.

Sincerely,
Sam and Nancy Smith

To: Sherman

From: Kate

Subject: heaps of thanks

Hey, just wanted to say thanks again so much for going with me to my sister's party, and sorry we walked into such a crazy scene—you're a good sport. It was so nice to see you! The rehashing of my unhappy months in the lab was incredibly therapeutic, so I have to thank you for that as well. And while your confidence in me is very heartening, I believe that Prof. Greene was not entirely wrong and, on some level, knew what he was doing, even if his manner was demeaning. Did he finally get your letter of rec written, or is he still caught up on the book tour?

On a brighter note, I'm so excited for you about Lakshmi—I always admired and respected her, and I think you guys are perfect together. She is one lucky lady because you are a total catch, my friend. I hope you guys have a smashing time at the renaissance faire. Sounds awesome.

Keeping my fingers crossed for you on the job front. Let me know when you hear.

Kate

Dear Ms. Pearson,

Thank you so much for interviewing me the other day. I really liked talking to you, and you were the best interviewer I have had so far! I loved everything you told me about the school. The students sound so nice, and I'm sure I would love taking science classes, meeting new friends, and reading all the good books you teach there.

Thanks a million for the time you took talking to me. I was nervous before I met you, but it turned out to be really fun.

Sincerely yours,
Claudia

P.S. Did you talk to your friend? I have been trying to think up a good reason why she did that, and I can't. Sorry.

To: Chloe

From: Kate

Subject: thank you

Thanks for the oatmeal cookies!—they were ridiculous. I shared them with everyone here and am getting very popular because of you. I wish I'd seen you when you came by, but as usual I was in the middle of an interview. I miss you, and I'm so disappointed that I had to cancel our plans last night. I thought the Hudson holiday party was just going to be some quick after-work thing, but it turned out that it's this major event, and it went on until after 10:00. Great food and so much wine—you cannot imagine how much high school teachers drink. Wow.

I assume you heard about the infamous party? Don't want to put you in the middle of things, but "Victoria" already did, and we need to talk about Robert. It's time for you to patch things up with him. I don't want you to stay mad at him because of me, okay? I know how close you two are. And I should have told you something a long time ago—my collapse, my meltdown, whatever it was, was not only about Robert. There was other stuff going on, and I'd like to explain it all to you someday. But meanwhile, don't be angry with Robert anymore. It's over and done with.

But Vicki? I don't get it. It's not like she and Robert were ever such good friends. Can you explain what she's up to?

I'm at work all the time, up to my ears in files to read. This job is way, way more intense than I thought it would be. I'd love to get together once we've finally sent our decisions out in February.

Oh, and why are you asking me about farms? Is this some volunteer thing, like growing vegetables for children who live in urban "food deserts"? I'm happy to help with a project if you need it although I'm not really into nature. Also, do you think it can wait until after the admissions season is over? I'm swamped.

Xoxo K

ISEE SCORES

Student: Dillon Blake

Verbal Reasoning: **1**

Reading Comprehension: **2**

Quantitative Reasoning: **1**

Mathematics Achievement: **1**

ESSAY: In the space below please describe your idea of a perfect day.

A perfect day for me wuld be hanging out with my friends and doing nothing but hanging out them. We wuld hang out, talk, and play video games.

We wuld hang out because my friends and me like to hang out together and laugh. At school we play chase in the yard and play tackel.

We wuld talk. I like talking my friends because it is fun. We say funny things and make jokes.

We wuld be playing video games the whole day. I am a leval 8 and I wuld kill evryone and beat my friends and say, "AAHHHHHHHH, I killed you!" re-ally loud.

That wuld be my perfect day.

January

"I love to cook," I told my date. "I would cook every night of the week if I didn't work so late all the time."

"I prefer to eat out," he said. I was clearly boring him, but I liked how polite he was about it. He hadn't checked his phone once since he'd sat down. "It's great that you have something you like to do."

"A home-cooked meal isn't your idea of heaven?" I asked.

"No, not really. All those dirty dishes to deal with."

"Would you ever want to live on a farm?" I asked.

He put his coffee cup on the table. "I'm afraid not. Sorry."

The "sorry" killed me because he said it so sincerely, like he felt really bad for disappointing me. What a nice guy. "I'd like to have a vegetable garden," I went on, and then I had to remind myself again that this wasn't about me.

"Not really my thing, gardens, yards, cooking, any of that. But, hey, kudos for finding a passion."

We'd been talking for over half an hour, and I found this man so appealing, in spite of the fact that we had absolutely nothing in common. He seemed mature in a way that I thought might be good for Kate. He was handsome and possibly a little uptight, but I couldn't tell for sure. He was grounded, that's what it was. Grounded. Exactly what Kate needed. He was a left-leaning, lonely doctor, finishing his residency at a psychiatric hospital. He had no time to meet women and spent most of his time with people who were either severely deranged or highly medicated. Kate would seem so stable in comparison. It was too good to be true.

"Can I come clean with you about something?" I asked.

"We have no chemistry?"

"Are you allowed to say that?"

"I think so, unless you think it's rude. In which case, I apologize."

"It's blunt, but it's okay." I took a deep breath, and plunged in. "I

want you to meet a friend of mine. She's smart and fabulous, and I think maybe you'd like each other."

"Do you always pass your bad dates along to other people?"

"You're not a bad date. And I don't ever do this. Ever. Her name's Kate."

"Another Kate?"

"Sorry, I'm Chloe."

"Your profile says Kate."

"Yeah, well, Kate's coming out of a rough patch."

"What's that a euphemism for? She's a recovering meth addict? A schizophrenic? How rough are we talking?"

"Nothing like that," I said. "She was just in a slump, and to be honest it was all my fault, so if I could set her up with you, and it worked out, then I'd be legit off the hook for messing up her life."

"Kate . . ."

"Chloe," I corrected.

"Were you planning to fix me up with her all along?"

"Yes."

"Doesn't that break some kind of Internet dating etiquette?"

"If you end up liking her, what difference would it make?"

"I'm not interested, but thank you."

"A few years ago," I began, knowing that this man was far too polite to walk out on me, "I introduced Kate to my cousin, and it didn't work out."

"Then maybe you should stay out of the matchmaking business."

"No—I didn't say I set her up with him. I introduced them the way you have to introduce two people when you know them both and they don't know each other. I never meant for them to get together. But they did, and it was a catastrophe, and now I want a chance to set her up with someone for real. It's kind of a long story."

"I need to get back to the hospital."

"My cousin, Robert, he's a very judgmental, critical person,

and Kate is open and understanding, and I just didn't think they made any sense together. But next thing you know, Kate's moving to France to live with him. She seemed really happy, so I was just hoping he would make himself worthy of her. Can I buy you another cup of coffee?"

"I have to go."

"The day before she was leaving New York for good, Robert called me from Paris, and he told me he wants to end it with her. He doesn't see it working out between them, he can't commit, he wants out. So I asked him if he'd been drinking, and he said yes. So I said, 'Just go to sleep. You're being a dick for no reason, as usual.' What was I supposed to do?"

He shook his head. "I have no idea."

"You think I should have told her?" I asked.

"How do I know? I don't even know these people."

"I didn't tell her." I waited for a reaction, but I got nothing. "I had no idea he would do something so terrible. He wasn't even at the airport when she got there. She called him, woke him up, and when he finally showed up, he dumped her right there in the international terminal. And then—to make matters worse—he asks her why she's surprised to hear it. 'Didn't Chloe tell you before you left?' "

"Okay, maybe the guy's a jerk, but . . ."

"You think I should have told her."

"I don't know. Maybe. Are you even trying to meet anyone yourself? Or is this whole thing a ploy?"

I shook my head. "I'm living with someone. No one knows about him yet, so don't tell Kate when you meet her."

"I didn't say I'd meet her."

"You should."

"I think—professionally speaking—you should stop feeling responsible for what other people do."

"You sound just like George."

"Who's George?" he asked.

"My boyfriend."

"Well, I can't speak for George, but I can tell you it's actually a form of egotism. You're making everything about yourself while you pretend to be thinking of others."

"No, not at all," I said, feeling suddenly defensive. "I'm being a good friend. And it's not easy given the cast of characters. I might not be responsible for Vicki's actions, but as her friend, I have to get involved when she does something stupid."

"Vicki?" he asked.

"She's our friend who for some reason showed up at a party recently with Robert. I can't imagine what she was thinking. I'm not even speaking to him, and somehow she thinks it's okay to take him to a party?"

"And she's your problem, too?"

"Obviously."

"This might be presumptuous, but I think you need to see someone about this."

"What's wrong with wanting to fix things?"

"Taken to the extreme it's a disorder. It's pathological egotism—you're playing God, meddling in the affairs of mortals. You don't trust people to do the right thing because you think you're superior to them."

"This isn't about me at all. Do you do this to all your dates? Psychoanalyze them? Because I can kind of see why you're single."

"Apparently we're not here for a date."

"Well, your diagnosis of me is way off. I am the least self-absorbed person you'll ever meet. All I do is think of others. I work on behalf of the homeless. Is that egotism? I don't think so."

"I see," he said, working that into the equation. "Then maybe you're bringing your work home; you're social-working your friends, and you haven't asked them if that's what they want. Let your friends be in charge of their own bad decisions.

What's-her-name? Vicki? She's obviously got something going on with your cousin, and that's her choice, not yours. You can't stop her from sleeping with someone, even if her actions are going to hurt your friend, that other girl—Chloe."

"Kate. No, wait, you're so off base here. Vicki is not sleeping with Robert."

"Of course she is. It's obvious. What other reason could she possibly have for bringing a guy who's persona non grata *to a party unless it's to bring him back into the fold so that he becomes acceptable again, so that she can sleep with him aboveboard, except that she already is sleeping with him, and now she wants retro-approval for that, probably from you because she clearly doesn't care about the other girl. Kate. Think about it."*

I sat there trying to process the information he'd hit me with.

"Oh," he went on, "and the girl? Vicki? She's not just sleeping with your cousin. She actually likes him. If it were only about sex or if it was a one-time thing, she wouldn't bother involving her friends. She's probably in a real relationship with him and wants it to become serious."

"What?" I asked.

"That's my opinion, anyway."

"No way."

"It makes sense, though, right? I'm only trying to help."

"Then stop speculating about all this, and meet Kate," I said. "That would be helpful. What's the harm?"

"I don't want any part of this mess. I work with crazy people all day long."

"Touché."

"So you don't work in admissions?"

"No, Kate does."

"And she wants to grow vegetables?"

"No, I do."

"We need to start over."

I felt encouraged. "Kate works in admissions. She's a city girl, smart as hell, and a total romantic. She's on my short list of favorite people in the entire world. She's a gem and you probably don't deserve her."

I remembered saying the exact same words to Robert on the phone the night before Kate flew to France, trying to talk him out of dumping a girl who was way, way too good for him to begin with. He was mumbling words at me I couldn't understand. "Speak up," I'd said.

"Eeet's just not going to work for me," Robert had repeated, and I could picture him shrugging, feet up on his coffee table, the stupid Seine out his window. "You know me, Chloe. Giving zings up for someone else? Eeet's not in my nature."

"Robert?" I had asked. "Why are you whispering?"

I smiled at my new friend, who was looking at me with a mixture of curiosity and amusement.

"This has been a very peculiar date," he said.

"So you'll meet her?" I asked.

"I'm not sure," he said, "but I'll think about it."

ISEE SCORES

Student: Annie Allsworth

Verbal Reasoning: **7**

Reading Comprehension: **8**

Quantitative Reasoning: **9**

Mathematics Achievement: **9**

ESSAY: In the space below please describe your idea of a perfect day.

There are many days I would consider wonderful, but on a perfect day I would spend time with family, read a good book, and help others.

I love to spend time with my family. There are so many activities we do together, like skiing, snorkeling, going to museums in France, and helping out at a soup kitchen. My mom always makes sure we do things that are a good use of our time, and she always tells me every day how special I am. When I am with my family, I feel very warm and happy.

On my perfect day I would find time to settle down with a good book. The Carcassonne Castle books are my favorite at the moment because I love reading about olden times and kings and queens. Reading makes me feel good and it is something that I do for at least twenty-five minutes every day. When we are at our house in the Hamptons, I get in the hammock by the beach and read for hours. A day without reading would make me sad because I love to read!

Finally on my perfect day, I would want to spend time helping others. There are so many people in the *world who need our help, like Africa, and I would spend time feeding children or cleaning a park or building a school or finding clean water or going to the soup kitchen. It is important for people like me who have so much to spend time with people who have nothing. That way you know how lucky you are.*

In conclusion, it would be wonderful to have a perfect day where I could spend time with my family, read a good book, and help others. That would make me very fulfilled.

To: Henry Bigley
From: Mel Branson
Subject: 6th grade applicant Gus Smith

Hello Henry,

I am writing regarding a wonderful student I am currently placing for 6th grade, Gus Smith. You will likely note in Gus's otherwise stellar first semester report card from Horizons (which you will receive sometime this month) the words "Three Day Disciplinary Suspension." There was an incident last week, and I feel—as do his parents, Nancy and Sam—that it is appropriate and fair for me to give you Gus's side of the story.

Gus has repeatedly told his teacher and the principal (this is documented) that there is a girl in his class who torments and distracts him during lessons. This girl has been continually poking at him, teasing him, and laughing at him. It was "harmless" according to the teacher, but beyond aggravating for Gus. The other day she was taunting him about his personal choice to wear pink socks to school, but this time she got a rather large group of girls to join in with her at recess and lunch. They targeted him throughout the remainder of that day and began again the following morning. He has marks on his arms from where they pinched him. The teacher did nothing to help him, and his patience finally wore out. He issued a stern ultimatum—in so many words—"please stop it or else." His teacher wrote in the report you will receive that she also heard expletives and insults, but it is hard for me to believe any young boy would use phrases like "vicious thug," "two-bit whore," and "dim-witted troglodyte."

The girl told her parents that she perceived Gus's ultimatum as a threat against her life. She "feared for her safety," which is beyond ridiculous. It was self-defense, nothing more. However, the principal decided that Gus would stay home from school for a few days to write a letter of apology to the girl. Gus was told that he will not receive such a letter in return as the girl's parents claim she has nothing to apologize for. In my view, Horizons handled this situation poorly, particularly as the teacher seems oblivious as to what goes on in her own classroom. I'm sure Hudson would have dealt with it in a more nuanced and just manner. I can assure you, Gus is a sensitive, unusually interesting young man, and I am sure he will impress you if you keep an open mind.

As Hudson is one of the family's top choices, I simply ask that you not hold this incident against him.

Please contact me if I can answer any questions regarding this or anything else in Gus's application.

Best regards,
Mel

To: Angela
From: Nancy
Subject: Your sister and Hudson Day School admissions

Hi there! Hey! Happy New Year! Wow, is it January already? Where does the time go?! I was thinking it would be such fun to get together sometime soon. This week would work for me.

On a different note—do you remember when you offered to have me meet your sister who works at Hudson?—Well, I would just really love to take you up on that! I can meet wherever you like—my treat, of course—whenever it is convenient for you! I don't work, so I can be very flexible, as long as it doesn't conflict with my personal training session. That's the only thing set in stone. Soon would be best simply because of the timing of the application process. Gus, Sam, and I have our interview there next week, and it would be great to pick her brain before then. Gus had a little hiccup at school, a minor misunderstanding with another student, and I'd like to ask your sister how best to gloss over it. I know you said she's new there and may not know too much yet, but I'd like to meet her anyway.

All the best for a Happy New Year!
Nancy

Kate, Henry, and Maureen were becoming a well-coordinated team, reading files, answering emails, updating the electronic tracker, and finishing up the last few weeks of interviews. It was halfway through the school year, and Kate was starting to feel like she understood how things worked. She handled phone calls with a professional and friendly tone and entered testing data with accuracy. She helped file away hundreds of packets of admissions materials and had the paper cuts to prove it.

She was gaining confidence, in large part because she spent frequent afternoons and occasional evenings with Henry, talking about everything from the kindergarten art show to the middle school musical to the college office. He seemed determined to get her up to speed.

Tours were now fun. Kate walked large groups of families through the school, introducing them to teachers and students, like she was a White House tour guide, running into the president himself. And the First Lady and the chief of staff. "Now isn't this a happy surprise? This is Ms. Banter, the head of our English department. She's an inspiring teacher who does a particularly fascinating set of lectures on Civil War poetry for our sixth-graders."

"Oh, look! Over here in the lab—this is an eighth-grade science class, preparing to do an astronomy lesson that promotes an understanding of the ratio of distances between planets."

"Hello, Coach Stafford! These families were just asking me about athletics offerings for middle schoolers. Anything you want to tell them about the PE program?"

"Hey there, Avery! Nice job in the basketball game yesterday—way to go! Oh—can you tell our visitors what you're doing in sixth-grade history this week? I heard something interesting about a civil rights debate."

Kate had a regular paycheck, a busy schedule, and lively

workdays that involved constant socialization. No more solitary, silent days of cleaning up raw data in a fluorescently lit lab space. No more solitary, depressing days of watching *Sex and the City* reruns and lolling on the couch. Instead, she was involved in conversations all day long, talking with kids, eating lunch with teachers, and spending hours with prospective families.

"How do you size people up like you do?" Maureen asked.

"What do you mean?"

"You talked to that family in the lobby this morning and said I better watch out for them."

"The short kid with the weird boy-bangs?"

"What a hairdo."

"I think he's trying to cover up his trichotillomania," Kate said.

"What?"

Kate shrugged. "I don't know. I was just guessing."

"I interviewed the family, and that poor boy is one screwed-up little psycho. And the hair, my God. What did you say he has?"

"Trichotillomania?"

"Is that a fancy word for hideous hairstyle?"

"Hair pulling. It's an impulse control thing. He had a huge gap in one of his eyebrows that was filled in with pencil. I'm thinking he got the bangs to hide it."

"That's what that was?"

"It's a pretty interesting disorder. I'm not being mean. I'm just being descriptive."

"I'm being mean. That kid is a freak, and he asked weird questions, like is anyone going to know what he keeps in his locker, and what kind of punishments do kids get for breaking rules, like he was hoping to hear bare-ass spanking. I got a bad vibe from him."

"Sounds like he has anxiety. Poor kid."

"Poor me. I had to spend half an hour with Spanky, trying to get him to say something normal, but he just twitched around in his chair and told me stories about his pet turtle."

"But he had a tic, didn't he? Made faces like he was yawning?"

"That's what that was? I just thought he was tired."

"Could be a neurological issue, like Tourette's syndrome. If that's what he has, a stressful situation, like an interview, can cause an increase in involuntary movements. And hair pulling might be his way of dealing with stress. I wrote a paper in college about some patients who pull out their hair and then eat it; they can actually get matted hairballs in their digestive tracts and die."

"Bullshit."

"It's true. I'll send you an article."

"Please don't. I've heard enough for one lifetime." Maureen looked through the stack of files she was holding. "You know, you're not nearly as bad at this job as I thought you were going to be." They'd gotten in the habit of visiting each other a few times a day to talk about anything from applicants to shoes to YouTube videos. "But I told you not to fall in love." Maureen found the file she was looking for and dropped it on Kate's desk.

"Claudia?"

"She needs a full ride. And she won't rise to the top."

"What does that mean?" Kate asked.

"You'll see when we go into committee."

"No, but I really want her to come here. And she's so smart."

"Don't fall in love."

"It's too late," Kate told her.

"Someone certainly likes you. Who sent those?"

Kate opened the box of handcrafted European chocolates on her desk and offered them to Maureen. "Chloe."

"That girl has a thing for you. Chocolates, flowers. Has she sent you lingerie yet? Because Valentine's Day is right around the corner." Maureen bit into a piece of chocolate. "Your girlfriend must have a lot of money."

"Not at all," Kate said. "She's just incredibly nice."

"No one's that nice. I told Henry I didn't think you were gay because you have a hang-up on that old boyfriend. Not that we were talking about you behind your back or anything, but we were." She put another chocolate in her mouth. "If you ask me, that girl is hot for you. If you're not interested, you should tell her so that she can stop running up her credit card on you. These chocolates are pricey."

"We're just friends."

"Then she wants something from you. Does she have a kid she's trying to get into school?"

"No, she doesn't even have a boyfriend."

"So what does she want, then? Think."

"I don't know. Maybe she just wants to make me happy."

"Wrong answer." Maureen ate another chocolate, and Kate had one, too, so Maureen wouldn't feel bad about it. They chewed while Kate thought that over.

"She shouldn't, but she blames herself for a little breakdown I had. He's her cousin."

"Who?"

"Robert. The guy who dumped me."

"I already told you," Maureen said, "I don't want to hear about him."

"I was only saying—"

"Breakup stories bore the shit out of me. If you meet a new man, I'm happy to listen, but I look forward, not back."

"There's nothing to say—I'm completely over him."

"Good, because I'm not going to sit around listening to you crying. You're young, employed, and thin, so don't feel sorry for yourself."

"I wish someone had said that to me a year ago."

"And never let some guy mess with your head."

"I don't. I didn't. I mean, I was feeling sorry for myself, but it wasn't only because of the guy."

"Good," Maureen said, "because I'm trying hard not to dislike you. No time for bullshit. January is the worst. And if you think this is bad, wait until we get to February. And March is no picnic, either. Henry and I refer to this as the dark time."

"You keep telling me that, and you're making me nervous."

Kate's phone rang.

"Back to work," Maureen said suddenly and walked out. Kate swallowed the rest of the chocolate and picked up the phone.

"Kate? Silvia Blake here. I'd like a word."

The name Silvia rang a bell, but she was over a hundred interviews into the season, and she struggled to remember who she was. Funny how some people assumed they were so memorable. She put her on speaker and checked her laptop to find the write-up. Ah yes, of course. Her very first interview. Silvia. Alum, old husband, Dillon's parents.

"We got the scores, Dillon's ISEE scores," she said and laughed uncomfortably. "I was wondering if you'd seen them yet."

Kate had seen them. Maureen and Henry had passed the report back and forth in fits of laughter. Maureen put Dillon Blake in first place for both world's dumbest child and shittiest essay of the decade, while Kate had said, "Ahh, come on. He's just a kid." Maureen had made a mad face at her and walked away.

"I haven't seen the report," Kate lied to Silvia on the phone, "but I'm sure it's in his file already."

"Well, Kate, let me just start by saying how much Kenneth and I enjoyed meeting you last October and how sure we are that Dillon would be a star at Hudson. He's a perfect fit for you. You said so yourself."

"I remember saying there's a process . . ."

"In any case, Dillon's having a great semester, but something seems to have gone wrong with the ISEE testing. His scores aren't correct." She laughed again. "I mean, they can't be. The machine or computer or something—it was off that day. On the fritz. There's just no way Dillon did poorly. He's very smart. Kenneth's daughter, Bailey, isn't *nearly* as smart as Dillon, and she got eights and nines. This just doesn't make any sense."

"Have you called the testing company?" Kate asked, recalling Henry's lesson on standardized testing debacles. "Sometimes students mismark their bubble sheets; they get off by one question and that throws off the whole test."

"That's definitely what happened. Definitely something like that. I knew you'd understand. I wondered if you could put a note in his file, a note explaining that the scores aren't accurate. Or even valid."

"I'd be happy to put a note in saying you're concerned about them."

There was a pause and Kate heard Silvia exhaling hard. "I'm not concerned about them," she said firmly. "Why would I be concerned? We just established that the scores are wrong."

"Well," Kate said, reading from her notes, "in this situation, in addition to contacting the testing company, some people—just to consider all possibilities—some parents take their child to an educational psychologist to get further testing, to rule out any sort of issue, learning issue, I mean."

"Are you saying you think Dillon's retarded or something?"

"Excuse me? Not at all."

"You wouldn't write off a kid over some stupid test," she said. "These scores are some kind of mistake. Besides, don't you read the newspaper? Standardized testing is meaningless anyway. Top universities are moving away from the SATs entirely."

"If the scores aren't in sync with what you believe are Dillon's abilities—"

"What I *believe* are his abilities?" Silvia asked. "I think I *know* my child's abilities."

"—with what you've observed," Kate clarified, "with how he does in school . . . then one option is a comprehensive evaluation. It could give us a better picture—"

"I don't believe this. I don't want *more* testing. I just want you to waive the scores. They're wrong—throw them out. Why is this a problem?"

Kate didn't say anything for a moment. She tried to imagine how hard it would be to receive your kid's scores and have them be *that* low. Terribly disappointing. And would you be disappointed in the scores or the child? Both probably. Or neither if you were Mrs. Blake, who was clearly in deep denial.

"You'll have recommendations," she was saying. "You'll have grades, you'll have all kinds of information on which to base your decision. You won't need some inaccurate, idiotic test score."

"We look at everything very thoroughly," Kate said, trying to sound reassuring, "and we discuss—"

"And as for this test," Silvia interrupted, "let me explain this to you clearly for the record: these numbers don't mean anything in Dillon's case. They're wrong. My son is terrific. People love him. He plays soccer like a pro and guitar like a rock star. And he's tall."

"I'm sorry, did you say 'tall'?"

"He's tall for his age."

Kate was stumped. "We can't really take his height into consideration," she said.

"It gets you somewhere in life. People respect a man who's tall."

"But wouldn't that imply that we would reject a student for being short?"

"That makes more sense than judging *my* son on some ridiculous fill-in-the-bubble test."

"I assure you, Mrs. Blake, as you said, the test is only one factor, it's just one part of the application, and we carefully review the whole folder . . ." she said, trying to calm her.

"I've heard enough," she said suddenly. "I want to talk to someone in charge over there. Transfer me to Henry Bigley."

"Of course," Kate sighed. "My pleasure," and she transferred the call.

Passing the call to Henry felt like failure. She hadn't handled it on her own, she'd made a parent angry, she'd screwed up, just when she'd thought she was getting the hang of things. She thought about going into Henry's office to sit with him during the call, but then that seemed weird, like she'd be eavesdropping or invading his privacy.

Her phone rang again.

"Hey." It was Angela, making a noon check-in call.

"Hey."

"How's it going?"

"Meh."

"You okay?"

"Medium," Kate said. "This job is hard."

"Just do your work and be professional."

"Duh. That's not even helpful."

"And don't have dinner with your boss again. Honestly, Kate. You know better."

"It was for work. I learned a lot actually."

"Don't be naïve. It's unattractive at your age. Clear boundaries. Please don't make me feel bad for introducing you to him."

"Give me a little credit, would you? How are you feeling?"

"Like God's joke on women. Girthy."

"I don't know what that means."

"Rotund. Doug made a joke about how I weigh more than he does, but it wasn't funny because it's true. I actually do. Did you get a chance to call my friend Nancy?"

"Not yet," Kate said, adding that to her to-do list.

"Please call her. She's not asking for special treatment or anything. She just wants a chance to say hello."

"I will."

"Did you ever talk to Vicki?"

"No. I don't want to, and honestly I can't be bothered right now."

"Just so you know—as stupid as that was—I think she was trying to help you put the whole thing behind you. You know? Forgive and forget?"

"Then she should have asked me first," Kate said firmly, "because I could have told her I look forward not back. I've already put it behind me. I don't think about him, and I don't need any more closure than I already have."

"Really, Kate?"

"Yes, really."

"You sound tired," Angela said, "but you sort of sound good. Do you know what I mean?"

"Yes, I do. It's exactly how I feel."

"Me, too," Angela said. "So no more dinners with your boss, right?"

"Angela, stop."

"I'm just saying."

They hung up, and Kate stuffed another chocolate in her mouth, just as Henry came to the office, looking grim. "Not an easy family," he said.

For a second, Kate thought he was talking about her sister until she caught on. "I'm so sorry about Mrs. Blake. Everything I said to her pissed her off. I wasn't sure how to handle it."

Henry shrugged. "You told her we don't waive scores."

"We don't, right?"

"Nope."

"Will she get Dillon tested?"

"Probably not. She's convinced there was something wrong with the test or the scanner. She'll make a call to the company, and they can take it from there."

"She sounded off to me."

"Off?"

"I feel bad for her."

"Don't, Kate. Let it go. It's not your fault that she doesn't want to accept that her son is so unbelievably dumb he needs to be watered. Can I have one of those?" he asked, pointing to the chocolates. "Poor kid is dumber than, what did Maureen say? Dumber than an empty box of hair. How about dinner again next Thursday? We can discuss what's going to happen in committee meetings next month."

Kate passed him the chocolates. Henry studied them closely, sniffed the box, and then handed them back. "Pat's got me off sweets," he said sadly.

"I'm on sweets," Maureen said, walking in and reaching for the box. "Sorry to be the bearer of bad news, but Annie Allsworth's grades and recs just came in—she's practically perfect."

"Damn!" Kate said. "I knew it."

"Who?" Henry asked.

"The girl Kate interviewed with the bulbous forehead, remember? The girl who looks like Worf from *Star Trek*? I call her Little Worfan Annie," Maureen said. "She's got a hideous, billboard-sized expanse up there. It's like the obstetrician pulled her out with a toilet plunger." She was using her hands to illustrate and then dropped them, staring at Kate. "What's the matter with her?" she asked Henry. "She's all sweaty."

"Dillon's mom called and gave her a hard time," Henry said.

"Dillon?"

"You know," Kate reminded her. "Dillon Blake, soccer player."

"Who?"

"Remember?" Kate asked. "The parents wrote in their statement that he would make an excellent politician because of his 'outstanding people skills.' "

"Doesn't ring a bell," Maureen said.

"Yes, you remember Dillon," Henry said. "Shockingly low ISEEs. Dumber than a loaf of bread?"

"Oh, you mean *Dillon*?" Maureen asked. "Dillon who wrote the essay?"

"Yes," Henry said. "That's the one."

"You've just insulted bread everywhere. Dillon's dumber than drywall." She looked down at Kate and waggled her finger in her face. "Don't take any of this to heart, Nellie," she said, "or you won't be able to stand it." She walked out of the office.

"'Nellie'?" Kate asked. "What's with 'Nellie'?"

Henry shrugged. "I have a spot on my tie," he said suddenly, looking down at it. "Is it noticeable?"

"Not really," Kate lied.

"Guess I over-margarined my bran muffin this morning," and he walked out whistling.

Letter of Recommendation: Claudia Gutierrez, applicant to grade 7

It gives me such pleasure to write on behalf of my wonderful student Claudia. When she asked me if I would be willing to do this for her, I assured her yes! It would be an honor. She then apologized if doing the task would take any time away that I might spend with my children. That is Claudia: modest, conscientious, and thoughtful of the needs of others. In all my years of teaching, I have never known a student to have such an innate concern for those around her.

I am well aware of Hudson's reputation as a tough, academic, and (may I say?) competitive school. Claudia is exactly what you need. While she is motivated to do her best and learn all that she can, she will stop to help a friend who falls behind. She is the quintessential community member. And more to the point: she is just plain smart. She will rise to the challenge of any work you put in front of her. She reads with the attention to detail I would expect of a college student. She thinks way outside of her own experiences. From playing a violin sonata to writing poetry, she pours her heart into every creative pursuit. She is well rounded and gifted. As corny as it may sound, I will say unapologetically: this girl is destined to do wonderful things.

Her personal life has not been easy, as you may have learned from reading her folder. Losing her father after a long illness was devastating, but she has managed to focus on her schoolwork and move forward. She was treated badly by some insensitive children at our school, and she handled it with grace and dignity. She was an example to us all.

If I had to come up with a weakness for Claudia, I would say that she doesn't give herself enough time to "play"; she uses her time almost too productively. However, given the demands of Hudson, I assume that would be an asset.

Please do not hesitate to contact me if there is anything I can do to help move her application forward and into your accept pile. Nothing would make me happier than seeing Claudia get what she has earned—a spot in a top-notch school. I'm aware that financial aid is limited, but I hope you will strongly consider awarding her as much as the family needs to attend.

Sincerely,
Elizabeth Fontain
6th grade English teacher and advisor

As soon as her 11:00 couple walked in for their appointment, Dr. Richards could feel the hostility. Nancy and Sam Smith were a lost cause, and Dr. Richards—if she were to be honest—wished she could coax them as quickly as possible toward a somewhat amicable divorce. The idea of counseling these narcissists for even another month was enough to make her want to quit the profession.

Sam arrived first, which was a surprise, and sat on the sofa, scrolling through messages on his phone and grumbling loudly to show that he'd rather be anywhere else. Nancy marched in five minutes later and refused her usual spot on the couch, opting instead for a straight-back chair closer to the door.

"So you had your first interview?" Dr. Richards asked. "How did it go?"

"How did it go?" Nancy fumed, still wearing her coat. "How did it go? Ha!"

"It wasn't that bad," Sam said, dismissing her as he always did.

"How can you . . . 'Wasn't that bad'? It was a complete disaster. And after all the strings I pulled? We had an interview at Hudson Day with the *head* of admissions, and you blew it. It was so embarrassing."

"Gus thought it went well."

"What the hell does Gus know?" Nancy yelled, saying his name like it was a bad word. "He wore pink socks to his interview."

Just get them to give up, thought Dr. Richards. *Put this marriage out of its misery and move on to custody counseling.* "Why don't you tell me about it?" she began. "Can you both recall what happened? What you each said?"

Nancy and Sam looked at each other.

"Yes, I remember perfectly," Nancy said, spitting a bit on the "p."

"Well, why don't we go over it in detail," Dr. Richards suggested. "How did Sam disappoint you this time, Nancy? And

Sam, how did Nancy's need to control you cause the interview to go so badly?" These were poorly worded questions, but Dr. Richards wanted to get the blame game going. She'd had enough of these people already. "Sam, if you could put your phone away for just a moment, I have an exercise I'd like you to try."

"I don't have all day," Sam said.

"This might be productive," Dr. Richards lied. "I want you to reenact the interview for me, just show me what happened at Hudson Day, and let's try to pinpoint exactly what went wrong."

"Act out the interview?" Nancy asked.

"As faithfully as you can," Dr. Richards said, standing up. She clasped her hands in front of her, cleared her throat, and said in her most professional voice, "Hello, Mr. and Mrs. Smith."

"He was a guy," Sam said. "Mr. Bigster."

"Bigsby," Nancy corrected. "What is *wrong* with you?"

"Just pretend I'm Mr. Bigsby, then," Dr. Richards said. "Now won't you sit down? And let's talk about Gus."

Sam rolled his eyes; he clearly thought the idea of playacting was childish and beneath him. Nancy, however, removed her coat, pushed up her sleeves, and came over to take her place next to Sam on the sofa. She reached over to hold his hand, looking as though she were hoping to get an A+ for her performance.

"Let's begin," Dr. Richards said.

"I'm sure I speak for both of us," Nancy said, with a fake politician's smile, "when I say how happy we are to be here."

Sam sat forward suddenly, as if—though annoyed—he didn't want to be outdone; he was competitive above all else. "You're saying *just* like it happened in the real interview? *That's* what you want to see?"

"Is there a problem?" Dr. Richards asked.

"No, no problem. I just don't think she's going to do it like it really was. No way she's going to be honest."

"I most certainly am," Nancy snapped. "Now I go: Blah blah blah . . . We're so pleased to learn more about Hudson. We both think it's extremely important—"

"Yes—" Sam started.

"We *both* feel it's so important to—"

"I canceled a meeting to be here," he interrupted.

"—to help you get to know our little Gus—"

"Three men to see me from Qatar—"

"And he canceled," Nancy said.

"I just told them, 'No. I'm sorry. My son's education is more important to me than some meeting.' "

"To both of us," Nancy added.

"And I sent them packing. All the way from Qatar."

"He canceled the whole thing."

"Well, I rescheduled really—"

"He prioritized."

"—until later this afternoon. I mean, *Qatar*. You can't exactly send them *back*, now, can you?"

Nancy turned on Sam abruptly. "I don't know why you felt a need to go on and on about that."

"What?"

"I'd already made the point that we were putting Gus first. Then you went off on your whole stupid Qatar thing. Who cares?"

"I thought it was worth mentioning. It didn't hurt anything."

"You make everything about you."

"Of course I do," Sam said, "and so do you, and so does everybody else. It's called having a *conversation*."

Oh yes, Dr. Richards thought. "Interesting," she said. "Let's keep going."

Nancy gave Sam's hand a little squeeze. "We feel that Gus would be perfect for Hudson."

"He's quite a kid," Sam said unenthusiastically. "He's something else."

"Very bright."

"Gus is sort of . . . what?"

"Adorable."

Sam shrugged.

"I'm a full-time stay-at-home mom, very devoted to my son. I've done my best to raise him well, teach him good values."

"So have I," Sam said. "I've always tried to impress upon Gus the importance of discipline. And hard work."

"Yes, we both—"

"I've always worked hard at what I do. I mean I *sweat* at what I do."

"Well . . ."

"What?" Sam asked. "I don't work hard?" He turned to Dr. Richards. "Do you see how she undermines me?"

"No, you *do* work hard," Nancy explained. "Of course you do. It's just that, you said 'sweat,' and I didn't want to give the guy the impression that you, you know, that we're one of those 'hard-working *and we need a scholarship*' kind of families."

"Oh, God no," Sam said. "I don't work *that* hard."

"We can pay."

"*Obviously*. Full tuition, all the way. Hell, we could throw in something extra. I mean, nothing about us says 'scholarship.' "

"You'll love Gus," Nancy said, getting back to the reenactment. "He's great. Smart as a whip. Things come very easily for him."

Sam looked irritated. "Sure, except for when they *don't*."

"Let me stop you for a second," Dr. Richards said. "Sam?"

"He always contradicts me," Nancy said.

"You were bullshitting the guy, and he knew it," Sam said. "There are plenty of times when stuff doesn't come easily for Gus. Besides, who wants to hear us brag about our kid? I hate that."

"In the case of a school interview, it seems acceptable," Dr.

Richards said. "So, Nancy, you were saying that Gus is smart. Sam contradicted you. And then what happened?"

Sam and Nancy looked at each other, thinking.

"Well," Nancy said, "then I tried again to say something about how Gus likes learning."

"And I said *no* kid *likes* learning," Sam said.

"And when Sam said that *stupid*, gratuitous remark I tried to spin it into something positive, so I made the point that Gus knows to ask for help when he needs it. That's a good attribute, isn't it?"

"Certainly," said Dr. Richards.

"I said that we're *always* there for him if he needs something."

" 'As long as we're around,' " Sam added. "You said 'as long as we're around.' That was a jab at me, of course."

"I just meant if he needs *anything*—"

"You just *had* to bring up that I travel," Sam said.

"And then *you* went off," Nancy continued, "talking about how Gus sucked at tying his shoes, like *that's* a way to impress an admissions director."

"Hold on a sec," Dr. Richards said, not wanting to miss out on the details that just kept getting better and better. "So, in an interview for sixth grade, you brought up shoe tying as an example of something Gus *couldn't* learn to do?"

"I was reinforcing her point," Sam explained, "because even though it took him *forever*, he finally learned how to do it."

"Sam kept saying things like, 'Gus just couldn't for the life of him figure it out, like, what kind of kid can't tie his shoes?' And '*How many times* do you have to show a kid how to do something?' So I explained to Mr. Bixby that of course I taught Gus how to do it because that's what mothers do: they show their kids how to do things over and over until they want to scream. And then Sam said, 'Well, thank God for Velcro or the kid would have spent his first decade barefoot.' "

"What?" Sam asked. "It was funny."

"It really wasn't," Nancy said. "I tried to laugh it off like he was joking, and I said, 'Of course Gus *did* eventually learn how to tie his shoes because *I* taught him how.' But then Sam suddenly asked me—totally seriously—right in front of the guy, 'When was that?' "

"Well, I'm sorry," Sam said, "I just don't remember you teaching him *anything*."

"Questioning me, questioning my parenting, right in front of the man, basically accusing me of *lying* . . ."

"It's just that I don't recall—"

"*Hours* I spent," Nancy said. "Hours and hours when Gus was sitting in that high chair thing. My God, I tied shoes until I thought I'd strangle the boy with his laces."

"I'm sorry, but I have no memory of that whatsoever. I guess I'm going senile already."

"I guess you are."

"Because I don't ever remember you sitting with him *anywhere*. That babysitter Olga—"

"She's a *nanny*."

"But *you*?" Sam asked. "Really?"

"Well, you're gone *all the time*, so of course you wouldn't remember."

"Yeah," Sam said to Dr. Richards, "and she keeps saying *that*, right in front of Mr. Bilbo, that I'm an 'absentee' father."

"I was trying to explain away the fact that you were calling me a liar . . ."

"What made you decide to emphasize Sam's travel?" Dr. Richards asked her. "Doesn't that go against the image you were trying to create of a cohesive family unit?"

Sam began imitating Nancy's voice: " 'He's *never* home, *ever*. Basically, I'm a single parent.' "

"Well, I am," Nancy said. She turned to Dr. Richards. "He

travels *constantly*. So I just explained to Mr. What's-his-name the *fact* of the matter, which is that Sam is sometimes gone for over a month at a time."

"I've *never* been gone for a month."

"About a month. Two weeks at time. Whatever. And then to defend himself Sam starts talking about how he's such a *devoted* father."

"I am. I provide. I email home."

"Oh, really?" Nancy asked. "Sending an occasional email makes you a devoted parent? And besides, you never email *Gus*. Ever. That's just a complete crock of shit."

"Which is *exactly* what she said to the interviewer," Sam told Dr. Richards. "She turned right to him and said, 'What a crock of shit.'"

"Is that true, Nancy?" Dr. Richards asked. "Did you say 'crock of shit' during the interview?"

"Yes, I may have felt a need to correct the record. Sam gave me no choice."

"Mind you, none of this was even relevant," Sam said. "Yeah, maybe I travel for work. So sue me. It's not like you or Gus even care. I mean, when I *am* around, I never see either one of you. Gus spends *all* of his time either stuffing his face in the kitchen or reading. He never wants to do normal stuff with me, like play the video games I bought."

"Did you say *that* in the interview?" Dr. Richards asked.

"Yes!" Nancy said. "He called Gus *fat*, while simultaneously complaining that he won't spend time sitting on his ass playing video games all day long. I'm sure *that* went over really well, so I jumped in, cut him off, and I explained that even if Gus *did* play video games, which he doesn't, *I* would limit the hours. I would be very strict about what *kinds* of games—and Sam just wouldn't drop it." She put on her Sam voice: "'There's this zone you get into, ya know? When you're blowing things up, killing people.' Then he started making *explosion* sounds and machine gun noises and saying stuff like, 'Ya know, it's fricking awesome shooting hookers and cops,' and I'm jumping in, trying to undo the damage, saying, 'No! But we would never allow *those* kinds of games.' But Sam just kept making it worse: 'Well, we own a stack of really violent shit, and it's fun as hell, and I wish Gus would get in there and play with me!' You think *that* made a good impression?"

"Did he actually say 'shooting hookers'?" Dr. Richards asked.

"I was explaining," Sam said, "that Gus *doesn't* play violent video games. And now *that's* bad? How is that bad?"

"Ever since you bought that Xbox," Nancy said, "you've been obsessed."

"It's an escape for me, what can I say. It helps me cope with my feeling that I'm utterly alone in my own house."

"And what happened next?" Dr. Richards asked.

Sam scoffed. "She goes into this bullshit perfect mother act." And he started using a falsetto voice: " 'Well, I always remind Gus while Sam is on the couch virtually shooting people—and he listens to me, Gus is *such* a good listener—that killing people is *bad*. That's what I say.' And all I asked her was, 'Really? You think he *listens*?' And I really wanted to know because I never get the feeling Gus listens to me. I can stand there yelling at the top of my lungs—"

"Yeah," Nancy cut in, "that was a great selling point: Sam said Gus must have ADHD since he doesn't pay attention when he's being shouted at."

"You, meanwhile," Sam said, "were actually trying to make the point that you're a good mother for teaching Gus that, in real life, murdering someone in cold blood would not be 'acceptable behavior.' And I'm like, 'Well, let's hope he knows *that*.' "

Nancy threw her hands up. "I didn't mean that he doesn't *know* it. All I was trying to do was fix the mess you were making, criticizing your fat, stupid kid."

"Gus spends a hell of a lot of time in the kitchen," Sam said. "That's all I was saying."

"And then—oh, and this was the real gem of the day, Dr. Richards—you know what Sam said? You'll love this: Sam leans forward, and says to the *head* of admissions: 'To be honest, Gus can be a complete pain in my ass.'"

"Really, Sam?" Dr. Richards asked. "Pain in the ass?"

Sam looked confused. "No. I don't think I said that *exactly*."

"Yes you did," Nancy said. "And when I gasped, you turned to me and said, 'Ah, come on. This man works with kids. He knows what little *fuckers* they are. Am I right?'"

"It was a *joke*," Sam said.

"It was totally inappropriate. And I was shrieking, 'Gus is *not* a little fucker. He's weird, sure, but when his behavior is challenging for us, as people who have no clue how to relate to him, we make sure he knows he's from a sound and stable family.' I was working my ass off to salvage the situation after all the shit you said."

"Let me stop you for a minute," Dr. Richards said. *So close to splitting up. They were so close. Time to drive it home.* "I'd like to hear the rest. But what I want you to do is, Sam, you be Nancy. And Nancy, you be Sam. Let's hear exactly how you sounded to each other. Can you do that?"

Sam stood up and, in a high, whiny voice, did his version of Nancy: "Ooooh, I'm the best mother ever in the whole wide world. I'm with my son every second of every minute of the day. Except for all the hours I'm getting felt up by my hot personal trainer."

Nancy followed by getting to her feet to do her best impersonation of Sam, lowering her voice as far as she could manage: "Gus is a shithead, and my family life totally sucks, know what I mean? But I don't even care because I'm too busy playing with myself and fucking my secretary every single night of the week."

Sam balked before he went on again in his falsetto voice: "I slam down my daily calorie allotment in Chardonnay and Xanax, but whether I'm bombed or not, I can't even pretend to give a fuck about my husband, because I don't."

Nancy dropped character for a second, as if she were ready to quit. But then in a final effort she clenched her fists and made her voice go even deeper: "I go out of town as much as I possibly can just so I don't have to spend a single minute with my old, boring, unsexy wife who I wish I'd never married."

They stopped and glared at each other.

"Well," Dr. Richards said, "are we done here or what?"

"You're not unsexy," Sam said quietly. "You're not old."

Nancy looked confused. "Well, you think I am," she said. "And I guess you found someone younger."

Sam shook his head at her. "That's just not true," he said. "I'm not fucking anyone. You're the one who avoids me. I come home from work, and you make me feel like I'm invading your space and irritating you just by breathing. You act like you can't stand me."

"That's because I know you sleep around, and I know you'd rather be somewhere else with anyone else. You come home from work, grab your 'gym bag,' and leave as fast as you can."

"I go to the gym at night," Sam said, "because I thought that if I got into shape, you might look at me and not get that disgusted expression on your face. But you never look at me."

"I don't want to look at you because I know you hate me."

He put up his right hand. "I swear to God on my life, on our town house, on my Porsche convertible, on everything I care about, which admittedly isn't very much: I'm not having an affair. I don't hate you."

Sam's BlackBerry buzzed in his pocket. He took it out, dropped it on the floor, and stomped on it.

What the fuck is happening? Dr. Richards looked at this

seemingly incompatible pair and saw that splitting up suddenly didn't seem so imminent after all. *Son of a bitch, they'll probably want to double up on sessions.* "Well, then," she said, taking a breath and inviting them to sit down again. "How many interviews do you have left? Five or six? I suggest we put this one behind us and move ahead. If the two of you teamed up, you could be quite a force. Are you willing to try? To see what you can do together?"

Dr. Richards watched while Nancy and Sam talked to each other, sitting cautiously side by side, pink-cheeked and turned on, and felt a pang of guilt for having rooted for their failure. She grabbed the notepad next to her and wrote a quick reminder on her to-do list (*Make appt w/ Dr. M*); even therapists need therapists from time to time.

Interview: Gus Smith, and parents Sam and Nancy
Date: January 12
Interviewed by Henry B. (Kate—conflict of interest)

This interview was beyond surprising. Gus is a most endearing child; smart, thoughtful, engaging and engaged. I give him two enthusiastic thumbs-up. He has many interests and was able to talk about them with passion and expertise. He reads a wide array of literature, as his nanny, Olga, has been taking him to the public library twice a week since he was four.

Gus is apparently a very good cook. His housekeeper initially taught him the basics, and since then he and Olga have been trying out recipes from all over the world, and in the process Gus has become somewhat of a master chef, making everything from crêpes suzette to baklava to Peking duck. And what a wonderful raconteur he is. When he described his pursuits in the kitchen, I quite felt like I was right there with him, smelling and tasting all that he created. He has read Julia Child's autobiography, and he's working his way through Peter Mayle "just for fun." Also he has started a club at school that raises money for a community garden.

Gus is indubitably a stellar student. If his grades aren't good, I'll eat my shoes because he struck me as reflective, industrious, and genuine, a child with a true yearning to *know*.

I asked him about his artwork, since his parents discussed his abilities at length in their parent statement, but he was baffled. Apparently he did some drawings in an art class a few years ago, but this is not a passion for him and never has been. Instead Gus enjoys reading (especially poetry), collecting pictures from the *New York Times* (in a scrapbook Olga got him), and playing with his beloved hamsters Gnome and Chompsky.

He told me the story about the fight he had with the girl at school, and I am willing to put the whole matter to rest. That girl who picked on him must indeed be "dim-witted," and good for Gus for using his words.

As for Gus's parents: I would be remiss if I did not mention that they are absolutely off their rockers. (I won't even attempt to describe their behavior because no one would believe me.) They are decidedly *not* hands-on, didn't even know Gus has hamsters; rather they were confused by his apparent "weird" interest in politics and anarchy. The good side of this is that I doubt the school would hear much from them, unless they're writing checks, so they can go off to Qatar and Equinox and leave Gus here with us.

While I am sure that he would be a quirky, delightful addition to our student body, my gut tells me he won't enroll at Hudson. This boy will likely have many excellent choices that will suit him well, schools like Graylon or Trevor, and my guess is that he'll want a school that allows for more creativity and individual expression while still challenging him at the high level that his sharp mind demands. If I'm right, it will be our loss.

In terms of rights and wrongs, given the details of this particular situation and the cast of characters involved, she was perhaps in the wrong. But whatever, she was already sleeping with him, and it's not like she could make that magically unhappen, and the truth was, she couldn't wait for it to happen again. Her behavior was possibly reproachable, but she felt entitled to feel what she felt and to do what she wanted to do, and she resented feeling that there were barriers to getting what she wanted.

So hard to concentrate on work. Designing the image of a new, handcrafted bourbon brand in her present wound-up state wasn't easy. She was . . . she was . . . What was she? Attracted? Obviously. Smitten? Too childish. Obsessed? Unhealthy, and moreover, it implied some kind of imbalance in affection, and she knew that wasn't the case.

Victoria was in love. Yes. That's what she was. In love. She was restless and peppy. Her face flushed out of nowhere, and her mind would wander off, remembering some moment between them, something that he'd said. Sometimes he called her "darling," and she thought she'd die. *Darling!* She thought about him all throughout the day and smiled accidentally. And to feel like someone cared about her, thought of her, to feel *not* lonely for once, it was unimaginably exciting.

Chloe was apoplectic. How she'd found out about Robert, Vicki had no idea, but a few weeks after the cookie party fiasco, Chloe had called to say she was coming over. Not thinking that it was anything other than a friendly visit, Victoria had quickly wrapped Chloe's birthday present and tied a card onto it with a ribbon: *I'll be waiting for you at the finish line, girl! Know you can do it!* It was a GPS running watch, a little token of encouragement for her friend's new hobby.

She handed Chloe the box as she came in, but she could see immediately that something was wrong; Chloe stood there in the doorway, refusing wine or a seat on the couch, refusing even to take off her coat.

"Please tell me you're not seeing him," she said. "Please."

"No," Vicki answered.

"No? No, you're not seeing him?"

"I mean yes. I am seeing him. I'm not ashamed to admit it."

Victoria was stunned by her adamant speech, none of which sounded like Chloe at all. Victoria had always counted on her for validation, so "I'm happy for you" seemed like a reasonable sentiment to expect from her. She was the kind of friend who would say "you can't help how you feel" and "it's not your fault" and "as long as you meant well" and anything that made you feel better, that let you off the hook, but that day she was different.

"End it!" Chloe demanded. "You have to stop seeing him right now. You're violating a code, and you can't do this to her."

"I'm not doing anything *to* her. I can't help it if I like him."

"Why him? Why does *everybody* have to fall for my cousin? He isn't even nice. How can you not see that?"

"You can't write him off like that."

"Well, I have—I haven't spoken to him even once since he broke up with her, and I don't plan to."

"That would hurt him so much, to hear you say something so hateful. He adores you and misses you terribly. Won't you even hear him out, *try* to be a little more understanding? He forgives you, you know. Will you at least put down your bag?"

"Forgives *me*? What did *I* do?"

"He called you that night, and you let him down," Victoria explained. "He was going through something pretty wrenching and didn't know how to end it with her, and he called you because he needed your help. And you—let's face it—you totally dismissed him, and you let Kate get on that plane. You set them both up for more pain than was necessary."

"I'm not God," Chloe suddenly said, "and I'm not responsible for his actions. Or yours, either."

"God?" Victoria asked. "No one thinks you're God, Chloe."

"What you're doing—it's awful. You're going to hurt Kate for nothing because this will never last. He's going to put you down and chip away at you until you don't know yourself anymore."

Victoria had to laugh at that. "I'm not exactly the kind of girl who gets 'chipped away' at by a guy. You should have a little more faith in me than that."

"He has a mean streak," Chloe insisted.

"Well, he has a nice side, too, and you know he does. Besides, Kate and I are nothing alike, and I would have thought you understood that."

"What's your problem with Kate?"

"There's no problem. I'm just sick of all the fuss everyone makes about her. You should have seen her brother-in-law, leaping to her defense, jumping over a couch to throw poor Robert out the door."

"It's called loyalty."

"It was a ridiculous display."

"Why do I have to be stuck in the middle of your mess?" Chloe asked.

"Why are you making this about you?"

"Fine. *You* would be better off alone than in a relationship with him."

"You and I are different, Chloe. Just because you get all of your satisfaction from saving the world, you should at least acknowledge that the rest of us might want to have some companionship and sex. It's called 'having fun.' "

"Fun? You think it's going to be fun? He's not going to turn into a different person for you."

"I would never want him to," she said, "but I will get him to behave. You'll see."

"I don't want anything to do with this," Chloe said. "I don't want to hear about it or talk about it. You're the one who has to live with yourself, knowing what this will do to Kate. You're being a bad friend, Vicki."

"Victoria."

Chloe had crossed her arms and said nothing.

"They broke up over a year ago," Vicki said. "Kate's moved on, and over time she'll understand. Actually, you should be the one to tell her. How did you know we're dating anyway?"

Chloe turned around abruptly, still holding the wrapped present, and walked out of the apartment. Victoria figured she was going straight to Kate to tell her everything. Even if they were both mad at her for a while, it would be a relief to have her relationship out in the open.

Victoria wasn't naïve. She knew Robert was a challenge, but it was one of the things she liked most about him; at least he wasn't boring. Victoria understood completely how his relationship with Kate had spun out of control when Kate started getting needy, suddenly willing to give up her whole life in New York. It was terrifying for him, and he hadn't known how or when to stop it. When he'd encouraged Kate to follow her heart, he hadn't meant she should follow it to *Paris*.

With Victoria and him, it was different. They had chemistry. They were alike. They looked good together and kept each other on their toes. He wasn't a perfect boyfriend, but Victoria planned to train him, no matter how much work she would have to do.

Turning her attention back to her work, she flipped through the new logo options for the bourbon label and took her time to determine which was the most appealing one, the sexiest. She narrowed in on one that was masculine and smoky, qualities she associated with Robert, and decided it would make even a non-bourbon drinker want to buy it. She wanted to talk to him. To call him. To text him? Or no, better to wait. It was his turn to get in touch, and she certainly didn't want to come across as needy. Victoria was not needy, never had been. Needy was unattractive and revealed a lack of independence, and Victoria was decidedly independent. She would wait to hear from him.

As the day wore on, she noticed an unfamiliar, sour feeling in her stomach. She was agitated, checking her phone every few minutes and snapping at people who came in her office to talk to her. She calculated the time difference in France and thought, *He should be home now, in bed maybe. Or out. Out where? Out with whom? Who is he with? Is she pretty?*

She closed her eyes. *Call me. Call me. Call me*, she willed. She opened them and checked her phone again. Nothing. The silence felt punishing. This was a game of some kind. An unpleasant game. And games are stupid. She was a grown woman, and she could certainly get in touch with a man she was sleeping with if she wanted. This was the twenty-first century. She wouldn't wait for him. Why should she?

Finally she sent a text that took over an hour to compose. She threw out the following drafts:

Thinking about you.

Miss you. Day okay?

Where are you? Can we talk?

Hope you like this pic, real thing when you get here.

Hey, how's it going?

Let's Skype. Sometime tomorrow?

It all sounded pathetic. She decided on:

Must see you. Next week works for me.

She held her breath and pressed send.

Silvia Blake stood at the gates of West Side Elementary, back to the wind, fur coat buttoned up, waiting for dismissal. She rarely had the chance to pick Dillon up because her work made it impossible, but when she had a free afternoon here or there, she would text the babysitter and go get him herself. She enjoyed taking him somewhere fun, like Shake Shack, or buying him treats at his very favorite place, Dylan's Candy Bar, and even reminding him to do his homework, which was a daily battle. But what energetic, sporty, fifth-grade boy doesn't fight homework? And what boy *wants* to sit down and write application essays and thank-you notes all weekend long? It was torture for him.

"Silvia! Hi!"

She turned to see Tess Allsworth, the mother of one of Dillon's classmates, running toward her with a panting little dog on a leash.

"What a surprise!" she said. "I never see you at pickup."

"Well, when you work full-time," Silvia said, "it's kinda hard to just take off in the middle of the day."

"I bet. So how's it going?" Tess asked. "Is the stress of all this admissions stuff just *killing* you?" Glowing with health from her run to the school, she stood on one leg and stretched out her quad. Lululemon, head to toe. Unlike Silvia, Tess didn't work; she worked out. While Silvia might have envied the bodies of women like Tess, she accepted her own wider ass in exchange for her wider life experiences. She was a wife, a lawyer, and a mother—she was one of those women who truly managed to do it all.

"I'm not letting it get to me," Silvia said calmly. "I know it's a lot to deal with, all the interviews, the applications, but at the end of the day, those admissions people will make the right decision. And I just want Dillon to be happy."

"Super attitude! Woo! I just keep reminding myself it will all be over soon. But it's always something. The *testing*! Oh my God! We got Annie's scores back. I can't say I'm too happy."

Silvia wanted to believe that everyone was taking this whole testing thing way too seriously. Even Kenneth was getting worked up about it. She told him that in Dillon's case, the other parts of his application would simply outshine his test scores; the admissions departments would focus their attention on Dillon's many wonderful qualities: personality, talent, athleticism, to name a few. "I wouldn't worry too much about it," she said. "I don't think schools weigh test scores *that* heavily. They're children, after all."

"But it depends on who you talk to, though, right?" Tess said, switching to stretch the other leg. "Some say one thing, some say something else. Who knows? But I sure hope you're right because Annie really didn't do as well as we thought she would."

"Don't feel badly. Dillon didn't, either."

Tess jumped up and down lightly to keep warm. "Annie cried when I told her she got eights on the verbal sections. She was *inconsolable*. I was, too, although I tried not to show it. At least her math scores were higher, thank *God*. How'd Dillon do?"

Silvia felt her briefcase strap digging sharply into her shoulder, and she shifted it to the other side. "Dillon," she said, "well . . . Dillon was about the same. Sevens, eights."

"Annie was so happy to get nines in math."

"Nines. Good for her." *What an unbearable show-off*, Silvia thought. The problem with mothers of daughters, Silvia had figured out long ago, is that they just don't understand boys at all. People like Tess were oblivious to how much more challenging it was to raise a boy, how difficult it could be to make a boy sit still to take a test.

"Yes, well," Tess said, "Annie's our little mathematician. She just gets it, you know? But you're legacy at Hudson, right? That's like a *guarantee*, isn't it?"

"That's what I've heard, but our real advantage is that Dillon interviews really well; he's such good company, and it's impossible not to like him. I've been told by a lot of people that it's a real strength for him, and the interview is pretty much the most important part of the process."

"So important! I mean it's that *and* the transcripts, right? And the recommendations? Oh, the things we put our kids through. And to lose their teacher halfway through the year? *Nightmare!* Was Dillon upset that Ms. Millner left? Annie was positively crushed! We went to the Hamptons, and she just cried the whole time we were there. She misses her so much."

Oh, the drama. Girls and their emotions, always so over the top. That was a problem Silvia didn't have. "No," she told Tess, "Dillon really didn't mind at all. He's sort of unflappable about that sort of thing. Just rolls right off him."

"How does he like the new teacher?" Tess asked.

"He doesn't. He says she's mean and overly strict and is always singling him out. She makes him stay in almost every recess, which is just cruel, I think, to do that to a boy. Boys *need* to run around, you know? Ms. Millner did that also, made him stay in and do math problems, like she just wanted to torture him."

"I'm so sorry to hear that. Poor Dillon! Annie *loves* the new teacher. Loved Ms. Millner, too, but, well, she just loves *teachers*. That's just Annie. Give her a book to read and when she's done, she'll sit down and write a report about it *for fun*. Teachers adore her."

"It's harder for boys," Silvia said, deciding right then and there to call the teacher and advocate for her misunderstood, mistreated, marginalized son. In spite of her strict, at times sadistic, teaching method, the teacher had surely highlighted Dillon's strengths in her letter for him. Isn't that the point of a recommendation after all? "Some teachers really discriminate against them. It's very unfair."

"How awful! I wouldn't know, but I guess boys *can* be a

handful, though, right? A little on the exuberant side? Rambunctious? At least that's what Annie tells me. A lot of them just can't sit still to do the work. Not Dillon, but I just mean some of the boys. Ahhh! Here's my girl!" Annie walked up to her mom, handing over her backpack and kissing her. Another boy-girl divide: Dillon had made it clear that there was to be no kissing in public, and Silvia grudgingly respected that.

Annie dropped down to the pavement, hugging the stupid little dog and talking to it in a baby voice. Silvia noticed for the first time that it was wearing little pink bows on its head.

"I wonder where Dillon is," Silvia mumbled.

"Playground," Annie told her.

"You see?" Silvia said. Case in point. "That's Dillon for you. I'll have a heck of a time getting him off the monkey bars."

Letter of Recommendation: Dillon Blake, applicant to 6th grade

I was Dillon's homeroom teacher until Thanksgiving when I made the unexpected decision to retire early for personal reasons. Dillon is now in the capable hands of my replacement who asked me to complete this form given that I have known him longer. Dillon's new teacher is less experienced, but her young age will be an asset, as Dillon has enormous energy. At my age, it was a struggle to harness his boundless zip, and I found myself eagerly waiting for the day to end so that I could go home and lie down.

At recess, Dillon is often a leader of various games, telling the other children what to do and then evaluating their ability to do it. He has a robust competitive instinct, which must help him tremendously on the soccer field. As I am not his coach, I do not know how he is as a "team" member. He can be creative when telling stories during share time, and while friendships often come with conflict, he seems to enjoy the company of other children. He is less receptive to the company of adults (i.e., me), as he does not like to be directed from what he wants to do to what is required (i.e., class time).

Math is a particular challenge although he certainly improved in his computation skills this fall. While subtraction was initially impossible for him, he was able to complete simple tasks using manipulatives (such as blocks or tiles which I borrowed from the first-grade classroom). His initial impulse was to "shut down" when confronting a difficult problem, but with firm guidance and input, he could rise to the challenge. Addition became quite easy for him over time, and I was proud of him for working with me on this important skill and becoming more independent when solving problems.

This was to be my thirtieth year in the classroom, and

teaching Dillon was a standout experience. He provided me with endless opportunities to seek new ways to explain concepts, and new ways to engage a student for longer than, say, a few minutes at a time. I wish Dillon all the best for his middle school years.

Ms. Millner
Former 5th grade teacher

February

Now I had two relationships to keep secret from Kate—easy since she was too busy to see me anyway, but stressful in that I worried about it all the time. When we talked on the phone, I never told her anything about George and me, about our joint checking account, our sex life, or even our rescue dog, Carter (as in Jimmy), who was a mix of Labrador and everything else, a breed George had dubbed "dogador." And I certainly didn't tell her the ugly, shocking news about Vicki and Robert. Once again, I was sitting on information. Why me?

"Victoria"? I couldn't call her that. And anyway, I liked the old Vicki better. I'd spent a whole summer traveling with her back in college, back when she was still my unpretentious, eager friend from Nebraska who'd never left the U.S.A. before, who was so gung ho to take trains all over Europe, staying in cheap, one-star youth hostels and getting by on forty euros a day. We were broke and without a plan, getting lost, sharing clothes, and meeting random people who would do absurdly generous things like invite us for dinner in their homes. In Munich we met cute German boys, and Vicki got bombed at a beer garden with them, while I tried to force-feed her big fat pretzels to get something in her stomach, to no avail. I zigzag staggered her back toward our cruddy room, and as we stumbled along, Vicki, without warning, went from laughing to crying.

"Oh no," she sobbed, burying her face in her T-shirt, which meant showing her bra to anyone walking by.

"You're okay," I told her, trying to pull her shirt back down. "Are you going to throw up?"

"I love you so much."

"Ohh, I love you, too. Keep going. We're almost there."

"Why do you like Kate more than me?" she asked.

"What? No, that's silly. I like you both."

"I'm a better friend to you, but you wanted her to come instead of me," she cried.

"No, I wanted you both to come, but this is great. It's the best trip ever. Aren't we having fun? You and me?"

"You don't even care that she always puts us last."

While it was probably true that Kate didn't put us first, we certainly were never last, and anyway it didn't bother me the way it did Vicki. That summer, Kate chose an archaeological dig in Mexico over our girlfriend trip to Europe, and while I may have been disappointed that she didn't go with us, I also knew it wasn't personal. If you wanted to spend time with Kate, you had to work a little harder for it. I would text her from outside the psychology building on a pretty day. She'd come out, blinking in the sunlight, and I'd have a coffee for her; we'd sit somewhere and talk for a few minutes. I would ask Vicki to come along, but she resented it when I indulged Kate that way. She thought Kate should come to us, not the other way around. "You're just encouraging her," Vicki would scold me. I couldn't understand why my relationship with Kate hurt her feelings.

Later it became hard to imagine that Vicki's feelings could get hurt over anyone. She changed over time, became haughty and cool. "Victoria" would have judged the boys who had bought us drinks and taken us dancing. She would have turned her nose up at the tinny beds and drippy sinks in the corners of hostel rooms. She would have criticized everyone who had reached out to us, offering directions, wine, and even sex, all of which we accepted at one time or another during those three months.

At the end of our trip, we went to Paris and stayed with Robert in his studio apartment in the 6th, not far from the Pont Neuf. I was excited to see him, but I remember warning Vicki, "My cousin can be a bit of an asshole. If he says something mean, just ignore him. That's just how he is." I was more than used to Robert's personality, having spent most of my summers in France with him when we were growing up. When I stayed with his family, we were inseparable, in spite of the fact that we had loud, vicious fights so often that one time my aunt declared that she couldn't take it anymore. She'd had it with us. She made me pack up all my stuff, and she put us in the backseat of the car with my luggage, taking us all the way to the airport before she revealed that she was only trying to teach us a lesson. We had physical fights when we were young, like the time he made fun of my French in front of a group of his friends and I punched him in the stomach, and political and philosophical fights as we got older, like the time we stayed up an entire night having it out over the issue of income inequality. I was the voice of the proletariat and he, of course, was the champion of the upper crust. We never resolved who won.

Our fights were always bilingual; I would shout at him in English since my French vocabulary in the fields of economics, civics, human rights, and any other serious subject was lacking, and Robert would yell back at me in French. While his vocabulary in English was admittedly impressive, his accent was an embarrassment, a problem he never rectified and, in fact, didn't seem to be aware of, even as an adult. In all the years we played, fought, drank, and laughed together, I never once made fun of how terrible Robert's pronunciation was, while he regularly pointed out my flaws in every conceivable category.

After we got to Robert's apartment, Vicki caught my eye when his back was turned and mouthed the words, "He is so hot," and she pointed—it seemed—at his ass.

"I am going to prepare for you a fabulous dinner," he promised and proceeded to whip up steamed mussels, sautéed asparagus, and potatoes au gratin with what seemed like no effort at all. "When you are with me in Paris, you are in very good hands," he said. Vicki smiled.

As we sat down to eat, Robert walked behind my chair to fill my wineglass, giving my shoulder a squeeze, forgetting his strength and gripping way too hard. His affection for me always came out in a brutal, physical way. He would give me a hug, knocking the wind out of me, bumping his head into mine accidentally and getting my hair caught on the clasp of his wristwatch. A hug with Robert often ended with me hollering in pain. For a suave, handsome guy, he could be astonishingly cloddish and lumbering, like he was my littermate in a family of big-pawed, uncoordinated Mastiff puppies.

Perhaps to counter his unchecked, unconditional attachment to me, he constantly made little judgmental remarks in a "we're so close I can say this to you" kind of way, and he was busy making them that night. We drank wine and told him stories about our summer, the time we this and the time we that: running out of money in Seville ("Chloe darling, will you always be my sad, destitute little cousin?"), dancing at a club until four in the morning ("I hope you can dance better than Chloe—she's quite embarrassing!"), giving our last euros away to a homeless woman we met on a train ("Chloe will never learn what a waste eeet eees to try to help those people."). I entertained him with a long story of an adorable boy in Portugal who fell in love with Vicki and followed us around for three days, offering to carry our bags or buy us dinner, anything to be near her. Vicki was modest and said, "How do you know it was me? Maybe he was in love with you."

"No, Vicki. I was there. He couldn't take his eyes off you."

"Then it was both of us," she insisted.

"I don't think so," Robert interjected. "I'm sure eeet was you, Vicki. Chloe doesn't have that sex appeal, that mystique that you have eeen abundance. Sheeeez cute but not beautiful. She could never drive a man wild."

"Fuck you, dude," I responded.

"What?" he asked. "We work with what we have, no?"

He had a harshness, a mean streak that he cleverly combined with an endearing smile and a boyish laugh, making me wish I were ten again so that I could still hit him.

"He's only teasing you," Vicki said, laughing.

"Really?" I asked. "Because it seems to me like he's picking a fight."

With no warning, he leaned in to hug me, accidentally elbowing me in the cheek as he reached his arm around me.

"There eees no person in theees world I would rather argue with than Chloe," Robert told Vicki, and then he added, in a faux whisper, "and we all know she eees an expert at concocting an argument out of theeen air."

I threw up my hands. "Seriously? I'm just sitting here. You're the one starting a fight."

"Perhaps in theees instance. Pardon. *But don't be angry with me; you know I love you exactly as you are."*

Sometime after midnight, we decided to go to sleep, since Vicki and I were flying back home the next morning.

"I inseeest you have my bed," Robert graciously offered. "You are my guests, and I will be very comfortable on the sofa."

Noises woke me up at around two, and I realized that Vicki was no longer with me. I could hear the two of them, sitting on the couch, talking quietly and laughing. It seemed ridiculous to feel hurt, but I did. Vicki was being disloyal, and Robert was stealing my friend. They had left me out, and I didn't like it.

I sulked over on my side of the apartment, straining to hear what I was missing, until I realized they were making out. Then I squeezed my eyes shut and faked sleep, pulling the thin blanket over my head and stopping up my ears, wishing I were anywhere other than in this nightmare.

But in the morning, in the rush of packing and calling a cab, I got over it. Maybe Vicki couldn't sleep, and there was no crime in hooking up with someone. Neither she nor I ever mentioned it, and I put the whole thing out of my head.

And later? When Kate and Robert started seeing each other? I never said a word about the one-night stand in Paris. I wasn't supposed to know, after all, and why was it my place to tell Kate? But it was one more thing that needled away at me. What if I had told Kate that Vicki had been with him first? What if I had been more honest about Robert's glaring flaws? What if I had told her that when he called me before she left for Paris, he told me all about the beautiful girl he'd met at a party, whispering because she was still asleep in his bed? At night, thoughts like these would spin through my head, keeping me from sleeping. What if I? What if I? What if I?

Maybe the good-looking psychiatrist's diagnosis was right; maybe I was egotistical.

I met the third Internet guy, a dental school student who was creepy and tried to make out with me right there in the coffee shop. I admired the enthusiasm but his breath was terrible. A dentist with bad breath.

Besides, I couldn't stop thinking about the handsome psychiatrist, and I was hoping to find a way to get them together casually. I took a chance and called him.

"Kate and I have plans to meet for drinks next week. What if you just happened to be there? I could introduce you to her." I was running a bath, straining to hear him over the sound of water pouring into the tub. My plan was that George would come home from work and find me there, a Valentine's Day surprise.

"But who am I at the bar with?" he asked. "I'm some creepy alcoholic drinking alone?"

"You could go with a friend."

"And then ditch him?"

"You're overthinking this," I said, lighting a few candles and dimming the lights. "By the way, you were right. I figured you deserve to know."

"Oh, good. Right about what?"

"Vicki's sleeping with my cousin, just like you said. I feel stupid that I didn't figure it out on my own."

"I'm sure you would have."

"Not necessarily." I held the phone, waiting for him to say something, looking around at the romantic scene I was creating in the bathroom. "It's Valentine's Day," I said. "Do you have a valentine? I'm not trying to be a jerk."

"We probably won't like each other."

"You don't like smart, beautiful women? It's not like you have time to find anyone on your own."

"Obviously, but—"

"Stop—you'll thank me for this someday. How about I'll meet up with Kate at her place, and you can just casually run into us." I added bubble bath and started taking off my clothes. The water turned blue.

"The timing won't be easy," he said.

"Whatever, so you'll circle the block a few times."

"Fine."

I gave him the address, and there was silence again on the other end.

"Hello?" I asked loudly.

"My address."

"I can't hear you." I turned off the water and tried again. "What?"

"You just said my address."

"How would I know your address?" I asked.

"You stalked me? I don't know."

"I'm not a stalker."

"You googled me."

"I didn't."

"That's your friend's address?" he asked. "What apartment number?"

"5C."

He groaned. "Oh God, forget it."

"You know her?" I asked. "You know Kate?"

"I'm 4C. Of course I know her."

"Kate? Kate Pearson—lives in your building?"

"Yes, and she hates me. She stomps around in her apartment at all hours, doing God knows what. It's like fucking Riverdance *up there."*

"Oh, come on."

"And when I complain, she gets louder. She's the worst neighbor, so inconsiderate."

"She's spacey maybe, in an absentminded professor way, but she's not inconsiderate."

"That doesn't make it any easier to sleep."

"Wait a minute—she works all the time," I said. I wasn't ready to give up. "I doubt she's throwing any huge parties."

"That may be," he admitted, "but she's capable of making plenty of obnoxious noises all by herself, believe me."

"Listen to you—you sound so hostile!" I told him. "Maybe she'd like you if you tried to be friendly. Have you ever done one kind, neighborly thing for her?"

"I'm perfectly friendly. She's not a nice person."

"You don't even know her."

"It's irrelevant, Chloe. She hates my guts. Okay? But thanks anyway."

There went my whole plan. I had stumbled upon more conflict when all I wanted was harmony. Happy fucking Valentine's Day. I drained the tub, put my clothes back on, and blew out the candles.

I sent Kate a giant Valentine's balloon bouquet to make up for it.

ROOFTOPS THRIFT SHOP

All proceeds from sales directly benefit the homeless population we serve. We rely on the support of our community and gratefully accept your tax-deductible donation of:

1 Garmin Forerunner GPS Fitness Watch

Market Value: $115.00

To: Angela
From: Nancy
Subject: No worries!

Hi there,

Huge congrats re: your new baby!! And please don't worry that you had to cancel our plans with your sister. I did get a chance to meet her the day we were at Hudson. She gave an opening presentation about the school and took us on a marvelous tour of the building—super-informative for Gus. Also I think she must have pulled some strings because we got to interview with the head of Admissions himself. Not that it helped because Sam and I managed to screw it up completely, but I will write to thank her anyway.

Since our Hudson visit, it's been a whirlwind. We toured Dalton, Trinity, Collegiate, Trevor, and Graylon, and it seems as though they all went fairly well, but who knows if he'll actually get accepted anywhere. At each school I watched Gus walk off with the interviewer, and I tried to imagine what in the world they were going to go talk about for thirty minutes. It's so weird when you realize that your kid is an actual person, and you suddenly think, "Who is that?"

Turns out, Gus fell in love with Graylon, so fingers crossed because we'll be finding out very soon! To be perfectly honest, I know he won't get into Hudson after our disastrous interview, so it's good that he prefers another school. Graylon has a beautiful, renovated building, and it's very artsy and nurturing—the complete opposite of Hudson in every way.

I won't be at yoga for a while. I'm taking a trip to L.A. with my husband for ten days—first time in years we've gone away together. Oddly enough, muddling through the admissions season has somehow been good for us—it got us talking. Sure didn't see that coming.

Congrats again on baby #2. Personally, I can't imagine.

Nancy

Kate missed her apartment. She, Maureen, and Henry worked long hours, reading through every file and preparing to discuss them in committee. One folder took Kate half an hour at least, and there were hundreds of them, packed tightly together in long file drawers that ran the full length of the admissions department back wall. February was turning out to be awful, even worse than January. It was dark when Kate got to work every morning, and dark when she left to go home at night. The dark time, indeed.

"When will it get better?" she asked Maureen. "I need to get a haircut. I need to buy groceries. I need to see my sister."

"You can catch up on all of that in June."

"I miss daylight," Kate said. "I want a window."

"Quit whining," Maureen said. She looked up at the bright red and pink balloons filling Kate's office. Albert had walked the giant helium bouquet from the front desk to the admissions area, awkwardly steering the balloons down the hall and around corners, reminding Kate of her dog walking days.

"Anything you need to tell me?" Maureen asked, reaching for a string and bringing down one of the balloons to her level. "I'm very tolerant."

"She's just a friend."

"If you say so," she said, walking out of the office. "Let me know when she sends you lingerie. Come on, time for committee. I hope you're hungry."

Kate wasn't sure what hunger had to do with it until she walked into the conference room and saw a buffet table piled up with snacks, chips, and chocolates mostly, but with a few grapes, celery sticks, and cheese cubes thrown in to mask the junkiness. The teachers who had been assigned to the admissions committee were already there, crowded around the food, piling it on their paper plates. The math teacher, Tim Mitchell, forgoing the individual plates, picked up several serving-size bowls of M&M's

and chips and moved them to the middle of the conference table for easier access.

Maureen had a cartful of file folders parked behind her spot at the table, and she sat with her reading glasses low on the bridge of her nose, organizing her papers. Kate handed her a Diet Coke and a bowl of nacho cheese Doritos and sat down next to her. Maureen took the soda but pushed the chips into the middle of the table, saying, "Get those away from me, bitch, my skirt's already unbuttoned." She ate a handful of M&M's instead.

Kate took a look around the room, noting the cast of characters. Janice, the school head, was there of course. Kate didn't know her well but had heard from Maureen that she was extremely opinionated and tended to slow the meetings down. Henry would see to it that every file got a thorough look, but he nevertheless would insist they keep things moving along at a reasonable clip. According to Maureen, things would get testy between them as Janice's penchant for wasting time clashed with Henry's need to get the job done.

Coach Stafford was there, hoping there might be an athlete or two he could fight for. He never read any files in advance, Maureen had told her, but he would perk up as soon as he heard words like "all-star," "trophy," or "tall for his age."

The English department head, Susan Banter, sat with an enormous binder of notes she'd taken on all the files she'd read. Tim Mitchell, after transporting ample food from the buffet to his side of the table, rolled up his sleeves and settled into his chair as though he planned to feast there for days. Next to him was Dr. Chen, head of sciences (one of the teachers who drank way too much at the holiday party), and to her left was the sixth-grade history teacher.

Henry, taking his place at the table, cleared his throat and welcomed them all to committee. He took a moment to explain the general procedures and to remind them that this was only the first of four meetings, each of which required their attendance. And then they got started with the files, beginning with the As.

Annie Allsworth.

"Annie has fabulous recommendations," Henry said, "top ISEE scores in math, and she plays the flute. Kate wasn't fond of her when she interviewed, but in terms of academic readiness, she's a definite yes."

"Whoa, whoa," Janice suddenly said, "slow down."

"Here we go," Maureen whispered to Kate. "That didn't take long."

"I have a problem with the application essay Annie submitted," Janice explained.

"What's wrong with it?" Henry asked. "Apart from being snobby?"

"That essay about her house in the Hamptons?" Janice said. "There's no way she wrote it. It didn't sound anything like a fifth-grader."

"Lucky kid," Mr. Mitchell said. "I'd love to have a house in the Hamptons."

Maureen handed Henry the file. "There's other evidence of her writing," Henry said, looking through it. "She has high marks in English. Her ISEE essay was fine, and she certainly wrote that on her own."

"How do we know that?" Coach Stafford asked.

"Because she wrote it at a testing site?" Ms. Banter said slowly.

"Well, excuse me," Coach Stafford said. "Just asking."

"I thought her ISEE essay was very simplistic," Janice argued. "She may have written it on her own, but she was clearly just following a formula she'd been taught."

"Exactly," Henry said, "and it was well-organized, and she used detailed examples."

"She could have delved a little deeper," Ms. Banter said.

"A lot deeper," Janice added. "There was no originality of thought."

Kate tried not to get too excited to hear a bit of pushback against Annie's application.

"We need exceptionally strong writers and thinkers at this school," Janice went on, "and I'm not convinced this girl can do either."

"Of course I agree," said Ms. Banter, "that students will struggle in my classes if they don't have well-developed writing skills, but having said that, I think Annie's admissible."

"I would argue that she's more than admissible," Henry said. "Her grades are outstanding. We simply can't determine the exact degree to which any parents have helped out on application essays."

"Helped out?" Kate said. "I bet her mom wrote ninety-five percent of it." She suddenly got elbowed in the arm by Maureen. "What?"

"She's getting in anyway," Maureen whispered. "Don't bother."

"Annie got nines on her math ISEEs," Tim said through a mouthful of popcorn, "so let's not forget about that. I vote definitely yes."

"Well, nines don't mean all that much given the amount of test-prep kids get these days," Janice said.

"Yes," Henry said diplomatically. "Annie may have had a tutor, I don't know. But the fact is she writes well, her math scores are very high, and her teachers love her, and, let's not forget, she's a full-paying student."

"Fine," Janice said. "I'm just raising questions before we leap to make a decision. Kate certainly didn't like her."

"Me?" Kate asked.

"I read your interview comments," Janice said. "You had serious reservations."

"Oh," Kate said, "but that was mostly on a personal level. It's not like she's applying to be my best friend."

"So we should ignore your notes?" Janice asked.

Kate looked at Henry and felt her face flush. "No, but I think the high level of her math skills and her reputation as a student are more important than my impression of her horrendous personality. She'll be able to succeed here academically."

"Thank you," Henry said. "Well put."

The discussion continued for several more minutes, and Maureen started sighing louder and louder.

"So," Henry said finally, "can we vote on her and move on, *please*? I'm afraid we're going to be here all night."

Annie was admitted, and while Kate was disappointed, she wasn't surprised. She leaned over to Maureen and said, "Guess we'll have to get all the doorways widened to accommodate her head size."

Maureen took her glasses off and gave Kate an approving nod. "Good girl," Maureen said. "Now you're catching on."

It took twenty-two minutes, but they were finally ready to move on to the second applicant. The second of four hundred applicants.

"Excuse me," the history teacher said, her first contribution to the meeting. "Can we take a restroom break?"

"Wow," Maureen mumbled. *"Already?"*

"Good idea," Janice said. "I've gotta make a quick call," and she left the room.

Henry put his pen down on the table and looked up at the ceiling with his eyes closed tight. Tim went back to the food table to refill his bowls of chips. He brought two cans of Sprite back with him. Maureen shook her head and made the face she always made when she was thoroughly disgusted with everyone around her.

"Hey, Maureen," Kate told her, "you're making that mad face."

"Yeah? You will be too by ten o'clock," she said.

The evening wore on, and eventually they made their way to the Bs.

Dillon Blake.

Bad scores, bad grades, bad recs. Just astonishingly bad. Kate felt sorry about it, but Dillon was an obvious no. After Henry quickly presented his notes, it looked as though it would be settled right away. Henry called for the vote.

"Not so fast," Janice said. "Aren't you forgetting something?"

"No," Henry answered flatly.

"Silvia Blake went here," she said. "Did you call the development office to ask what they think?"

"I didn't."

"Because we always check with development."

"Not this time," Henry said.

"Why not?" Janice asked.

"This is a clear-cut rejection. This boy would fail out of here within a week."

"Well," Janice said, "I think we should discuss him first, instead of just writing him off. I read Kate's write-up, and she said, and I quote, 'maybe structure is exactly what a boy like this needs.'"

Kate looked up to see that everyone was staring at her. "Yes, but the thing is I interviewed him way back in October," Kate explained, "before his grades and scores came. As it turns out, structure is probably the *last* thing this boy needs."

Maureen took Dillon's file out of the cart and handed it to the teachers to peruse.

"In any case," Janice went on, "we should certainly consider wait-listing him so that we don't anger an alum unnecessarily."

"We can't," Henry said. "No way."

"Why not?"

"We can't wait-list a kid who is this many miles outside of the acceptance norm. It makes no sense. We wait-list him, and then reject some other kid who is stronger in every respect? No, there has to be some consistency."

"That may be," Janice said, "but I'm simply bringing to the table the fact that his mom is possibly a generous donor. And we have to tread carefully."

"Even if his mom is Melinda Gates," Dr. Chen said, flipping through the file, "we're going to have to say no. There's no way he could keep up with the demands in science." She passed the file to Tim.

"I read this one," Ms. Banter said. "He can't write a complete sentence."

"He can't add or subtract, either, according to his math teacher," Henry said.

"Holy cow," Tim said. "Check out his grades," and he handed the file to Coach Stafford.

"I know that his mom is an alum," Henry said. "And *if* she's a donor, I'll call her personally to give her the news."

"Fine," Janice said.

"So it's settled?" Henry asked. "We can move on?"

"Wait!" Coach Stafford suddenly said. "He plays soccer!"

By now it was 8:30. Maureen poked Kate on the shoulder and asked for the chips. Kate passed the bowl, but it was empty. Maureen made the face.

The committee meetings were tedious at some moments and contentious at others, but mostly they were long. Kate saw very quickly that everyone had an agenda. Henry's was to give every applicant a fair but efficient review. Coach Stafford's was to fight to recruit a few athletes. The science teacher was primarily interested in finding kids with an interest in robotics, saying things like, "Can you imagine what this girl would do if we let her loose on our 3-D printer?" Janice's mission was to please the development office. She would flip to the preliminary application and say greedily, "Oh, goodie, a hedge fund guy!" or "This mother has her own *foundation*," and Kate's favorite, "A Tony winner could easily be persuaded to outfit our theater with cushier seats." Maureen's goal was to move things forward to the vote, and when time was wasted, she would get hostile and make sounds under her breath.

Kate realized on day two what her own agenda was, once they reached the Gs.

"I interviewed Claudia," Kate said proudly, "and believe me, we really want this girl."

"Claudia," mumbled Janice, as she scanned through her notes. "Claudia. Claudia. I don't think I read this file."

"I love her," Kate said, and Maureen kicked her under the table.

"Okay," Janice said. "Can you tell us why?"

"She's a terrific girl," Kate told the teachers. "She's intelligent, and she's a good citizen. Nice to people and unusually empathetic." No one said anything. "She's very smart," Kate went on, turning to Dr. Chen. "She loves studying biology, such as plant life and human anatomy and things like that. She wants to be a doctor. And she's so interesting to talk to," Kate went on to Ms. Banter, "about poetry or literature or history or anything. She's mature, and she's a model student. Did you see her recommendations? Her teachers love her."

"Kate had a very positive impression of her," Henry said. "Claudia is solid academically, and her teacher did write a very enthusiastic letter."

"Do I remember reading something about a cookie party?" Tim asked.

Kate suddenly felt flushed. "It was a hypothetical scenario," she said. "I probably didn't need to include that, but I was trying to give an example of her emotional intelligence."

"Does she do sports?" Coach Stafford asked.

"She's more into academics."

"Huh," he said and got up to get another Coke.

"How are her scores?" Janice asked.

"Not so hot in math," Tim said. "Middling."

"They're good enough," Kate said defensively.

"Fives and sixes? They're pretty low," he said.

"Well, it's not like she has the resources to prep for months and months like all those other kids."

"We've got other financial aid applicants whose scores are higher, and they presumably didn't have tutors, either," Tim said.

"Did you read her essay? Her 'perfect day'?" Kate asked.

"Can I see it?" Ms. Banter asked.

"It's this clever take on the prompt, because she didn't make something up like most of the kids did; her perfect day actually happened. It was a well-written, practically poetic description of a day she spent with her dad."

"Who died," Maureen said suddenly. "Her father died. This girl has been through a lot."

That prompted an "Ohhhh" in unison around the table.

"Well, that's very sad," Janice said, "but it doesn't change the fact that she's just not that great. Not if she needs the whole thing. Does she?"

"She qualifies for full tuition," Henry said.

"I'm sorry," Ms. Banter sighed, "but there are so many applicants needing FA who are better."

"Better how?" Kate asked, getting worried. "I don't understand how anyone can be better than Claudia. There's nothing negative about her."

"I think your perception's a little off on this one," Janice said. "She's weak."

"She's actually remarkably strong," Kate countered. "She's a very hard worker, and she's organized, like she has a whole system of color-coding her different classes, and she would never in a million years go to school without her homework done." Kate noticed that no one was looking at her. Ms. Banter was pretending to read Claudia's file, Tim was cleaning his glasses on his shirt, and Janice was checking her phone. Kate kept at it, saying, "She's so excited to do experiments in the science lab. I'm telling you, she would appreciate everything Hudson has to offer, every single day, and she'll involve herself in school life. I can imagine with her leadership potential, she'll probably join the student council, and she'll want to play in the chamber ensemble. Oh, and she *wants* a school with a uniform. I'm telling you, she'd be fabulous here. We would be so lucky to get a student like this, a girl who wants to be here as much as she does. How can we possibly tell her no?"

"Let's vote," Henry said. "Accept?"

Kate raised her hand high and looked around the table. "She's a wonderful girl, so well rounded," she pleaded. "Really. You'd all love her."

Maureen raised her hand, as did Henry, just out of solidarity. And much to her surprise, Dr. Chen raised her hand as well. No one else. It was 5 to 4, against, and Kate realized she was about to cry. Maureen leaned over to say something to her, and Kate prepared herself for a big "I told you so."

"Look forward, not back," Maureen whispered. "I know it hurts, but you'll have to let this one go."

Henry patted her on the shoulder.

At 11:00 p.m. on day four, they reached the end of the alphabet, and Kate was delirious.

"I'm going home," Maureen said. "It's late, and I gotta get out of these Spanx."

Kate dozed on the subway and almost missed her stop.

Stepping out onto the platform at Broadway-Lafayette, she took in the overwhelming stench of urine; that woke her up. She walked past a man who was fixing his shoe with packing tape and two women who were wasted, wearing slutty Mardi Gras costumes.

Once she made it to her building, her stomach made a junk-food growl, and it occurred to her that—as usual—she had no good food in the apartment. Another night of ramen. She got her mail and found a postcard with a picture of a capybara lounging on a raft in a swimming pool.

She started the long trek up the stairs. Ever since Maureen had told her not to get sick, she'd stopped using banisters, and though she longed to put her hand on the railing and haul herself up, she made her legs do the work instead. She read the postcard as she climbed:

> *I am aghast. Your former mentor has somehow found fame and fortune with his ludicrous, hollow best seller. Jordan Greene has written, by all measures, the most trivial embarrassment of a popular treatise I have ever had the displeasure to endure. There is no irony in this "book" which is part self-help, part pseudo-science, part sedative. The stupidity is truly staggering. He has sold his soul for millions in revenue. Self-promotion/whoring of this magnitude is more than a full-time job. (So much for professoring.)*
>
> *Do not purchase.*
>
> *Disgusted,*
> *your father*

Just as she got to the fourth-floor landing and took a moment to catch her breath, her neighbor opened his door.

"Kate? Hi."

"No," she begged, "please don't give me a hard time! I wasn't home all day, so if Stella was making noises, there's just nothing I can do about it."

He looked at her like she'd punched him.

"I'm sorry," she said. "I thought . . . Usually when you stop me on the stairs it's to reprimand me for, well, for existing above you."

"I'm sensitive to sound. And you used to be home a lot, if you don't mind my saying. There was a lot of marching back and forth."

"I walk."

"I only wanted to tell you that the meowing stopped. Your cat must have gotten used to spending more time on her own."

"She's not really my cat," Kate told him. "She comes with my sublet; she's only mine until the real tenant comes back."

"Oh," Jonathan said. "That's too bad."

"I'm sure he's a better neighbor than I am. He's studying to be a librarian, so my guess is he probably meets your standards for quiet."

"I'm sorry I come across as a curmudgeon."

"I think at our age it's called something else."

"Anyway, I got her a toy," he said, and he handed Kate a plastic fishing pole with feathers tied on the end of a long string. "I thought it looked like fun, but then again I don't know much about cats."

Kate was completely floored. "You bought this for Stella?"

"I'll get you one, too, if you want, but yeah, I thought she might like to play a little once you come home at night."

"Thank you. Stella thanks you. That's so nice."

"Your job must be really nuts, I guess. You're never here."

"Quieter now?"

"It's too quiet in fact," he said, shrugging. "I feel like I'm the only person in the whole building."

"Now I'm too quiet?"

"How's the job going?" he asked. Kate didn't answer right away. She was trying to figure out how he would twist this into something she'd done wrong. "You were a bit worried before you started, as I remember," he went on. "I didn't think you needed to be. I mean, you seem, well, you always seem capable. Like a capable person. Even when you were wearing pajamas all the time."

"Thank you. It's going well."

"No one died, right?"

"Died?"

"I told you no one would die because it's a school, not an ER, remember?"

"Yes," she said, snapping her fingers, "and you were right about that."

"Do you like it there?" he asked, sounding earnest, but Kate was still skeptical.

"It's not the best month to ask, actually. I have no life. My sister just had a baby, and I've only seen it one time, for, like, five minutes."

"It?"

"Her, sorry. Grace. But things will settle down soon, at least that's what I hear. And not to freak you out or anything, but I get four weeks off in the summer, and I'm really looking forward to spending some time at home. But I'll wear socks no matter how hot it gets."

"No socks, please. I, well, I miss your footsteps, to be honest."

This was a radical departure. Kate wasn't sure how to respond. "I could stomp around in boots tonight. If that would help," she said.

"Or tap-dance maybe?" and he began a clunky dance move ending with "Cha!" It was surprising and awkward, and his face suddenly went red.

"Well, I can't top that," Kate said, turning to leave, "but if I can muster up the energy, I'll jump rope. Thanks again for the present, Jonathan."

"Funny thing," he said, stopping her. "Do you know we have a friend in common? Chloe."

"You know Chloe?"

"Long story. Sort of. Through various social media connections. People we know who know other people. It's complicated."

"I haven't seen her in ages."

"We had coffee not too long ago," he said. "She's a big fan of yours."

"We were supposed to get together last week, but I had to cancel."

"She's wrapped up in things, too, I think."

Were they dating? Kate wondered. Was he hoping for an endorsement? Now that he'd dropped the whole dorm-master persona, she tried to see him in a new light, and she decided that Chloe would certainly find him attractive. "Maybe we should all do something together sometime," she suggested, "as soon as I make it through the admissions season."

"I'd like that," he said, hand on his heart.

"You, me, and Chloe."

"Sure. Or even just you and me, if Chloe's too busy."

So maybe they weren't dating after all.

"Are you hungry?" he asked. "I was about to order sushi."

HUDSON DAY SCHOOL

Dear Mr. and Mrs. Blake,

Thank you very much for your interest in Hudson Day School. We truly enjoyed getting to know you and Dillon through the admissions process. Dillon possesses many wonderful qualities, and we are confident that his middle school years will be happy and engaging ones.

Due to the large number of highly qualified candidates who applied to Hudson this year, we are unable to offer Dillon a place in our sixth-grade class. We know this comes as disappointing news, but Dillon will surely enjoy his learning experiences and find great success wherever he decides to go.

We wish you and Dillon the very best for the future.

Sincerely,
Henry Bigley
Director of Admissions

To: Kenneth Blake
From: Henry Bigley
Subject: Re: Dillon Blake

Dear Mr. and Mrs. Blake,

Thank you for your email. While we appreciate your continued interest in Hudson, we cannot accommodate your request. We do have a waiting list, but Dillon did not get a place on it. Therefore, there is no possibility of a space opening up for him.

Your comments about your interview have been noted. I'm sorry if you were under the impression that Ms. Pearson gave you a "verbal acceptance" during your interview. This was certainly not her intention, as we would not and could not make an informal offer before the official date. We make all decisions as a committee. In addition, as a member of the Independent School Collaborative (ISC), our school follows all of the organization's rules, which include issuing decisions on an agreed-upon date in February, and not a day sooner.

While we very much appreciate your wife's status as a Hudson alumna, we cannot go against the decision of the committee for that reason.

We wish you and Dillon the very best.

Sincerely,
Henry Bigley
Director of Admissions

HUDSON DAY SCHOOL

REPLY CARD

My son/daughter: Annie Allsworth

____ will attend Hudson Day School in the fall. (Contracts due 4/12)

____ will attend a revisit day on 3/15 3/18 3/21 3/24

(Please circle one)

____ will not attend Hudson Day School. He/She is enrolling at

________________________.

Please return by March 7th

To: Tess Allsworth
From: Kate Pearson
Subject: Annie's acceptance to Hudson

Dear Ms. Allsworth,

Thank you for returning your reply card. Could you please clarify: will Annie be attending a Hudson revisit day? I would be happy to sign her up for any of the four days we offer (3/15, 3/18, 3/21, or 3/24).

I look forward to hearing from you.

Sincerely,
Kate Pearson

To: Silvia Blake
From: Henry Bigley
Subject: Re: Admissions policies at Hudson

Dear Mrs. Blake,

The way the admissions process works is that we have one round and one round only. There is no "second round." As I mentioned in my last email, our decisions are made by committee, and we do not change the decision once it has been made. I'm sorry that I cannot honor your request for an "appeal." I can assure you that Dillon's file was given thorough and thoughtful consideration. We do not give reasons for rejections, so I ask you to accept the decision as it stands.

While we appreciate your continued interest in Hudson, we hope that you will understand that we cannot make exceptions to our policies.

All the best to you and Dillon,
Henry Bigley

To: Kenneth Blake
From: Henry Bigley
Subject: Re: Appalling treatment

Dear Mr. Blake,

You are welcome to meet with your lawyer if you choose to do so, but we are an independent school and reserve the right to make decisions as we see fit. I would urge you to look at the procedures detailed on our website. The process is clearly outlined, including materials we require, important deadlines, as well as official dates for decisions. We would never and have never made an offer to a student without a complete file to review. On the day you interviewed, early last October, Dillon's file was empty.

I have complete confidence that my colleague Kate Pearson behaved professionally and kept to our procedures. If you took her friendly, welcoming demeanor as an offer of admission, then you were mistaken.

While I am sorry to hear of your wife's deteriorating mental health, I dispute your assertion that the actions of our department had anything to do with her condition. We do, however, wish her our best for a speedy recovery.

As you have threatened legal action, this is the last correspondence you will receive from me or anyone in my department. Any future letters will be forwarded to our legal counsel.

Henry Bigley

To: Kate Pearson
From: Tess Allsworth
Subject: Annie Allsworth NOT attending Hudson

Dear Ms. Pearson,

As I indicated on my reply card, Annie will not be attending a revisit day or accepting your offer of admission. We appreciate your interest in having her attend Hudson and understand that this comes as disappointing news; however, we have decided for a number of reasons that it is not the right place for her. She was accepted into every single school to which she applied, and it has been very difficult to make a choice. We have definitely ruled out Hudson as a contender, but thank you anyway.

Regards,
Tess Allsworth

Dear Ms. Pearson,

Thank you so much for everything. You were my favorite interviewer of everyone I met. I'm writing to tell you that I want to keep my spot on the wait list. Thank you very much. I am keeping my fingers crossed that something will happen, and you will tell me I can come to Hudson.

Thank you for putting me on the wait list.

Yours truly,
Claudia

March

George and I moved to a new apartment in Alphabet City, had sex without condoms, and took a romantic trip to Cape Cod, and my friends still didn't know he existed.

In early March I got the flu. I was achy and weak, recuperating slowly, and I called Kate to cancel plans we'd made for the following day. She assured me that rescheduling would be easier now because she was close to coming out of what she called "the dark time." She thanked me again for the gifts, the notes, the candy. I guess I did those things out of guilt, but I like to think it was also nobler than that, that I was trying to be a good friend.

"It's after seven," I told her. I was sitting on the floor of our new place, sipping ginger ale and trying to empty a book box. Carter was lying down next to me, his tail thumping even though he was sound asleep. "I can't believe you're still at work. Are you doing okay?"

"Better than okay. It occurred to me the other day that I'm feeling great," she said. "I was walking to school, and I suddenly had this thought, 'I'm a person who has her act together,' and I don't know how it happened. I pay my bills. I'm punctual. The people I work with think I'm reliable. If I keep this up, I'm going to be employee-of-the-month material."

"They're lucky to have you."

"But I've been such a terrible friend; I don't know anything that's going on with you. I feel completely out of it. How's your life? What's happening with you?"

"Same old, same old," I said.

"Really?"

"No, not really." How could I possibly fill her in? "When I see you, I'll tell you everything," I said, "starting with George."

"Who's George?"

"He's a guy I'm dating. We're kind of serious, actually. Very

serious." I got up to join George on the bed. He had caught the flu from me and still had a fever. He was sitting up with an ice bag on his head, holding our rescue kitten Tutu (as in Desmond) in his lap.

"George?" she said to me. "I love his name. It's so earnest."

"You have to meet him," I told her. "It's impossible that you won't like him."

"And Vicki? How's she?"

"Oh, fine," I said vaguely. "I'm sure she's fine."

"Well, we should make a plan, the three of us. Or just you and me maybe, so we can really get caught up."

"And Jonathan?" I asked, making room for Carter, who jumped up on the bed and planted himself right between us.

"We've had dinner together almost every night since we stopped hating on each other in the stairwell. He waits until I get home before he orders takeout."

"That's neighborly," I said, nudging George and giving him the thumbs-up.

"You should have seen the look on his face when I told him the librarian is coming back, and I have to move out during the summer," she said. "It was kind of adorable."

"He really likes you, he told me."

"We'll take it slow, see how it goes."

I appreciated her caution. We agreed to get together in April, after the last group of accepted students visited Hudson to decide if they wanted to attend. Kate said she was nervous. She had schedules to make, sample classes to organize, and buddies to assign.

"It might not sound like much, but every student who attends a revisit day is expected to leave wanting to enroll," she explained, "and I have to set up all four days. If anything goes wrong, it's on me."

"What could go wrong?"

"A lot, because now the tables are turned. All year these students have been trying to get us to like them and now that we've told a

select group of them that we do *like them, suddenly everything's flipped the other way around: we need them to like* us. *So let's say they don't, and they choose another school; then we won't hit our eighty-five percent yield, and Henry will lose his mind, which I've never seen him do, and the board of trustees will be really pissed. And if we're actually under-enrolled for the fall, we'll have to keep seeing kids through the summer, pretending every time like a spot just happened to open up because some beloved Hudson family was unexpectedly 'transferred to London.' I have to make sure that the accepted students have the best, most stimulating, friendliest day a child could possibly have at Hudson. There can't be any mishaps. What if a visiting kid feels sad and lonely during lunchtime in the cafeteria? Or a couple of Hudson high school students are making out in the stairwell just as my visitors walk by? There could be an accident, like an explosion in the chemistry lab or a child could trip and fall into the ceramics kiln."*

I stopped her. "I'm sure none of that is going to happen."

"Last year the guy who had my job, Nathan, lost a kid."

"He what?"

"He had around twenty-something students revisiting the first day. Somehow, in the middle of all the chaos, there was a mix-up with the buddies, and one kid didn't know where he was supposed to go, so he wandered around alone and ended up in the high school video production room. It was empty, so he got on one of the computers and played Miniclip games."

"For how long?" I asked.

"A couple of hours. He had a great time, chilling by himself. All the parents arrived to pick up their kids, and Nathan suddenly realized he was missing one. He ran around the middle school floors, checked every bathroom, every classroom, every closet, and came back to the lobby, completely freaking out, which didn't help the situation. The mom started screaming at everyone, and she tried calling her kid's cell. When he didn't pick up, Nathan actually started

crying, making a huge scene. You've met Albert, right? Our security guy? He assured everyone that the boy hadn't left the building, but Nathan couldn't pull it together. Eventually the film teacher found the kid playing Club Penguin *and brought him to the lobby. The whole thing was a huge mess. Anyway, I want everything to go smoothly on my watch."*

She had one more hectic, nerve-racking month before she could finally relax a little.

"Can I bring you anything?" she asked. "Soup? Saltines?"

"No, no. I have everything I need," I told her. "I'm fine."

"And Vicki?" she asked again. "What's going on with her?"

For half a second I considered telling her the truth, the story of another terrible, messy situation, but found I couldn't get the words out. Why spoil a nice conversation? Instead I sent her a fruit basket. I felt guilty, plus I knew she didn't have time to shop.

Victoria noticed with horror that she had a small pimple on her nose. It was stress, and she didn't appreciate it. Whipping this boy into shape was proving even harder than she'd anticipated. When Robert was in town, they were together every night, but when he left, he wouldn't call for days at a time. He was inconsistent. She had a long way to go to get him to do things her way.

And it was hard dating a man that handsome. Everywhere they went, girls gawked and made eyes at him. Walking into a restaurant, she would see a pretty blond head turn, and then she'd watch him intensely to see if he made eye contact with her. On her way to the ladies' room one night, she stopped at a table of college-aged girls, leaned in to one in particular, and said, "Back off, bitch." The girls looked at each other and laughed, and Vicki stormed off to the bathroom in a rage. She couldn't recall a moment that humiliating. Standing at the sink, she looked in the mirror, asking herself, "Who am I? Who am I?" She arranged her beautiful hair, put on lipstick, and said, "I'm a girl who gets exactly what she wants."

And, in fact, it seemed she had him, with all of his flaws. Chloe was right: his judgmental comments were irritating. They weren't insults exactly, more like little put-downs, about the fit of her pants, the size of her apartment, the seriousness of her job. He was astonishingly self-satisfied and had something to say about everything. But on the plus side, his apartment in Paris was to die for, his skill in bed remarkable, and she didn't expect him to be perfect. They would have these amazing nights together, and she would forget all about the opinions he flung around. Besides, she often agreed with his opinions, many of which were quite sensible. Flying first-class, for example, is always worth the money, but excellent wine doesn't have to be expensive. Absolutely true. Robert appreciated good design, whether in clothing, furniture, or hotel lobbies, and respected it as an art form just like she did. And he could be thoughtful in the most remarkable ways, remembering the details of everything she said and then acting on them. She had mentioned offhandedly that she'd bought a cool, sexy IRO dress at Barneys, so Robert surprised her during Fashion Week with an IRO jacket and an invitation to a private party with the French men behind the label, the Bitton brothers themselves.

He was so ridiculously French, which was somehow an asset and a defect at the same time. The beautiful, heavy accent and the embarrassingly deep V-neck T-shirts, the smoking that she'd thought was social and turned out to be addictive. Wine ditto. Espresso ditto. His obsession with soccer. His attitude about Americans who make a crisis over every little thing when all they need is a nice dinner with friends and an easy solution that is probably staring them right in the face. "What eeez ze problem?" was his usual response to any problem, which felt undermining every time she presented a goddamn problem. But then again, maybe he was right? What *was* ze fucking problem, after all? She just needed to stop being insecure. Self-loathing didn't suit her. Although self-admiration didn't suit him so well, either; she never knew any man could spend as much time as he did primping and studying his face in any reflective surface he could find. One night at a restaurant, he tried to check his profile in a spoon.

If Chloe knew how much time she spent either arguing with Robert or stalking him, she'd give her a big I-told-you-so lecture because she wouldn't understand that it was complicated. She and Robert had grown-up issues. They would iron them out eventually, and once they did, it would all be okay. Victoria expected that one day, Chloe and Kate would be happy for her. The past simply made for a funny story. A slightly awkward but nevertheless hilarious wedding toast. Bygones.

Neither Chloe nor Angela knew that the miserable breakup

Kate endured, the infamous airport dumping, had made Vicki ecstatic. She kept that to herself, of course, and had taxied with Angela out to the airport, letting Chloe take the fall, while she had feigned an outpouring of sadness and concern when she was, in fact, privately elated. It was a triumph, a score for Team Vicki. It was restitution for that night, that graduation dinner, that was supposed to be the moment when she and Robert reconnected, a year after their Parisian fling, when instead, he'd gotten caught up with Kate, with the wrong girl, and Vicki stood there watching while her soul mate flirted with her friend.

Fucking Kate.

Victoria—taking her usual peek at Robert's laptop when he was in the shower—discovered that Robert had contacted Kate. He'd sent an email saying he wanted to see her, talk to her. Victoria wished she'd never suggested that he apologize. It was supposed to be a way of smoothing things over, of allowing them to go public, but now it seemed like he really wanted to connect with her. Recently, on a one-week vacation from his job (that didn't actually seem to be much of a job, in that he never actually needed to be anywhere), Robert came to New York and talked about Kate more and more, dropping her name, remembering things, telling stories about her. "*Quel dommage*, that Italian restaurant eeez closed. Kate and I had a marvelous dinner there one night." "Kate bought me theees book; I always meant to read eeet, and she was right—eeet's wonderful." "I hope Kate eeez enjoying her work; eeet was clear to me ze life of a professor was not ze right choice for her." He lit a cigarette and opened a window, as if that would help.

Victoria answered with a jab. "Chloe acts like Kate's job is such a big deal. Even if she had potential, a long time ago, she threw it all away. You do know that she's just an administrator, right? She's a glorified secretary. Whatever."

He shrugged and said, "Certainly they figured out how intelligent she eeez and how very personable."

"What good does it do anyone to be intelligent or personable when it doesn't materialize into real success?"

"Eeen any case, I'd like to see her sometime," he said casually, exhaling a plume of smoke all over Vicki's white walls, carpet, and couch, "just to catch up, you know? As I said before, we should all be friends again."

"Why?" she asked, teeth clenched to the point of breaking. "What do you want to know? I mean, yes, she's doing swell without you. She has a job, she's probably seeing someone, whatever, why do you even care?"

Robert stood there, glass of wine in his hand, skinny jeans on his ass, and said, "Victoria, what eeez ze problem?"

"Nothing. There's no fucking ze problem."

He flicked his ashes into a saucer, saying, "Jealousy doesn't look good on you, darleeeng. Eeet makes you look ugly."

"I have a boyfriend," Kate announced.

Maureen was in the middle of printing out the final RSVP list of families who had signed up for spring tours. "So?" she asked.

"Well, you said once that if I met a new guy, you'd be happy to hear about him."

"You misunderstood."

"He lives in the apartment below me."

"Does your girlfriend know about this?" Maureen asked.

"All this time," Kate said, "we've just bickered in the stairwell. I thought he was uptight and stodgy; we couldn't possibly have gotten off to a less passionate, less amorous start. And the thing is I always thought it was important to get crazy and carried away over someone right from the beginning. But Robert swept me off my feet and look how badly that turned out. With Jonathan, I find the more I get to know him, the more I like him, and do you know what happened last night? He said the exact same thing about me."

"Your phone's ringing."

"Jonathan is thoughtful and a little nerdy in the best way, and he loves to talk to me."

"He sounds weird."

"I can be myself around him, which is such a relief. He's smart and funny, and it turns out, he's the most romantic guy imaginable."

"And the sex?"

Kate smiled. "You are too nosy, do you know that?" she said, turning to go back to her office. "Just prying in my personal life all the time. Stop getting all up in my business."

"Your business does not interest me," Maureen called after her. "You don't even have any business. Like I don't have better things to be doing?"

Kate went back to her desk and saw she had, in fact, missed a call. She listened to the voice mail and then played it over again at least ten times. It was the saddest, most desperate drunk-dial message she'd ever heard. She played it for Maureen, who didn't find it sad at all.

"Scary maybe," she said, "but not sad. Silvia Blake has gone off the deep end. I told you New York City parents are batshit crazy."

Henry listened twice and contacted the school's lawyers, who archived the clip and issued Silvia and Kenneth Blake a cease and desist order.

> "You think you're really something, don't you? You think you're so powerful? You're just some stupid bitch *girl* who goes around ruining people's lives. You think you're God, don't you? You think you're God with your little computer, sending your stupid letters like you're in charge of everybody and [*indecipherable*] key to the gate, like you're some goddamn bouncer bitch who gets to decide, and you're standing at the door choosing [*indecipherable*]? Well, you lose, lady, because Dillon would have been the best thing that ever happened to you and you're too dumb to get it. I hope you get hit by a cab. Good. Bye."

Huge mistake. Angela got a stupid, springtime idea in her head that she would look like a younger and cuter new mom with a short, pixie haircut. It turned out she didn't. She was on maternity leave with too much unstructured time on her hands, most of which she spent looking in the mirror, tugging on the ends (as if that would help), and begging it to grow in faster. Turned out it didn't.

When she first walked in the apartment with the new hairdo, Grace started crying. Angela locked herself in the bathroom and started crying, too, which made Emily cry. Doug stood in the midst of all the tears, telling Angela how much he liked it, how pretty she looked, which was a big lie, one she could see right through because Doug never knew when to stop talking. He stood at the bathroom door making choice comments like "Of course I love it, sweetheart; it's the same haircut I always get." She wrapped her head up in a scarf and emerged from the bathroom, only to hear, "Wow, honey—you look exactly like your mother."

It was a hideous haircut, boyish and severe in the worst way. One needed serious cheekbones to pull off hair this short, and Angela didn't have them. *It will grow back* became her mantra. In the meantime, she just didn't want to get stuck thinking about it every time she was sitting on the couch breastfeeding. She needed to keep her mind occupied on something else. As much as she appreciated the time at home with Emily and Grace, she missed her bustling, productive days in the office. She missed having a project to keep her busy, so she decided to come up with one.

Project #1: Kate. Angela suspected that she had something going on with her boss, and it had to stop. Kate always denied it, but she talked about him all the time. Henry this and Henry that. She had spent the month of February "working late" with him every night. She'd accepted not one, not two, but three dinner invitations, and those were just the ones she'd told Angela about. She was rushed every time they spoke, like she was avoiding talking to her, and even when she came by to meet Grace, she had some excuse to leave after only a few minutes. Angela knew what Angela knew. This man who was so "supportive" and full of compliments was obviously trying to get in her sister's pants. How could Kate not understand the implications of something like that? Why didn't she have better judgment?

Angela felt a need to develop a Plan B, in case the entire situation exploded and Kate either quit or got fired. She wanted to plant a seed of ambition, get Kate thinking about an eventual return to academia. She got on her computer to search the NYU anthropology website to see what would be involved in the process of reapplying, when she noticed that her father was online. He was a newcomer to Facebook, and he had gotten thoroughly carried away posting selfies, poems, and random observations from wherever he happened to be on his sabbatical. Angela thought it was embarrassing, because who cares about his thoughts on the founding of the National University of Córdoba? And who wants to see pictures of a bookstore in Buenos Aires? A *bookstore* that looked to Angela like every other bookstore she'd ever been in. She was planning to instruct him on better Facebook practices, until she saw that he had 1,184 friends.

In taking charge of Kate's future, Angela figured it made good sense to get her parents on board, to enlist their help. After all, they had every reason to want to see Kate launch a successful return to their professional world.

She clicked on his name.

hey dad

Ahoy there, Angela. Greetings.

all ok?

Magnificent. How are your little ones?

great. and mom?

A dynamo.

i was thinking . . .

A worthy activity.

maybe time for kate to start
thinking about grad school
as in again
back on the horse
hello?
dad???

Yes?

could you make some calls, see if you can
connect her w someone you know in her area?
get her motivated, excited to go back?

Mmm, don't think so.

i know she's been out of academia awhile,
but I'm sure there's something you can do

Eu não entendo.

what?

She likes her job, yes?

it's not something she'll want to do forever.
isn't a return to anthropology the long term goal?

For whom?

? for kate who else?

No, I don't think so.

why not?

She's happy.

maybe now, but down the road . . .

If it ain't broke . . .

don't you think she should go back?

To bio-anth?

yes

No.

wait why not?

She hated it.

what? no she didn't

She did.
And to be honest it wasn't her strength.

meaning . . . ?

She lacked the requisite skills.

???????????
not what her college profs thought

That was college, not life.

what's the difference?

The quality of the food.

dad. be serious.

In that case: she'd be better in something related
to social psych. More human, with a focus on
the present. She needs to share ideas and be
engaged with people, living ones, not dead ones.
Analyzing dry bones makes for a very solitary life.

Why not stay where she is now?

i just assumed

Is a return to anthropology her idea or yours?

mine

Ah. I see.

?

Let's let Kate take charge of her own journey. She is navigating through obstacles, and she may get tripped up on them, but I assure you she will make it through in the end.

not sure what you mean by any of that but i disagree. strongly

At every meal in Deutschland they ask if you want your water flat or "mit Gas." You my dear are flat. Kate has gas. We need both kinds. We need loan analysts as well as carbonated people who jazz around. The bubbles may look out of control, but ultimately they know in which direction they're going.

i'm flat?

As am I. Your mother on the other hand . . . She is highly effervescent.

Must locate her as it is time for tea. Eu te amo, dear.

Excuse me??

Até a próxima vez.

huh?

Over and out.

Incomprehensible. Misguided. And possibly insulting. But in any case, none of that talk solved the problem that Angela saw looming.

She didn't want to, but she called Victoria to ask what she had heard about Henry, which turned out to be absolutely nothing. She and Kate hadn't spoken in months. Victoria sounded oddly pleased about the news of a possible affair, even after Angela explained that he was married.

"But at least she's moved on," Victoria said. "That's a very promising step."

"But this guy is old and has a wife, and he's her boss. It's a disaster."

"Aren't you the one who introduced her to him?"

"What? No, I only connected them. Professionally."

"Well, it shows she's over Robert. Isn't that what we wanted?"

"I guess I wanted more than that," Angela said. "Didn't you?"

Over her better judgment, Angela decided to call Chloe as well, but Chloe refused to believe that Kate was involved with her boss in any way that wasn't professional. "Certainly not," she said plainly. "It's not true."

"How do you know?"

"Because she isn't dating an older, married man she considers to be her mentor. No, it would be completely out of character for her. She has better sense than that and a conscience, too. And besides—she's dating someone else. A guy I know."

Angela allowed a pregnant pause. "Chloe. The last time you set her up, it didn't end well, to say the least."

"I *never* set her up!" Chloe said. "I *introduced* her, but thanks for bringing that up again, with all your facts messed up. This new guy, Jonathan, happens to be very nice, and he really likes her, and from what I understand, it's mutual."

"It can't be serious or I'd know about it, wouldn't I?" Angela snapped back. "Kate would have told me. And I think—given what happened before with your despicable relative—it would be best if you didn't meddle in her life."

The speech Chloe delivered next felt to Angela as though it had been rehearsed a few times over: "Listen to me—I fucked up. I wish I'd told her what Robert said to me before she got on the plane, but it's not my fault he broke up with her. And it's not my fault that he did it in such a terrible way. It was a long time ago, and I'm sick and tired of you blaming me for the whole thing. I happen to be a very good friend to her, and I always have been. She's not dating her boss—I don't know where you came up with that stupid idea. She's working her ass off, she's doing a great job, and she's met a terrific guy who happens to live in her building. I know you don't want her to be friends with me but she is, and we are, so get over it." Just before the phone went dead, Angela heard a man's voice saying, "Finally, babe! Good for you!"

Dear Ms. Pearson,

I apologize for the voice mail my wife, Silvia, left you. She was understandably very upset. She is taking some time to recuperate from the stress of the admissions season and is feeling much better now. I hope we can start again fresh.

We need to talk to you, to hear from you what happened with Dillon's application. All we need is a few minutes of your time. We have decided not to sue you or the school for your actions, although we probably could.

Given what happened and the situation we're now in as a result, we're certainly entitled to an explanation. I'm sure you would agree that this is a fair request. Our family got completely screwed over, so I think you owe us at least that much.

I would prefer you not mention this to Henry Bigley, as we have been asked to stop contacting anyone in the school.

Kenneth Blake
CEO Universacom

To: Sherman
From: Kate
Subject: bon voyage

May I congratulate you, good sir? I'm sorry that the position at KU isn't what you were hoping for (tenure-track wise), and I'm shocked, to be honest. But still, I'm happy that the Jayhawks recognized the value of you two lovebirds ;-) and that they snatched you both up in whatever way they could. Please tell Lakshmi congratulations on her Asst Prof post. As for you, I know that adjuncts are not treated as well as they should be, and I'm sorry they're not offering benefits (yay, Obamacare), but you are a determined, passionate, invested, promising researcher, and I'm sure over time they'll find you indispensible and, at some point, they (or another institution) will offer you the job you deserve. Yes, I promise to visit if I ever get to Kansas, and please, please look me up the next time you're back in New York.

Meanwhile—I hope the next 5 months of fieldwork at Laetoli yield fabulous data and some good memories as well. Godspeed!

Be safe out there! And please keep in touch.

Xxxooo
K

To: Kate Pearson

From: Office of Kenneth Blake

Subject: Meeting request

Dear Ms. Pearson,

I am the administrative assistant for Mr. Blake. Please call or email me as soon as possible regarding the appointment Mr. Blake and his wife Silvia requested over a week ago. Mr. Blake is very busy, but he has asked me to find a time that is amenable to you.

Sincerely,
Sandra

Picking Dillon up from school was the last thing Silvia planned on doing that day or was fit to manage. She was sprawled out in bed, watching episode after episode of *The Real Housewives of Who-gives-a-fuck*, having taken an indeterminate amount of time off from work to rest her tormented mind. That's what the psychiatrist prescribed, rest and calm. And a cocktail of calming meds to take the edge off. No thinking about her clients, no thinking about anything at all. Silvia was in a nice, blank, bleary state, where she could exile the crisis and all of its hideous details to some unknown place in her mind, a place she could stay the hell away from.

In the lovely haze of the afternoon, the babysitter called, saying she had the flu and couldn't pick Dillon up from school.

"You're fine," Silvia told her. "Just go get him and take him to the park. You can lie down on a bench."

"No way," the babysitter said, hacking into the phone, "I can't work today."

Silvia thought of calling Kenneth to explain the situation but decided against it. He didn't need to be bothered with this nonsense. She was his young, energetic third wife; she was someone who could do it all. Being worried over, like she was some kind of invalid or something, felt all wrong. Kenneth used to brag about her being efficient and accomplished, but lately he'd been describing her with words like "fragile" and "unstable," and she didn't want to be those things. So to prove she wasn't, she somehow got herself up, ordered an Uber, and arrived at the school gate, just as Tess jogged up wearing teensy shorts and a spray tan, dragging her stupid little dog behind her.

"Hey, Silvia! *Bonjour! Wow*, you're certainly dressed for winter." Silvia had pulled her long fur coat on over her pajamas, assuming no one would notice that she hadn't exactly groomed that day.

"Yeah, well, I've been in meetings, so how am I supposed to know spring came when no one bothered telling me?"

"You okay?"

"Of course," Silvia said, pulling her coat around her. "Why wouldn't I be okay?"

"No, I just mean that *I'm* certainly stressed out—poor Annie has been to one school revisit after another, just wearing her out. I know it sounds spoiled, but it's a burden to have so many choices." Arms over her head, she stretched to the left side and then to the right. "And the pressure of deciding, of choosing the *one*, it's just so hard, you know? She's leaning toward Chapin right now, but other days she thinks she wants coed, and I'm hoping for Spence, but then again we both loved Riverdale. Oh! What to do?!"

"Sure, yeah, I hear you."

"We're going to our house in France for spring break, just to recover from all the stress! Has Dillon made a decision?" Tess asked, jogging in place.

"Nah, I'm not pressuring him, you know?"

"Right, but the deadline is coming. What's he leaning toward? Hudson?"

"I'm sorry," Silvia said, "but can you stop jumping around like that? You're making me spizzy. Dizzy."

Tess stood still and stared at Silvia.

"I've had a flu," Silvia explained.

"You poor thing," Tess said, taking a step backward.

"And I really don't care all that much about the school stuff. I mean, fuck it, you know?"

"Wow, okay. I wish I could be so cavalier. I just want us to pick the right place for Annie. Dillon got into Hudson, right?"

"He did, but somehow they lost my metal in the mail. Lost my letter the mair. I need to call them."

"The schools did email acceptances. Annie got her acceptances at nine a.m. sharp on the day. Same as everybody else."

"Well, I mean, he's *in*, obviously. They told me so to my face when we were there. I don't really need it in writing."

"My God, Silvia. That's really . . . That's the weirdest admissions story I've heard all year. Have you paid your deposit? And what about the contract? You need to sign the contract."

"I'm going to talk to them," Silvia said. "I called them already."

"And what did they say?" Tess asked.

"Nothing. I left a message."

"I don't understand. You're an alum there. I mean, you should go talk to them about it. Get some answers."

"I know!" Silvia said suddenly and way too loudly.

"Even if it turns out . . . I'm sorry, I'm still confused, though," she said, crossing her arms in front of her. "Where did Dillon get in *exactly*?"

"Where did Annie get in *exactly*?" Silvia said, crossing her arms and mimicking Tess's voice.

"*Silvia!*"

"*Tess!* Ya big show-offy bitch."

"Okay," Tess said, holding her hand out in front of Silvia's face. "I don't know what's going on with you, but you're a little scary, and you're wearing bedroom slippers, okay, so I really don't know what to say to you. Ah, here comes Annie. I'll see you."

"*Annie,*" Silvia scoffed as Tess started to walk away. "Puh-lease."

"Excuse me?" Tess asked, taking Annie's backpack from her, while Annie started baby-talking and kissing all over the dog.

"No, nothing," Silvia said. "It's just that, *Annie's* not as awesome as you think she is." Silvia nodded, letting that sink in. "She's not all that *special*, you know? Hate to break it to you, but someone had to."

"What?" asked Annie, eyes wide, looking up with the little dog in her arms.

"I beg your pardon?" Tess asked.

"I think someone should tell you that Annie's got a very weird-shaped head. Look at that thing. It's always bothered me, since first grade. I just thought you should know, in case a doctor didn't tell you already, you should get her checked out because she's borderline syndromish."

"Mommy," Annie said, starting to cry.

"Silvia! What? What is wrong with you?"

"Oh, pooh, take a joke. Ha! I have to go get Dillon down off the jungle bars. He just loves playing, you know. You could learn a thing or two from him, like you shouldn't be so fucking serious all the time." And she walked away, leaving Annie in tears, and Tess in a pink-faced rage.

The previous September, on the day he interviewed Kate Pearson, candidate for the assistant director position, Henry talked about her in great detail with Pat, whose opinion he valued greatly. Pat was wise in a way that he wasn't, could see things before they happened. Henry appreciated that about him and brought his problems home to him every night. He figured if he were president of the United States, Pat would be one of those First Spouses who advised him on matters like foreign policy, and he'd be criticized for it, but he would ask for his advice anyway because his judgment was spot-on.

Pat was the guidance counselor at a large public school, so his world, although also in education, was nothing like Henry's. Some people may have thought it was strange that they both worked in schools, having never had children themselves. They spent their days with other people's kids, they had their evenings to themselves, and they never felt they'd missed out on anything. They both looked young because they didn't have children to age them prematurely. They slept well, and they had money to spend on vacations. This past summer they had taken a trip to Italy; they had seen it all and done it all, from the Duino Castle near Trieste to the vineyards in Tuscany.

When they returned from their trip, rested and ready to begin another school year, Henry had gone into work to find the following letter on his desk:

> Hey Henry,
>
> I hate to do this to you last minute, but I quit. I spent a lot of time soul-searching over my break and decided I can't hack another season. I don't know how you and Maureen do it. All the judging, rejection, and injustice have left me drowning in a cesspool of negative energy, and I owe it to myself to be in

a healthier place in my head. I still have recurrent nightmares about losing that child.

I wish I had Maureen's ability to make jokes about the kids and keep it light. You guys are able to keep a healthy distance from it all, and, hey, whatever works, man. But I can't be down with that; it's not who I am. I have to honor my feelings and step out of this profession.

I'm moving in with my mother so I can get my degree in computer programming. As you would say, it's a better fit for me.

Peace
Nathan

Having to fill Nathan's position on such short notice was the worst possible way to start a new year. Hudson's online student application would be going live in a matter of weeks, so there was barely enough time to post the job opening, review résumés, and schedule interviews. Henry spent a few days seeing a handful of applicants, none of whom was even remotely qualified, and one of whom was a registered sex offender.

When Henry came home the day he interviewed Kate, his final applicant of the batch, he walked into the apartment utterly defeated and said, "What am I going to do?"

Pat picked up two sets of hand weights and suggested they discuss it during their walk around the reservoir in Central Park; the temperature had finally dropped below 85 degrees, and they could talk while they enjoyed a beautiful fall afternoon, getting their heart rates going at the same time. Power walking was a new activity. Before their big trip to Italy, Pat and Henry went for their annual checkups, and Henry's ECG showed a weird dip in his T wave, an inversion, an abnormality. He was sent to a cardiologist for a follow-up, and Pat went along because if Henry was having a heart problem, he needed to know how to fix it.

The doctor prescribed daily aerobic exercise, whole grains, low fat, and Lipitor, all part of what she called "necessary lifestyle adjustments."

"How's your stress level?" she had asked. "Are you sleeping?"

"No stress at all," Henry had said. "I'm on vacation, actually, heading to Italy in a few days."

"But when you're not on vacation?" she pressed. "Do you eat well? Exercise?"

"No," Pat said, "he doesn't."

The doctor frowned. "That's going to have to change."

"And his job is very stressful. There are three people in his department, doing the work of five."

"It's not that bad," Henry said.

"I didn't say it was bad. I said you're overworked."

"I always sleep well."

"You have to start taking better care of yourself, Henry," Pat insisted. "Tell him."

"He's absolutely right," the doctor said.

Henry started to feel ganged up on.

"Your ECG shows some kind of cardiac episode," she went on, "and it may be an anomaly, but you should take it as a warning sign. You need to lose ten to fifteen pounds, get at least thirty minutes of exercise every day, and take your medication."

"I'm fat?"

"And don't overdo," Pat added.

Henry liked Pat's attention and concern, but he didn't like the idea of being told to alter his habits or food intake. He didn't like the idea of getting old.

"This interview was actually funny," Henry said as they headed out to the park for their brisk walk, pumping their weights by their sides. "I don't mean good funny. She was so bad, it was laughable, or at least that's what Maureen said. I'm in such a panic, I can't even be amused by it."

"Don't be mean," Pat said. "What was so wrong with her?"

"I wish you'd been there. Maureen made fun of her all afternoon. I nicknamed her the Kate-astrophe, but Maureen calls her Nervous Nellie. Or Seventeen."

"Why Seventeen?"

"That's how old Maureen thinks she is."

"You and Maureen are vicious."

"It gets us through the season. And we need nicknames; how else can we keep track of the hundreds of people who walk through the door every year?"

"So what actually happened?"

"Aside from shaking and sweating and talking about nudity, using the word 'asshole,' and wearing a skirt that's too short? Not a thing. She was *fabulous*. Ideal."

"Sarcasm," Pat noted. "Nice."

"Well, she's out. I'll start over again tomorrow and try to find someone tolerable before things get too busy."

"Because she used a bad word?"

"Among other things."

"I hate to remind you, but you need to find someone in a hurry. You can't possibly do without a third, so before you rule her out, you better at least give me a good reason."

"She's too young," Henry explained, "too self-deprecating, and frankly too . . . flustered."

"So?"

"Pat, she was terrible."

"Why?"

"Because she was rambling."

"What's wrong with being talkative? You're rejecting this woman because she was flustered? And young?"

"I was with her for quite a while. Believe me, I gave her a chance."

"It sounds to me like she was just anxious."

"No. I mean yes, she was, but it was the content of what she said."

"Like what?" Pat asked.

"She was inappropriate, politically incorrect, and incapable of lying even for the right reasons. She's totally inexperienced. I'd have to teach her everything."

"Training someone can be much easier than retraining," he said. "Can she pick things up quickly?"

"Maybe," Henry admitted, "because she must be at least a little bit smart."

"Sensible smart or brainy smart?"

"Brainy smart, but it doesn't matter—this was without a doubt the worst interview ever in the history of interviews."

"Hyperbole."

"Well, I'm sorry, but she said things that no one in her right mind would say when trying to get hired." He could feel himself getting winded already. "She got very sweaty at one point. Like drippy sweat. It was painful to watch."

"Poor thing."

"Do schools smell like bologna sandwiches to you?" he asked.

"Yes."

"This girl—Kate—actually said outright that she's unqualified for the job. Oh, and that she's not even punctual! Who admits to that?"

"Either someone who doesn't really want the job or someone very honest."

"She wants the job. She practically begged."

"Huh. Would parents like her?" Pat asked.

"She's smiley and chatty. Attractive. Yes, I think they'd like her, especially the lecherous dads." He reached his arm out in front of Pat as a bike went by fast and uncomfortably close.

"How do you know she's smart?" Pat asked.

"She's Seven Sisters summa cum laude smart. That's why I interviewed her in the first place."

"Really?" he asked. "Impressive. That must have come across."

"Mixed in with the nonsense, she said a few observant things, about fit, about the kind of kid who would do well at Hudson, even something about uniforms. Out of curiosity I called her only reference—her undergraduate thesis advisor at Wellesley. She was a dual anthropology/psych major and wrote a senior thesis that got published in an academic journal. This professor raved about her intuition, her keen observational skills, her sophisticated writing style. He used the word 'astute' about a hundred times."

"Why does she want a job in admissions?"

"I don't know," Henry said. "She said she needs a chance. Something about walking dogs and coming out of a funk. Being disconnected. What does that even mean?"

"Something or someone threw her off track," Pat said. "An illness? A death in the family maybe?"

"It's almost impossible to reconcile the girl the professor described—reliable, perceptive, confident, full of potential—with the one who showed up for the interview."

"Psychology major, huh?"

"Here we go," Henry said.

"No, think about it, Henry. I think she sounds great. Perceptive? Intuitive? That's a glowing reference. She's clearly capable of doing excellent work."

"We don't know that."

"She got a solid education, and best of all, her academic background is in two departments that focus on what it means to be *human*."

"Now you're just reaching."

"I was a psych major, and it certainly helped me."

Henry looked over and saw that Pat had barely broken a sweat. He was tanned from their trip, and he looked like a boy in his fitted T-shirt.

"In your case, the connection between psychology and your job is a little more obvious," he told him, "and fitting."

"In your job, too, don't kid yourself. You assess and evaluate personalities all day long. Anyway I don't believe in writing off a young woman with potential just because she didn't come across as perfectly polished," Pat said. "And please keep in mind that if you don't hire someone soon, you're going to start the year a whole month behind. You and Maureen can't possibly do this on your own."

"I don't know if she could do the work."

"It's not brain science," Pat reminded him.

"No, but it's relentless and exhausting. Is she good with details? Planning? Communication? Because according to her, she isn't good at anything."

"She's insecure. Somewhere along the way, she lost her confidence. You asked me what you should do. I think you should take the risk and hire her."

"Seventeen couldn't handle it," Henry said bluntly.

"My God, you're acting like you need a NASA engineer to do the job. Be fair, Henry. She's plenty smart, so she can learn your little admissions process."

"*'Little'?*"

"She's young, which means she's energetic and knows how to use a computer a hell of a lot better than you or Maureen. She's eager to get back on track, so she'll work hard because the last thing she wants is another setback. She published something, so she can obviously write well. And—best of all—she's inexperienced, which means you can tell her to do things exactly the way you want them done. And think about it this way: she wants the job *so* badly, it made her sweat. You should hire her."

"No, no, no, no," Henry said, "you weren't there. You didn't experience the Kate-astrophic, flop-sweating debacle firsthand like I did."

"Something or someone damaged a promising, smart young girl, and then you demean her and call her names? Shame on you, Henry. How soon can she start?"

"Immediately."

"Perfect. Take her under your wing, get her back on her feet. She may need extra support, so tell her what a good job she's doing at least twice a day. Treat her like a grown-up, an equal. Invite her to working dinners to discuss strategies for the year. Let her know you trust her opinions and instincts. If she does well, she'll be grateful to you for the rest of her life, and she'll bend over backward to do a good job for you." Pat stopped walking and put his hands on Henry's shoulders. "I don't want you wearing yourself out this year, okay? You have to be around next summer to take me to Scotland, or I'll kill you."

"I'll be around."

"You better be. Hire that girl."

"Are you being serious?"

"Entirely. If I'm wrong about her, you can let her go in the spring."

"So—for the record—you're encouraging me to work with a young, unqualified, troubled, sweaty person? Maureen will think I've completely lost my mind."

"You and Maureen could use a shake-up. I bet she's going to do you both good."

April

One year ago, George and I met at a conference on hunger in Washington, D.C. It was a beautiful spring day, and we were assigned to the same breakout group in one of the afternoon sessions on the impact of food stamp cuts on working-poor families. Every time I looked over at him, I caught him watching me. When the conference ended, we took the same bus back to New York together, and from then on everything moved smoothly and very quickly. This relationship was easy. It wasn't fraught with conflict; it was perfect for me. We came into it with such balance. Our thoughts on topics across the values spectrum were perfectly in tune:

Religion—atheist
Politics—progressive
Finances—almost equal amounts of debt and almost equal salaries (high and low, respectively)
Biggest problem our country faces—greed
Allergies—none
Vision—nearsighted
Etc.

I'm not saying we've never had an argument, but when you start out with so many of the big topics as nonissues, you've got a pretty heavy advantage going in.

There was a bar in our neighborhood that George and I had decided was our "local." It suited us. It was a bit of a dive, but the drinks were cheap, and it was dark and homey, with pretty votive candles on the windowsills. We were meeting Kate and Jonathan there, and we arrived first to get our usual table. I hadn't seen Kate in so long, I felt almost giddy waiting for her; I couldn't wait to talk to her, to have her meet George, and to see the chemistry between her and Jonathan.

To: Angela

From: Nancy

Subject: Thanks to you and Kate

Angela—

A million thanks to your sister—would you believe?—Gus actually got IN to Hudson! I can't imagine how, but he was accepted! Kate clearly went to bat for us because between Gus getting suspended from school and Sam and me ruining the interview, there was NO WAY. Even our placement specialist told us to forget about it. So thank you for putting in a good word, and please thank Kate for doing the impossible. She is one powerful lady!

Gus decided on Graylon Academy in the end. Something about he wanted "experiential learning," "creative expression," and "collaborative circles," whatever the hell that all means. But it was great to be able to tell everyone he picked it over Hudson. Ha!

I'm sorry I didn't share the news sooner, but things have been really busy. Sam and I are taking a big summer trip together, a private cruise in the Mediterranean. I've got gobs of shopping to do.

Thank God for nannies, right? :)

Nancy

Ms. Pearson,

Silvia is distraught at your refusal to do the humane thing and talk to us. All we want is to know what happened. We have to apply all over again next year, so it would be helpful to know what went wrong so that we can receive a better outcome next time. Even as I write this, it does not sound like a lot to ask. It is astonishing to me that you remain unwilling to help.

Kenneth Blake

"So Maureen comes into my office," Kate was saying, "and looks in the Victoria's Secret bag and says, 'Ha! Lingerie! I told you! I told you that girl is hot for you.' "

Angela was struggling to focus on Kate's litany of work stories, but she somehow couldn't keep up. "That who's hot?" she asked.

"No, she's . . . It was just funny."

"And Maureen knew that?"

"Never mind," Kate said cheerfully. "You probably had to be there."

Angela had come uptown to a restaurant near Hudson to meet Kate for lunch. She had arrived ten minutes late, and Kate was already there, waiting for her, engrossed in *The Tenant of Wildfell Hall*. "I'm rereading every Brontë novel by the end of the summer," she had said, putting the book away in her bag.

They were sitting outside at a table on the sidewalk, pretending spring had arrived, taking off their coats but keeping their scarves on as they waited for the food to arrive. The place they'd chosen was packed with people in oversize sunglasses who were drinking iced tea and shivering.

"I might get a coffee," Angela said suddenly. "Pep me up a bit."

"Does Grace sleep through the night yet?"

"Ha. No."

"I'll start coming over more now," Kate said. "I promise. I have four weeks off, and I can help out anytime you want."

I'll believe it when I see it, Angela started to say, but instead she smiled. "That would be great."

Doug had suggested a form of behavioral therapy: suppress the urge to make a disparaging remark by saying something positive in its place. Angela was doing her best, but it was a challenge. She found it so hard not to find fault, not to foresee disaster. She had come to lunch with the goal of putting a stop to her habit of criticizing, giving her sister credit instead, trusting Kate the way Chloe did, the way her parents did.

Angela had a list of apologies, and she was prepared to talk through each one, starting with "I have this tendency to underestimate you." Her little sister was—what had Nancy said?—powerful? She could do the impossible. Her boss liked her because she worked hard, not because he wanted to sleep with her. Angela felt like a huge ass.

"It seems like you're a pretty big deal at Hudson. Getting Nancy's kid in?"

"No, don't get carried away," Kate said. "I had nothing to do with Gus getting accepted, so don't give me too much credit."

"She said you pulled strings, got your boss to interview him."

"I just thought it would be awkward to interview him myself. She's your friend, and what if we didn't take him?"

"We're not really friends, and I think I was just trying to impress her—having an 'in' at one of the best schools in New York? I was trying to be cool."

"Cool? You?"

"Right, hilarious," Angela answered. Having her hair chopped off and getting told off by Chloe had made the past few weeks hard but enlightening.

"Have you considered hair extensions?" Kate teased.

"Yes, and I've been buying up hats all over town." Angela tried to tuck her hair behind her ear, another old habit. In spite of the incontrovertible evidence—her head—Doug was still insisting that she looked pretty, always trying to compliment her, telling her sweetly that she looked just like his handsome hero, Stephen Colbert.

The waiter came with a bread basket, and Kate checked the time on her phone.

"Are you going to be late?" Angela asked.

"It's fine, as long as the food comes soon. Hey," she said

suddenly, "in another month we'll have parents again. Finally, right?"

"It's about time."

"*Willkommen! Tervetuloa!*"

"God help me," Angela sighed.

"It'll be good, though, right?" Kate said. "Grandparents would probably come in handy."

"I'm trying hard to put aside my resentment toward them for their neglect and abandonment."

"They'll make up for it: prepare to be subjected to a thirty-part PowerPoint lecture series, full of anecdotes and fun factoids. I'm not sure if I'm ready for all of that."

"I've always been the odd man out in the family," Angela confessed, "but it looks like I've finally won you over to my team."

"What if I want to be on both teams?"

"Meaning?"

"Turns out my job is a little like applied sociology. I was thinking, maybe someday I'll get a degree in social psychology. Or pedagogy. Or maybe even educational policy. Or maybe not. I don't know. No need to decide now." She shrugged.

"What?"

"Or maybe I could be a school guidance counselor someday, like Henry's husband. When I meet him, I'm going to ask him about it."

" 'Husband'?"

"Pat."

"Who? What are you talking about?"

"My future. It's a lot to think about. Doors just flying open everywhere I look, you know?"

Angela just sat there, adjusting to Henry's sexual orientation and to her own apparent inability to be right about anything anymore. At the same time she couldn't help marveling at her sister's lack of direction. Despite her father's metaphor about carbonation, the one in which he made the claim that Kate had some clue where she was heading, it was hard for Angela to see anything other than random, chaotic movement.

"So, are you seeing anyone these days?"

"Yes!" Kate said. "As a matter of fact, I'm dating my neighbor."

"Is it serious?"

"I hope so."

"When were you going to tell me?"

"I just told you."

"Well," Angela said, "that's wonderful." *Be positive. Be positive.* "And work is still going well?"

"I love it. You were so right: you were the one who said a school would be a good fit for me. You must want to send Henry a gift basket for taking me in." She looked at Angela and smiled. "I know I was a serious pain in your ass for a while there. You hid it well, but you must have been really sick of me."

"No," Angela said. "But I've missed you the last few months. I thought you were avoiding me."

"Not at all. I was just busy, making rookie mistakes."

"I doubt that."

"It's true. Okay, here's one that weighs on me: I begged Henry to let me wait-list this one girl, Claudia, since she didn't get in, because I thought it would be kinder to cushion the blow, rather than flat-out reject her. He said it was a bad idea, but I insisted. And now I realize he was absolutely right, because all I did was keep her hopes up for another month for no reason at all. It was cruel."

"But you're right that a wait list is nicer than a rejection."

"No. Nicer on me maybe. But if you know it's going to be a rejection anyway, you're just prolonging the agony for the other person. I should have listened to Henry."

The waiter came with their food and took a moment to deliver condiments and refill their water glasses. Kate looked up at him and said, “Can you please bring the check as soon as you get a chance?”

In terms of maturity, punctuality, and responsibility, Kate had certainly made impressive and unexpected strides. “I’m proud of you,” Angela said, “and I hope that doesn’t sound condescending.” It was true that she was proud; Kate was doing well, and she was energized in a way that Angela found comforting and reassuring. However, she couldn’t help but notice that Kate’s shirt was unbuttoned one button more than it should have been, and she was itching to say something. *I can practically see your bra, Kate. My goodness, don’t you ever look in the mirror?*

“Pretty blouse,” she said instead.

May

It was the week's Breaking News, or "Afternoon of Terror!" as one news program coined it. When it was all over the board of trustees ordered a review of the school's security systems and protocol in order to evaluate exactly what went wrong and to prevent anything like it from happening again.

The event—or "School Scare!" as another news program called it—left Albert sad and shaken. He felt the whole thing could have been prevented had he only been more vigilant and forceful, had he only stuck firmly to the Guest Identification Guidelines as he'd been trained to. He wasn't held responsible because the security footage showed a scene far too chaotic and congested for one guard to handle alone, so new procedures were established to stagger dismissal times by division, thereby decreasing the flow of human traffic over a thirty-minute period. Furthermore, Albert was assigned a partner for the two busiest times of day, mornings and afternoons, and additional security cameras were installed on the school's exterior. A big debate followed on the pros and cons of installing a metal detector in the school's entry, and the parent body voted it down, feeling it would look too threatening and might upset the children.

The episode—or "Nightmare on 84th Street!" as yet another newspaper headlined it—began when a couple entered the building at 3:15, just as school was dismissing. They were heading in as 250 students were heading out.

"Excuse me," Albert said. "ID please."

"We have an appointment," the older gentleman said over his shoulder. "We're just dropping off some papers for Kate Pearson," and he and his wife pushed through the swarm of kids and past the indoor park benches to the admissions department. Albert should have gone after them, but they were so well dressed and sure of themselves, so moneyed, that he didn't. The woman was wearing enormous dark glasses, and the man was in a pinstriped suit. They knew their way around, and Albert accepted their air of privilege as license to skip the red tape, a mistake he forever regretted.

Kate saw the couple walking down the hall, and she stopped them in the sitting area of the admissions department. She noticed right away that Silvia Blake was not in her right mind. She was sloppy, listing slightly to the side, like her Xanax had been sloshed down with a glass of gin. She looked older, worn, and her roots needed serious attention.

"Can we talk?" Kenneth said.

"I'll get Henry," Kate told them.

"No," he said. "You."

"That's a pretty party dress," Silvia said, trying to focus in on Kate's buttons. "So pretty. What is that?"

"Sweetheart—let me," he said, and he propped Silvia against the wall. "We need to talk to you," he told Kate. "You know what went wrong. You're someone who understands this impenetrable process. You have to help us."

Silvia wagged her finger. "I remember he said you have a leg in, or a foot on, or whatever he said. Ah! You have the smell of all this—something about smell."

"You screwed us over," Kenneth said. "You liked Dillon when you met him. You were very enthusiastic, too enthusiastic apparently, and then out of nowhere you dumped him."

Kate stopped him. "Mr. Bigley—and the school—they've already told you multiple times that we can't discuss decisions once they've been made. I'm sorry I can't help you. I'll walk you out."

"Excuse me, Miss. Lady," Silvia slurred. "Don't think you can just do that, just blow us off like that, like we're nobody. We're here now, and you better show us some respect," she demanded. "I want to know why you hate my son."

"No one hates Dillon, but we can't discuss decisions," Kate repeated.

"Yes you will. You will. You have to," Silvia insisted.

"No, you have to leave," Kate said.

"Calm down," Kenneth started, "all we want—"

"You will too talk to me!" Silvia cut in, stomping her foot and pulling a shiny silver handgun out of her Louis Vuitton. It matched her chunky platinum rings. "I'm an alum here, goddamn it. You can't tell me to leave."

"Are you shitting me?" Kate asked, throwing her hands up in the air.

"Easy now," Kenneth said, and Kate wondered which one of them he was talking to. Silvia's Chanel sunglasses, which she had propped up on her head, dropped down over her eyes, and she seemed confused as to why she couldn't see. She pointed the gun randomly at the ceiling, and then the floor, the file cabinet, and then the ceiling again. "Okay, doll, why don't I hold on to that," Kenneth suggested.

"Oh, psshhh," Silvia said, carelessly dropping the gun in her bag like it was nothing but a pair of cheap reading glasses. "Take a joke. Everyone's so serious all the time. I need to sit down."

Kate went into a sort of role, like she was playing a part. All she had to do was get through this, handle it, by acting like she understood more of the situation than she did. She had gotten good at that after nine months at this job. Just another interview.

"We'll talk," she said, pointing toward her office. "Let's go talk." She walked backward to the file cabinet and pulled Dillon's folder, fat with school reports and letters. "The thicker the file, the thicker the child," was what Maureen always said.

"Can I see that?" Kenneth asked.

"No," Kate said, hugging it to her chest. "You're not allowed. We have strict rules here, like no weapons of any kind in the building. Is it real? Is it loaded?"

"Oh, please," Kenneth said. "It's not like she's going to use it."

"That's not what I asked," Kate said quietly, wishing she knew how Henry would tell her to deal with an angry, psychotic couple wielding a gun, with people who can't take no for an answer. *We never went over that scenario at dinner*, Kate thought, but she knew what he would say; it was obvious: *Make a run for it. Run away screaming. Run for help.* It wasn't that she didn't want to haul ass out of there, but she could so clearly imagine a bullet hitting her right between the shoulder blades if she were to turn her back on them. She was too afraid to do the one thing that made the most sense.

Instead Kate followed her own instincts and entered her office with Silvia and Kenneth, closing the door behind them. They all sat in the same spots they had during the interview the previous fall.

"*Humiliated*," Silvia belted out. "That's what you did. You humiliated us. It's been a nightmare, everyone else's kids getting into school after school, and then there's us. I want to know how come you think those kids are any better than my Dillon. You just went out of your way to screw with us. I keep remembering at the end of the tour here, someone said—what did he say?—we should try to 'enjoy' the process. I don't even know what that means. Enjoy what? It's been a nightmare. I have a muscle thing in my left eye that never stops, I can't sleep—they put me on all kinds of pills."

"We don't understand what happened," Kenneth said. "How come no one wanted our kid?"

"Ten schools," Silvia suddenly shouted. Her bag was in her lap, and Kate kept her eyes on Silvia's hands; she was holding them out, fingers spread wide, to make her point.

"Silvia, please," Kenneth said.

"We applied to ten schools! And got ten rejection letters."

"Maybe you should wait outside," he suggested.

"Or at home," Kate added. "I could call a cab?"

"Do you have any idea what that looks like?" Silvia went on. "Ten rejection letters filling up my in-box? Dillon has no place to go. What's he supposed to do now?"

"You should have accepted him," Kenneth said. "You made a big mistake."

"You sure did," Silvia added. "You all did. I know a conspiracy when I meet one."

Kate had studied enough psychology to understand the basic problem: Kenneth and Silvia were delusional. In the Abnormal Behavior course she took at Wellesley, she'd learned that people suffering from delusions aren't swayed by evidence that contradicts their beliefs. You can put facts in front of them, but facts won't change what they perceive to be true. In this case, they believed that Dillon could succeed in a school like Hudson, an opinion that defied all logic. Silvia also seemed paranoid, convinced that there had been some kind of orchestrated effort to sabotage Dillon's application. Kate wondered if she could somehow get them to accept the truth, a risky and likely futile idea, but she couldn't think of what else to do. *No one will die*, Jonathan had told her, *no matter how incompetent you are*. She hoped he was right.

"I'll talk to you," Kate said, "but I need to make sure you understand that there's nothing I can do to get Dillon in here next year. You can force me to explain our reasoning, but Henry says that once decisions are made, they're final."

"Oooh, la-dee-da," Silvia chimed in. "*Henry.*" She started coughing.

"Are you okay?" Kate asked her.

Silvia reached for a tissue and blew her nose. "No, I'm not *okay*. I'm sick, obviously. I took an antihistamine with my Zoloft before we left. With a swig of cough syrup." She jammed her hand into her bag, and Kate held her breath; Silvia pulled out an Altoids tin. "This whole thing has made me ill. And we're going to have to go through it all over again next year. I can't stand to even think about it. I feel like I might actually throw up."

Kate passed her the garbage can.

"We need answers," Kenneth said. "What happened?"

"One thing I've learned," Kate said, "is that admissions is about fit, so I'll try to explain why we feel that Dillon and Hudson are a bad fit."

"I object to that," Silvia said, "fundamentally."

"I haven't started yet," Kate said weakly. "Let's go over what was submitted." She opened the file. "So first of all," she began, "you already know this, but Dillon's test scores were really low. Dillon and I had a nice conversation when he interviewed, but as soon as the scores came in, I knew there was a problem. And then when you called about it, I suggested that you have him tested for a possible learning issue or even test anxiety, just to give us a better understanding of why he did so poorly."

"Oh, come on," Silvia said dismissively, sucking on a mint. "You put too much *empathis* on that stupid test."

"Maybe we do," Kate acknowledged, "but in this case he scored, sorry, at the rock bottom of every percentile in every category. Hudson can't accept a kid with scores that low. It's a big red flag. It shows that there's something wrong."

"There's nothing *wrong* with him," Silvia said suddenly, clenching her teeth. "I think there's something wrong with *you*." She turned to Kenneth and mumbled, as if Kate couldn't hear her, "I might just shoot the bitch after all."

"No one's shooting anyone," he responded.

"My wording was bad, I'm sorry," Kate said, feeling herself getting sweaty. "I didn't mean *wrong*. I only meant that his scores indicate that he would have a hard time managing the curriculum here. There's an incompatibility."

"I do not believe he did that badly," Kenneth said, very plainly.

"But he did," Kate said. "The scores are right here," and she held them up. "You've seen them."

"I think they're someone else's scores," Silvia said. "They got the test swapped around with some other kid."

"Stupid machines," Kenneth added.

Oh my God, Kate thought, *classic delusion*. "Maybe you're right," she said hopelessly. "I just thought that more thorough testing could help you figure out what happened."

"Dillon doesn't need any more testing," Kenneth said.

"You're so dumb," Silvia said, "making such a big deal out of some random numbers. He's just a little boy. I figured you'd see this test for what it is: *irrevalent*. A bleep. A blip. A blotch."

"Well, I want to agree with you, believe me, I do, except I can't because, well, because the scores were in line with everything else in his file," Kate said tentatively.

"Nuh-uh," Silvia said.

"That's impossible," Kenneth added.

"Have you talked to Dillon's teachers?" she asked. "He struggles in school."

"No, *he's* fine. It's just that his teachers don't like him," Silvia explained, "and they pick on him. It's not his fault that they like girls better than boys."

"His teacher—his very experienced teacher—was working with him to teach him basic subtraction. In the fifth grade," Kate explained.

"Well," said Silvia, "as long as we're spilling all the beans here, let me tell you what I know about math: ten rejection letters, taking over my whole goddamn Gmail account. And guess how many acceptance letters," and she made a zero with her hand and squinted one eye to see through it.

"He lacks basic skills," Kate said slowly. "He would need nonstop individualized attention to get caught up."

"Let's say you're right," Kenneth proposed, "and I don't think you are . . ."

"Okay."

"Then we would need a top-notch school like this one. If Dillon needs the best teachers money can buy, fine. We have money."

"This school—" she said clearly, "I'm assuming you know this already since Silvia went here—this school is rigorous and competitive and highly stressful. The students here do three to four hours of homework every night, hard homework, stuff I can't even do. And we don't do remedial help. We don't accommodate individual student learning needs because Hudson students don't have any. It's not that kind of school, and it doesn't pretend to be. There's no recess here, and the list of rules is a mile long: sit still, tuck in your shirt, don't talk out of turn. It's an amazing place for certain types of kids, but tell me truthfully, can you picture Dillon sitting down to do an hour of grueling Latin homework every night?" Kate asked.

"I can picture him looking adorable in his little blazer," Silvia said, her eyes glazing over. Kate wondered if she might pass out.

"Personally, I think he would rise to the occasion," Kenneth said. "He's getting older and more mature every day. You're not giving him credit for the strides he's making, every day, big strides. By the fall, he would be fine."

Nothing she said was getting through to them. They wanted answers, but if they didn't believe or trust her, then what good was it to go through this exercise? How could she possibly get them to leave? "Should we talk about extracurriculars?" she sighed.

"Absolutely, Dillon plays guitar like a—" Kenneth said.

"Rock star?" Kate asked. It came out bitchy and sarcastic, and Mr. Blake was taken aback.

"Excuse me? Are you saying he doesn't?"

She started to apologize when she recalled that in the interview they had said they wanted to talk to someone in charge. They were used to going "to the top." She wondered if she were tougher and more confident, if she were more like Vicki, would they respect her? Could she school them then? *Who am I?* she thought to herself, sitting up taller. *I'm God with my little computer. I'm the bouncer bitch.* If facts wouldn't sway them, maybe bullying would; it was a method they likely understood. "You know, that rock star line, it isn't . . . It's . . ."

"It's what?" Kenneth asked.

"That rock star line is *bullshit*," she said and swallowed hard.

"Excuse me?" Kenneth asked.

"You showed me that talent show clip. That was *air* guitar, for God's sake. Tell me truthfully—can Dillon play? Or does he just fake it and put on a show?"

The Blakes looked confused.

"Does he take lessons? Can he read music? Does he even want to *learn* how to play?" she asked. "I'm going to go out on a limb here and say probably not, given that he has a guitar without strings."

"You're a very mean person," Silvia said.

"No, I'm asking a question: can Dillon play the guitar?" Kate asked.

"Only a little," Kenneth admitted. "Maybe a chord or two. We may have overstated his abilities."

"Okay," Kate said, feeling emboldened with her new tack. "Dillon is no guitar prodigy, so let's not pretend he is. You're padding his résumé instead of presenting his qualifications. It would be better to stick with his strengths."

"I see," Mr. Blake said. "Point taken."

"Is there anything he can do well?"

"You are so rude," Silvia said.

"No, I mean, tell me what he's passionate about. What are his actual strengths?"

"How about the pretty picture we sent?" Silvia asked. "The landscape."

Kate looked through the file. "Ah yes," she said, finding the artwork and looking Kenneth directly in the eyes. "You want my advice for next year? Don't send in stuff like this. What were you thinking when you put this in an envelope and mailed it to us?" she asked. "I mean, what are you trying to *say* with this? That Dillon's an artist? First of all, we're not an art school. And second, unless your kid is da Vinci, and—trust me—he's not, you have no business sending your kid's doodles to an admissions department, and certainly not *this* admissions department. This picture shouldn't get sent further than your own refrigerator, and even then, I'd think twice." Kate noticed that their posture had changed. Kenneth looked angry, but he was leaning forward, actually listening to her, and Silvia, struggling to focus, had put her bag down on the floor. Kate's adrenaline kicked in, and she kept going. "This scribble? That *Dillon* has somehow titled, 'Upstate Farmhouse #7'? Come on, as if I'd believe that he even knows what 'upstate' means. Oh, yes, Dillon, tell me what you mean by 'upstate'—oh, wait, you can't because you have some kind of undiagnosed processing disorder. And '#7'? Are you kidding me? This drawing is part of a series? A *series*? Like Monet's haystacks? And by the way," she said, holding up the drawing, "this does not even call to mind a farmhouse. Where's the farmhouse? Hm? Where exactly on this piece of paper is the farmhouse? And don't tell me it's Dillon's abstract representation of a farmhouse because I'll puke."

"Jesus Christ," Silvia said loudly.

"I'm not trying to be mean," Kate said truthfully. "You're here, asking me what went wrong, and I'm telling you how this works."

"So what do you want us to say when you ask about what activities a little kid likes to do?" Kenneth asked.

"It's not a trick," Kate said. "Be honest. What does Dillon like to do? Reading? Legos? What?"

"Honestly? I don't know. He watches TV?" he said.

"What else?" Kate asked. "How does he spend his time?"

"Monkey bars," Silvia said. "He's very at home on a jungle gym."

"Okay, good, monkey bars. Anything else?" Kate asked.

"Soccer," Kenneth added. "The kid can really run."

"Great," Kate said. "It sounds like Dillon is very athletic."

Silvia perked up suddenly. "Tape!" she said. "He likes tape. He likes tape a lot. He makes things out of tape, and he likes to tape things together. And wrap things up in all kinds of tape, but especially duct tape and red masking tape. You can't imagine how much tape we buy."

"He does like tape more than the average person," Kenneth admitted reluctantly.

"Okay. Then you need to find a school that embraces a kid who struggles with subtraction, loves sports, and is creative with duct tape. I wish you'd told me about the tape thing when you were here. You say that I misled *you* during the interview? Well, maybe I did but at least it wasn't on purpose. You intentionally misled me."

"Wait a minute," Kenneth said, "so I'm supposed to believe that if we had walked in here and said, 'Take our kid; he loves tape,' you would have accepted him?"

"Absolutely not," Kate said emphatically. *Final arguments*, she thought. "That's precisely my point. Hudson is decidedly *not* a tape-friendly school. It's serious and demanding, and no one gives a shit about tape. And the sports program is totally mediocre because it's just not a priority here. If you had thought about it and thought about who Dillon really is, my guess is you would have crossed Hudson off your list."

"And send him where?" Kenneth asked. "I'm not sending *my* son to some second-rate, lousy school."

"This isn't the time to be a snob, Mr. Blake, honestly," Kate said. "It's not about that, first-rate or second-rate. It's about Dillon. Do you want him to thrive in school? Or do you want him to feel every single day that there are expectations put on him that he can't possibly meet?"

There was a loud knock on the door that startled Silvia and made her jump. Henry walked in, wondering who would be having a closed-door meeting with Kate at the tail-end of the season. He looked alarmed when he saw who it was.

"Henry, you remember Kenneth and Silvia? Dillon Blake's parents."

"What is this?" Henry asked sternly. "I explained to you repeatedly that we don't change decisions, or explain decisions . . ."

Kate wondered if he was addressing her or the Blakes or all three of them.

"Oh, ppsshhht," Silvia said, spitting a little. "We're in the middle of something here." She grabbed her bag again and reached her hand in, as Kate considered the option of tackling her onto the floor. This time Silvia pulled out an empty bottle of Smartwater.

"It's okay," Kate said, wondering if her armpit sweat was actually visible through her dress. "They just want to talk. We're wrapping things up."

"I don't know about that," Silvia said. "Don't be rushing me, lady. Could I get a drink around here?" She shook the empty bottle. "I'm thirsty."

Henry looked at Kate and started to say something.

"Trust me," she told him. "It's fine."

He stepped back and made a weak version of his chivalrous arm gesture, allowing Kate to go on.

"No, I mean, would you mind excusing us?" Kate said.

Henry looked stunned. "You're asking me to leave?"

"Could you please go refill Silvia's water?" she asked, taking the bottle from Silvia and handing it to Henry. Anything to get him out of the room. Kate felt she was close, so close, to getting them to understand, and the last thing she wanted was for Henry to get in the middle of this mess and end up getting shot.

Henry looked furious, but he walked out of the office and closed the door behind him. Kate figured he was either going to tell Maureen to post a job opening for Kate's position or, more likely, he was going to alert Albert; either way she knew she didn't have much time to end this meeting in a peaceful and even positive way.

"You guys seem like good parents," she said sincerely, "to be advocating for Dillon like this, and I know you want him to be happy."

"I want *this* school to make him happy," Silvia said sadly. "This is the school we want," she said.

"I know you think it is. But you need to understand that it's the wrong school for Dillon." Kate scooched her chair closer to Silvia and spoke slowly. "Think of it this way: it's like when you're crazy in love with a guy, and you try really hard to be what he wants, but he treats you like shit and rejects you. And you're completely devastated about it, you're so sad, until one day you wake up and realize, 'Wait a minute, that guy is a total dick,' and then you think about it a little more, about how bad he made you feel, about how he wanted to change you into someone else, and then you think, 'That *asshole*? He's not my type at all. I wouldn't go out with *him* if he were the last man standing.' Finally you see it, and—even if it's too late—you're like, 'Oh my God!' And *you* reject *him*."

Silvia leaned in and tried to take in what Kate had said. "Ohh-hhh," she whispered.

"Right?" Kate asked.

"Right," Silvia said. "I reject *you*!"

"Yes! Exactly! *You* reject Hudson, because for Dillon, Hudson *sucks*. It's the last place you'd want him to go."

"You *suck*," Silvia said.

"I see what you're saying," Kenneth agreed.

"Exactly," Kate said. "Hudson *sucks*. Screw Hudson. What you want is the *best* school for Dillon, the right school," Kate said, "and I'll help you find it. I'll sit down with Henry tomorrow, and we'll come up with a list for you. I'm sure we can help find a good solution for this fall." She wasn't actually sure of that at all, but she felt there was momentum; she was making progress with them and didn't want anything to mess it up.

"That's so sweet," Silvia cooed. She looked sleepy and was slouching sideways in her chair.

"That would help, yes," Kenneth said. "I admit my knowledge of private schools is pretty limited to the top tier."

"Why don't we do this: I'll call you tomorrow afternoon," Kate suggested. "That will give us some time to pull together a good list of options for Dillon. I can also put you in touch with Mel Branson. He's a school placement guy. He'll take a lot of the pressure off of you and Silvia because he can handle most of the details."

"That's an excellent idea," Kenneth said.

"By this time tomorrow we'll be well on our way to solving this," she said, speaking more quickly now, placing her hands on her thighs, and starting to get up, a move she hoped signified the end of the meeting.

"Just as long as it's all over soon," Silvia mumbled. "I can't take any more of this, I swear. It's killing me."

"I'd better get her home," Kenneth said, getting up and helping Silvia to her feet. "So did you say you'll call me, or I should call you?" he asked.

"I'll call you," Kate said.

Kenneth let go of Silvia and shook Kate's hand. "This has been so eye-opening," he said. "I mean it, I really appreciate this. You're very good at what you do."

Silvia wobbled and tried to steady herself. "I reject *you*," she said emphatically. "I like that. It's so much better than the other way around." She hauled her purse up on her shoulder and turned a sickly shade of gray. In no particular order, she threw up on the carpet, dropped her bag, and the gun fired.

June

In less than a year, Kate went from catatonic loser on the sofa to local hero and celebrity. She claimed everyone had the facts wrong, but the news anchors said she wrestled a gun away from a lunatic woman, saving countless children and teachers from imminent death. I was proud of her, I'm not going to lie.

"They're making such a fuss about it," Vicki said. "It's not like she got shot in the face."

"What are you saying?" I asked. We were having drinks with Vicki and Robert, for what I hoped would be a chance to salvage some remnant of our relationship. It might have been a lost cause, but it was important to me to try.

As I sat there in our favorite bar, holding George's hand under our usual table, I wondered if there was much of anything the four of us had to talk about. Vicki was in a fierce mood, and Robert was, of course, Robert.

"Chloe, Chloe. I can't believe you would pick theees bar of all ze places in New York City for us to have our reunion. A 'dive'? Eeez that what you called eeet? I would like to say eeet has character, but eeet's too sticky to be charming." He was using a napkin to wipe the grime off his elbow.

"This wine is god-awful," Vicki remarked. "Tastes like Welch's grape juice."

"Do you want to send it back?" George asked.

"I can choke it down," she said.

"We met Kate and her boyfriend here not too long ago," I told them. "Before the incident."

Vicki threw her hands up. "Kate's upset, Kate's depressed, Kate's employed, Kate's a goddamn hero. I get it."

"Anyway," George said, trying to change the subject. "So whew, Paris to New York, New York to Paris? You two must have some carbon footprint."

"And since when does getting shot make you a hero anyway?" Vicki went on. "Dodging a bullet should make you a hero. And it's not like she sustained some sort of permanent injury. It barely grazed her calf. It's a flesh wound. Why do we have to make a saint out of her?"

"What's the problem?" I asked.

"Nothing," she said.

"Kate was eeen ze hands of a maniac," Robert said, "and a centimeter away from certain death. You can't eeegnore a beeeg story like that."

"It was more like three feet from fatal," Vicki argued.

"Let's just talk about something else," I proposed. "How are things with you?"

"Everything's fabulous," she said and moved her chair a little closer to Robert's.

"I have stuff to catch you up on," I told her, "about me and George, some really good things."

"Speaking of catching up, let me ask you something," Vicki jumped in. "What did Kate say when she heard about us?"

"I thought you didn't want to talk about Kate."

"That's what she says," Robert laughed, "but then she always does."

"I don't want to talk about her. This is about us*," she said.*

"Kate was surprised," I told her, "and incredibly understanding."

"You see? Ancient history, what did I tell you?"

"Except that she doesn't want anything to do with you anymore. With either of you."

"Kate will come around," Robert said casually. "We are all adults, after all. I don't see ze problem."

"Well, I do," I told him. "I think it's a big problem. You two didn't give her even the slightest consideration before you . . . you . . . She's not your friend anymore, you know." I winced at how childish I sounded.

"We are civilized people," Robert said. "All except for Doug, who proved himself to be an absolute brute. But Vicki and I will *be friends with Kate again one day, you'll see."*

"That would be nice," George said, "I think."

"What do you want me to do?" Vicki said. "Break up with him? Some of us want what we want, when we want it. Maybe that's hard for someone like you to understand because you're always so fulfilled doing everything for everyone else in the world, passing out blankets and free fucking sandwiches, while you practically starve yourself, but some of us are a lot more selfish than that."

"Good grief," George said.

"That's really . . . bitchy," I told her, "on so many levels."

"I'm only trying to make a point," Vicki said.

"Well, thanks for the critique. Maybe we should just call it a night?" I suggested.

"Oh, come on, Chloe," Robert said. "Seeet down. Victoria eeez only teasing you, and we are so happy to see you finally. You have no idea how much we miss you and how often we speak of you. There's no need to have an argument."

"What are you so mad at me about?" I asked Vicki. "I didn't do anything."

"Because you won't even try to see this situation from my point of view. You two always take the same side; you gang up against me."

"No we don't."

"She's jealous," Robert said, chuckling. "Sometimes eeet's hideous, and other times eeet's adorable."

"I am *jealous," Vicki said. "I admit it. It's very upsetting that you refuse to be happy for me."*

"I'm trying. Why do you think I'm here?" I asked.

"Try harder," she said. "I'm your friend, and you're not allowed to be mad at me anymore. Whenever you want something, I

always encourage you, don't I? I wouldn't tell you you're an asshole for wanting to run a half marathon."

"Sure, but who am I hurting if I run a half marathon?"

"You're running a half marathon?" George asked.

"Even if you trampled over someone in the marathon," she said, "and you just kept on going, I'd still cheer you on. I'd still be your friend. I wouldn't sit there and make you feel like a bad person."

"But it's Kate you trampled, and it's not nice."

Vicki looked at Robert and rolled her eyes.

"But hey," I went on, "I saw her, and she's fine, so it's fine, whatever. I'll try to be happy for you, just like I'm happy for her. She has a boyfriend who adores her."

"Jonathan, yeah," George said, nodding. "Great guy."

"I'm relieved to know she's doing well," Robert said. "After she threw a suitcase at my head eeen ze airport, I really thought she had lost her mind for good."

"Can you blame her?" I asked.

"Mmm, no, not particularly."

"Good. Because you were a total asshole as you well know."

"Coupable," he said.

"Did you ever officially apologize?"

"Officially?"

"At all?" I asked.

"I would like to, but how can I apologize eeef she won't speak to me?" he asked.

"You could write a letter," George suggested.

"I don't see what he has to apologize for anyway," Vicki said. "It wasn't entirely his fault."

"Well," Robert said, "I don't know about that."

"She acted like he proposed or something," Vicki told us, "like, officially."

"Pardon?" Robert asked. "Why is everything 'officially'?"

"I mean a ring, an actual proposal," Vicki said. "That's the only *thing that would justify anyone acting so rashly." She stood up and smoothed down the front of her linen skirt. "Where's the ladies' room in this place anyway? Is it revolting?"*

Robert turned to watch her walk away. "Perhaps I deeed propose," he said. "Not 'officially,' as she says, but of course Kate and I talked about a life together. But then one day somezing occurred to me, struck me on ze back of ze skull," and he patted his head lightly to illustrate.

"Was it Kate's suitcase?" I said in my snarkiest voice.

"A realization," he stated. "It came to me, all at once," and he snapped loudly. "You understand?"

"No," I said bluntly.

"No? Then I ask you, George. Yes? If a woman walked up to you tonight, and she wanted to make love, would you do eeet?"

George blinked a few times. "I don't understand the question."

"Imagine: Chloe is away somewhere, out of town, and a beautiful woman eeez propositioning you. For sex, oui*?"*

"Non. *That kind of thing doesn't happen to me."*

"But you would not," Robert said, pointing a finger at us. "I can tell by looking at you. But when Kate and I were seeing each other and I would go back to Paris *on my own, many women approached me, and I always said yes. Every time, weeezout exception."*

"What?" I asked, thoroughly disgusted. "It was more than once?"

"I confess, eeet was often."

"Oh my God."

"And then one night after many hours with a Russian sweemsuit model, I got up out of bed, and I asked myself, what eeez the meaning of theees? And then suddenly I knew: Kate deeed not love me. She was not moving to Paris *to be with me; she was moving because she needed somezing to do.* Paris*," he said sternly, "eeez not just a thing to do."*

"Oh, you poor thing," I said sarcastically. "But you really loved her, I suppose?"

"Non, *I deeed not love her either. I discovered that as well."*

I took a sip of water and put the glass down hard, causing the table to wobble. "What is wrong with you?" I asked. "You couldn't have had your epiphany, like, six months earlier? Or twelve sexual encounters before?"

"No, but as soon as I understood the truth, I knew we could not go on as before. The next day I woke up refreshed, unburdened, and the moment I saw her, I deeed what I had to do, and I told her everyzing."

"About the Russian swimsuit model?" George asked.

"Certainly not. There was no need to be cruel."

"Oh, please!" I said. "You don't get points for that. You handled the situation horribly, and you were most certainly cruel. Don't kid yourself."

"Touché. *But why must you always make a situation weightier than eeet needs to be? Life happens ze way that life happens. I don't see why eeet should to be any more complicated than that. You agree,* non?"

"Oui," *said George, "but not entirely."*

"I was not as kind to Kate as I should have beeen, I'm aware of that. But, I was not all bad for her, either; because of me, she did not continue with her studies, which was an excellent outcome," Robert added. "Work should be fun. I encouraged her to quit because she was miserable with that lifeless, boring job."

"I agree," I said reluctantly, "that she needed to find a way out."

"Ah, so, you see?" Robert exclaimed happily. "Everyzing for ze best. So don't be angry with me anymore over Kate. We have always had our fights, Chloe, but we always make up, and theees time eeez no exception, d'accord? *You know how much you mean to me."*

Vicki returned from the bathroom and sat down. "I think I caught a disease," she said.

"And the bullet wound?" Robert continued. "Eeez she going to fully recover?"

"Seriously?" Vicki asked. "Are we still on the shooting?"

"I simply want to know if Kate will be disfigured or walk with a limp. She eeez a nice girl, and I don't believe in eliminating women out of one's life after the sex eeez over. Why should we do that? It's very foolish if you ask me. I have fond memories of Kate. So, I'm giving her time to be angry with me, and when she's ready, we'll be friends again. I am friends with all of my former lovers."

"Robert," Vicki said calmly, "you and I can be friends with all kinds of people, but if you think I'm going to have dinner every other night of the week with random sluts you've dated in the past, you are out of your goddamn mind."

"But why? What is ze problem?"

Vicki took a full breath, all the way in, and all the way out. "You might be French," she explained, "but I'm very American."

"I don't know what that means," Robert said.

"It means we're doing things my way. End of discussion," and she gave him her most stunning smile. Just when I thought they were starting to have a big fight, Robert pulled her close, and she kissed him. I wondered how she would feel if she knew just how incapable of monogamy Robert really was.

"My Victoria eeez like a terrorist, you see?" he told us proudly. "You don't negotiate weeeth her. You do exactly as she says, and nobody gets hurt."

"At least I'm myself with you," she said.

"And I'm myself with you, my love. And I will tell you honestly that when you get that bossy look of a bulldog in your eyes, I can't decide if I want to walk out on you forever or throw you on ze bed."

"I don't look anything like a bulldog, and I'll tell you honestly that I want to stab you with a fork every time you say something idiotic like that," she told him.

Under the table, George squeezed my hand, hard.

"I believe you," Robert said. "Nonezeless you know perfectly well that Kate eeez not a random slut, and I plan to see her and attempt

a reconciliation. If I fail, then I fail. But when I succeed, we will be better for it. No one needs more enemies than necessary in the world. Even a terrorist knows that."

"Fine," Vicki said, sighing. "Out of respect to Chloe, I'll try to make up with Kate, get us back on speaking terms, anyway. Maybe someday she'll get our children into that fancy school of hers."

"Children?" I asked.

"I'm living eeen Victoria's apartment now, deeed we tell you already?" Robert asked.

I was floored. "You moved to New York?"

"Too much flying back and forth, landing in JFK, a véritable *nightmare. I couldn't bear eeet any longer. And Victoria, she couldn't tolerate the distance between us. Theees beautiful woman becomes wildly suspicious if she calls and doesn't hear back from me in precisely five minutes. She once sent me fifty-four text messages in the course of one hour. I counted. I thought to myself: I can, of course, keep my apartment in Paris, and I can work as well from here as anywhere else. And eeef I move in with her, that will shut her mouth for good."*

"I don't know about 'for good,'" she said. "My next demand is that you have to quit smoking all over my expensive upholstery, or I'll send you straight back to Paris."

He looked startled and then suddenly laughed at her. "That eeez not going to happen. So you can get all red in the face like you do and throw yourself on the floor and cry like a baby, and you can even send me back to Paris. You asked me to move, and I moved. I never said I would give up cigarettes, and I won't do eeet."

"We'll see about that," she said firmly. "You might look sexy when you smoke, but you won't look sexy to me when you're dying of emphysema."

"I'd rather be dead, darling, than quit." He took her hand and kissed it.

"I'm so confused," George whispered.

"So, Robert," I said suddenly, deciding I was through keeping secrets, "that's a pretty big admission, to say that you cheated on Kate over and over again with who knows how many swimsuit models. I'm just curious, how often do you cheat on Vicki? Is it weekly, or monthly, or what?" I waited for an eruption.

"Oh, sweetie," Vicki said to me, like I was a child afraid of monsters in the closet. "That's not going to happen."

"Cheat on her?" Robert asked. He looked truly baffled by the question.

"If he did, it would be all over, and he knows it," she said, and she leaned back and punched Robert hard on his arm.

"Oww, I wouldn't dare, never," he laughed, rubbing his bicep. "No, I would never behave that way with her. Do you know what theees insane woman would do to me?"

"Make you very, very sorry," she said.

"She would castrate me. She would murder me in cold blood," he said. "And you, Chloe, you will give the eulogy at my funeral. And in that moment I hope you will be glad that before my untimely and violent demise, you and I were on speaking terms again. I, for one, am extremely happy to have you back eeen my life where you belong. You are toujours compliquée, *but you know I love you just as you are." He grabbed me and hugged me hard, bumping his big head squarely into mine.* "Pardon, cousine," *he said, handing me an ice cube from his water glass.*

"I'm not at all complicated," I told him. "It's everyone around me causing problems."

"What problems?" he asked. "We're having a marvelous time together, non?"

"Whatever," I said, giving up any further attempt to make him understand. "Your accent seriously sucks," I added.

"Now zat eeez categorically false. I have beeen told I have no accent."

"You've been lied to."

"George," he said with the softest "G" possible, looking for an ally, "tell her my English sounds like British aristocracy. I speak as eeef I am ze love child of Hugh Bonneville and Princess Diana."

Vicki saved George by sticking to the topic of killing Robert. "I hope you know that no one will go to your funeral because I'll bar the door."

"How will you bar ze door to my funeral from your jail cell?" he asked.

"Jail? I'm not going to jail. I'll outsmart the police."

"Chloe, after she kills me, you will have this woman arrested. Swear it. Your allegiance eeez to me."

"No, Chloe, tell him. You tell him you expect him to pay the ultimate penalty if he betrays me or disrespects me in any way. He listens to you."

It seemed they both had their hands full. At that moment I had to admire Vicki for her tenacity and passion, and, whether I liked it or not, I knew I had no choice but to love Robert who, with all of his many flaws, was part of me, and all there was left to do, I realized, was to have hope for them. Kate was right—they did make sense together. And I was and would always be a fixture in each of their lives, whether they were together or not, dysfunctional or madly in love, happily single or miserably lonely. What a surprise it was to find myself truly wanting it to work out for them.

"Vicki can be very determined," I told Robert. "You may lose more than a few battles with her. And I know neither one of you likes to lose."

"I am willing to accept defeat from time to time," he said, "but only because she eeez a magnificent and terrifying opponent."

"Enough about us," Vicki said. "We want to hear about you. Tell us all the ways the two of you are going to save the world together, while we selfish people are busy enjoying ourselves. When did you meet anyway?"

*

"They're scary," George said to me as we walked home that night, "but you matter to them; they'll never give you up."

"I know," I agreed. "So I guess we're keeping them?"

"Of course, as long as you promise you won't take it upon yourself to clean up any messes they make."

"Never again," I vowed. "But I do want to be in their lives, especially for the important, complicated moments, the big events like Robert's funeral or Vicki's murder trial."

"Or something more positive," George suggested, "like a wedding."

"It's a damn good thing you didn't get yourself shot in January," Maureen said. "We wouldn't have had time for this kind of bullshit then."

"I'm not even complaining," Kate said.

"Oh, please," said Maureen. "I broke my toe once and didn't carry on like you're doing." They were making their way up the three steps to the conference room, where Kate had a meeting with the school lawyer.

"I can totally walk without you," Kate told her. "You're the one chasing around after me all day. If you want to be my best friend, just say so."

"You're a pitiful, cast-wearing, limping, fat-legged version of your former self. And don't think you can get away with any of that PTSD shit. When this is over, it's over. And I told you—you remember?—I told you, you wear your skirts too short."

"You never told me that," Kate said. "What's my skirt got to do with it?"

"If you'd had a longer skirt on, the bullet would have had some material to bounce off of. It's your own fault."

"Isn't that, like, blaming the victim?"

"Victim? No one feels sorry for you."

If the gun hadn't fired, the crisis would have evaporated very quickly; Hudson certainly didn't want any negative publicity. However, with a puncture right through the Louis Vuitton, a gash on the side of Kate's leg, and a hole through the office wall, the school couldn't possibly sweep the incident under the bloody, vomit-covered rug. Kate understood perfectly well that something serious had happened, but when Henry told her the severity of the charges Kenneth and especially Silvia were facing, she didn't think it was right. Silvia had suffered a mental collapse, and was currently an inpatient at Payne Whitney, getting evaluated and medicated. Kate felt she'd been punished enough.

Maureen left Kate with the lawyer, who explained the situation from Hudson's perspective. A gun had discharged in a school zone, even if by accident. Silvia had brought the weapon into the school knowingly and under circumstances that made her no friend to the school and certainly no friend to the admissions department. Her actions reeked of malicious intent. She had broken the law and would now face jail time, along with community service and, of course, money to cover medical costs, pain, and suffering.

"I'm not suffering," Kate said. "I'm going to be fine."

"That's not the point," the lawyer said. "She held you hostage, and she could have killed you, not to mention a student. You're owed something, and the school is owed something because she's damaged our reputation; we're a school with a shooting incident on our record. Your job of selling this place will be a lot harder next year given that parents really don't like crazy people shooting guns off where their kids go to school."

"But I'm telling you, she never planned to use it. She was just a medicated, desperate mess."

"And him? What's his excuse?" the lawyer asked. "As soon as he knew she had the gun with her, what prevented him from trying to get her off school property right away?"

"Stress?" Kate suggested.

"The bullet went clear through the wall; what if it had killed a child? And Kate, you got lucky. You could be a quadriplegic in a hospital bed right now, needing around-the-clock care for the rest of your life."

Kate imagined Angela feeding her with a baby spoon, day in and day out. Angela would give up everything to take care of her, no matter how big a burden she turned out to be. And Chloe would be there, too, buying her stuffed animals and making her pudding.

"And what about Henry?" the lawyer continued. "He's a

husband and a pillar in this school. What if the gun had gone off while he was in the office?"

All the blood that ran down her leg, soaked her shoe, and puddled on the carpet could just have easily been Henry's. Kate pictured him drenched in it, gasping for breath, and the idea of him dying suddenly brought on an unexpected rush of tears.

"Or Maureen?" the lawyer went on. "What if something had happened to her? I'm not trying to upset you," he said, passing her a box of tissues, "but you have to consider the heinousness of intentionally bringing a loaded weapon on school premises. A *school.* Children with no way of protecting themselves, teachers, staff, people you care about. Something much worse could have happened."

"I understand," Kate said, trying to dry her face while the tears kept coming. "So what do we do?"

"That's what you need to think about. These people have a lot of assets, and you're entitled to compensation. The school is considering its options, and you should consider yours."

After the meeting Kate slowly made her way to Henry's office and stood in the doorway. "Silvia didn't aim it at me. You know that, right? That the whole thing was an accident?"

"We don't know what she had planned," Henry said, getting her a chair to sit on and another to elevate her leg.

"She didn't intend to hurt anyone."

"I don't care. She was reckless, and she could have killed you. That's enough for me. Honestly, Kate, how did you stay so cool? Why didn't you run or scream for help? I could have done something. I could have tried to help you."

"No point in both of us getting shot," Kate said. "What would you have done if you were me?"

"I don't think I could have handled it half as well as you did.

And after what they put you through, I want them to pay, I do. She could have killed any one of us, even if it was by accident. Do you have any idea how furious Pat would be if I died?"

"I know. And I accept that there should be a stiff punishment for what they did. But I've been thinking about it, Henry," she said, "and with your permission, there's something else I really, really want to get from all of this."

HUDSON DAY SCHOOL

Dear Claudia,

We are very pleased to inform you that our wait list has finally moved, and we can now offer you a place in our 7th grade class. We know this news comes late, and we hope we can convince you to consider attending Hudson in the fall, in spite of whatever plans you may have made for your education next year. We are certain that at Hudson you will find the rigorous curriculum you're seeking, as well as a strong community filled with new friends who share your interests and worldview.

The admissions committee was enormously impressed with every aspect of your application, and it is with great pleasure that we offer you the first-ever Blake Prize, an academic scholarship that extends beyond tuition to cover any other expenses you will incur every year that you will be a Hudson student. This scholarship includes full yearly tuition, weekly private music instruction, and the cost of any academic, artistic, or athletic summer programs in which you choose to participate. Based on your fine academic achievements and your outstanding attitude toward school, learning, and community, we can't imagine a worthier student to be a Blake Prize recipient.

Please let us know if you will be able to accept our offer.

All the best,
Kate Pearson

"Doug!" Angela called. No answer. "Doug!" she tried again, louder this time. She put down the lamp she was carrying and tried to tuck her hair behind her ear. It was still too short to stay put. Why wasn't he answering? She wandered into the kitchen and leaned out the back door: ah, there he was, holding a garden hose, filling up the plastic baby pool for Emily, while Grace sat on a picnic blanket watching them. Funny that there were so many objects that had no place in Angela's life until now: garden hoses, picnic blankets, baby pools, and baby gates. "Suburban trappings," her mother called them.

The day her parents arrived back on American soil and began unpacking their Austrian etchings and Peruvian textiles, Angela made a panicked call to tell them that Kate had just been shot in the line of duty. Some homecoming that was. They heard the story and were horrified. Their daughter was the victim of a crazed, gun-toting citizenry, of an elitist system that ostracizes the weak and favors the wealthy, that judges children using all the wrong metrics, that clearly drives well-intentioned, over-achieving, misguided parents to complete madness. Angela was in the waiting room when they bumbled into the hospital, looking lost and jet-lagged, and on seeing them after such a long time, on feeling that Kate wasn't her responsibility alone, on realizing that help, that family—in whatever form—had arrived at last, Angela, thirty-one-year-old mother of two, threw herself onto her parents and sobbed.

"Darling daughter," her mother said. "Whatever did you do to your hair?"

More people arrived and waited for Kate to come out of surgery: Henry and Pat, Maureen and Albert, Doug, Chloe, and Jonathan. They were all somber and stunned, having never been so close to an act of violence. Angela went up to Henry, who looked down at the floor and said in the most avuncular way, "I'm so sorry I let this happen." It was astounding to see this group of strangers, so devoted to her heroic little sister who, though wounded in the act, had ultimately succeeded in helping a pair of unyielding, unreasonable parents yield and accept reason.

⁂

A few weeks after the shooting, Angela hosted a multigenerational family dinner that she cooked in her new kitchen. The party of eight took their seats around the dining room table and got reacquainted. Angela's daughters had mistakenly believed that their grandparents lived full-time inside a laptop screen, until that day when they met them in real life, back from the field, dressed in peculiar getups, and aged from travel. They brought gifts to the little girls, a menagerie of balsa wood animals from the Amazon and a team of Dala horses from Sweden that Angela lined up and down the center of the table in a parade.

Kate brought Jonathan, a brave move considering the cast of characters, but he didn't seem put off by it, even after Kate, Doug, and Angela tricked him into playing a drinking game: take a shot every time their mother used a foreign word. He got bombed, and during dessert he stood up at the table and asked Kate if she would move in with him.

Angela was flabbergasted. Too soon! It was way, way too soon! Surely Kate knew better. She wouldn't do something so rash and impulsive, just when she was finally putting her life back together.

She felt Doug sliding his arm across her shoulder, and she thought of the countless times he'd said to her, "You need to let go a little. She's okay, Angela. You can let go."

"When I said she should see a psychiatrist," she whispered to him, "this wasn't quite what I had in mind."

"Maybe this is even better," he said.

"Alles Gute! Parabéns! Felicitaciones!" her parents declared, lifting their glasses.

Even if they weren't perfect, even if they were different from Angela in almost every respect, they were present, and at least for Angela, the relief was palpable. She raised her glass as well and silently wished Kate a smooth trip and a clean landing.

She had choices: she could go upstairs to continue unpacking boxes in one of the bedrooms, go to the basement to put the wet laundry in the dryer, or go outside and get used to more new trappings in her suburban life—folding chairs and sun umbrellas. She got two beers out of the big side-by-side fridge and went outside to sit on the patio with her family.

Returning to the lab where she had struggled and failed to become a budding anthropologist felt stranger than Kate had imagined.

The graveyard. Even the smell of the place gave her a creepy flashback of missed deadlines, skull-crushing migraines, jagged pieces of bone, and impenetrable spreadsheets. Dr. Greene's office door was open, and Kate stood up straight before she knocked.

"I don't believe it," he said.

"Sorry to barge in."

"No, it's nice to see you. I heard about the incident," he added quickly. "Come in, can I get you something? Sit, please." He was wearing his usual black skinny jeans, T-shirt, and blazer. Dr. Greene was a brand, and the product was brains, hipness, and a ton of ego. The rumor, according to Kate's parents, was that he had gone to the set of *Good Morning America* with an entourage; his stylist had brought, among other things, a nail buffer, bronzer, and a selection of breath mints. "Does it hurt?" he asked.

"I'm fine," Kate said, sitting across from him and setting her bag down.

"Frightening what you went through. What was it like?"

"Surreal."

"I heard you grappled with that psychotic woman for the gun. Have you considered writing a book about it? People would eat that up."

"It really wasn't all that dramatic," Kate explained. "And she wasn't psychotic."

"Too bad," he said. The window behind him was open, letting in the sound of jackhammers and a view of ugly steel scaffolding. "Do you have a copy of *my* book?" he asked.

"Not yet, no."

"Ah, allow me." He went to his bookshelf and took a copy. "I'll even sign it for you," he said. "How are your parents? Have they retired yet?"

"No," Kate said. "Never. I can't even imagine."

"Let's sign a book for them, too, shall we? It's always nice to have one that's been autographed." He sat at his desk and selected a pen. "And how are things with you, since you moved on from this house of horrors?"

"Something surprising happened when I was in the hospital, recovering: I couldn't stop thinking about this place, about my experience here."

"That's nice to hear."

"Sorry, I don't mean that in a good way."

"Ah. So you're still sore that I had to give you the boot," he asked, raising one eyebrow, "after all this time?"

"No, no, I've moved on. But I felt this need to come back here because I wanted to remember how it felt at the time, how disempowering it was to get judged so negatively. My new job is all about that, evaluating children and often rejecting them, and I wanted to be reminded firsthand of what the aftermath of that feels like."

"Well, it's an unpleasant business, but there's no point deceiving people, is there?" He blew on the ink of his signature, snapped the book shut, and opened the next one. "The world is a tough, competitive place, and the sting of rejection is something one has to learn to live with, preferably with a modicum of dignity."

"So how do you deal with it?" Kate asked. "What is it like for you?"

"What is what like?"

"Say, when you get a bad book review?"

"That's different. Those terrible reviews? Those are nothing but bitter remarks made by jealous academics trying to take me down a notch because they can't stand to see a colleague succeed. I don't allow any of that to penetrate."

"So you've never fantasized about bringing a gun into the offices of that reviewer who called your book 'an epic waste of paper'? Or that woman who said, what was it again? That your book is 'a misguided dung heap, with content so incongruous and immaterial, it can't even be considered wrong.'"

Dr. Greene winced for a split second, but then quickly waved his hand around as if to shoo gnats away. "I don't even read them. What could I possibly get out of it? No, I choose to focus on the good reviews, and fortunately for me, there are many, *many* more of those." He pushed the two books toward her, all the way across the desk, and then stood up to close the window, muffling the sounds of construction.

"I see your point," Kate said, "but I can still understand how a hurtful rejection like that *could* make one go completely berserk, out of despair and panic. And I know I went a little nuts when you gave me mine."

"I'm sorry to hear that," he said, sitting back at his desk.

"Oh, it's okay," she said, raising her hands up. "See? No gun."

He smiled at her. "Yes, well, lucky for me."

"I'm learning to place more value on the good things people say about me. But I still feel I need to process the bad ones somewhere in my mind. Don't you believe there's something to be learned from a harsh critique?"

"I'd say that depends on how much respect you have for the person who's giving it."

"Ah," Kate said, leaning back in her chair and nodding. "Well, now *that's* a very good point. You know, the other day I was remembering when you told me that, among other qualities, this field requires precision, intuition, and grit. You said to me, 'Now you, dear, are careless with details, fail to have insight, and you give up too easily—you're zero for three.'"

"I apologize if I was hard on you," Dr. Greene said, "but I was relaying what I observed. At the time you agreed with me."

"I don't think either one of us knew me well enough to sum up my weaknesses in such a sweeping, unnuanced manner, but I did listen to everything you said. I have no regrets about leaving this field behind, and I can say with absolute certainty that my current boss would use much kinder words to describe me."

"In that case I'm glad you've worked on improving yourself."

"My current boss is approachable, supportive, and invested. Forgive me," she said, "if I tell you that—as a supervisor—you were zero for three. I thought you should know."

"Kate." He got up again, walked around his desk, and leaned against it. Arms crossed, hair shaggy, gaze penetrating; he was doing a perfect imitation of his own book jacket photo. "It's disappointing to see that you have a chip on your shoulder. Lots of people fail in this field; you're not the only one."

"That's true."

"Lots of people can't cut it."

"Like Sherman?"

"Well, Sherman," Dr. Greene said, chuckling. "Adjuncting is the best someone like Sherman can do."

"Meaning?"

"Let's just say the job market is really tough these days."

"I was wondering—how come you never brought Sherman along to conferences with you? It seemed like you kept him in obscurity."

"I was as supportive of Sherman as I am of any of my grad students." He leaned in toward her. "But there are some people you simply can't have as the 'face' of your department. Sherman, and you can't deny this, is eccentric and even embarrassing. He hath the tendency to maketh people uncomfortable."

"Did you put that in his letter of recommendation?"

"No, of course not. I also didn't mention that he often wears bow ties with his T-shirts."

"I've read hundreds of letters of recommendation this year," Kate told him, "and I know now how important they are in helping make a case for a candidate. So I'm only wondering, given that, let's be honest, you don't really like Sherman personally and given how incredibly busy you've been with promoting your book, if maybe, just maybe, you rushed it? Maybe, inadvertently, you sent off a lame, generic, half-assed letter that didn't adequately highlight Sherman's strengths."

"I think I've been in academia long enough to know how to write a recommendation, and I certainly wouldn't sabotage anyone."

"You're right," Kate said, shaking her head, "of course not. I owe you an apology. I'm upset about Sherman's situation, and I'm sorry for trying to put it on you."

"You're clearly emotional," Dr. Greene told her.

"Is that what it is?" Kate asked. "Maybe so. I just didn't want to believe that a best-selling author, top mind in his field, highly respected member of the anthropological community, could write a strong letter of support for an outstanding candidate, and yet be completely ignored like that."

Dr. Greene took a deep breath. "They simply didn't offer him the job. It happens."

"Of course, but that's pretty rude, isn't it? Insulting? The opinion of a professor of your standing should be worth *something*." She got up to go. "My parents are not going to understand this."

"Why?"

"I wouldn't be surprised if they call up their friends at KU to find out themselves what the hell happened there."

"Your parents know Sherman?"

"They met in Berlin last fall and were so impressed with him. I mean, talk about high praise: my father wrote me, calling him brilliant, passionate, and charming, and he said that 'Herr Doctor Gregson' will chair a department by thirty-five. And then my mother called his recent paper a game changer in terms of data analysis methodology. They love him. They'll definitely want to get to the bottom of why he couldn't land a tenure-track job *anywhere*."

"But there's no point second-guessing these things," Dr. Greene said.

"As if I could stop them," she said, laughing. "Well, it was good to see you again, Dr. Greene." She picked up her bag and shook his hand. "And if I can make a suggestion: I'd take a good, hard look at all your negative reviews. See if there's anything to learn from them, anything at all. You might be surprised by what you find out."

"What would I possibly find out?"

She walked out of the office, leaving the signed books on his desk.

To: KU Search Committee

From: Jordan Greene

Re: Applicant for Assistant Professor Position, Department of Anthropology

---

I am attaching a letter in support of the application of Dr. Sherman Gregson, my former graduate student. I believe our department secretary may have inadvertently sent you an incomplete draft of a letter intended for someone else. I ask that you please read the attached recommendation and reconsider Sherman for your tenure-track position.

If you have any further questions, please do not hesitate to contact me.

Dr. Jordan Greene

Professor of Biological Anthropology
Author of *This Little Piggy Went to Market: How Grocery Stores Are Making Us Fat and Why Grazing Will Make Us Fit*
(available on Amazon, iBooks, Google Play, and at bookstores everywhere)

Hudson was closed for the summer, and Kate was surprised at how different it felt without the students and teachers filling up all the rooms, giving the place life. In the classrooms, chairs were placed upside down on desks, and the hallways were empty and dark. Starting tomorrow, Kate would be gone as well, taking her four-week paid summer vacation, during which she would move downstairs one floor, keeping Stella close by while distancing herself from the couch she'd relied on for far too long.

Her office felt like a second home now, and she spent her last day there organizing and getting prepared for the upcoming season. She shredded hundreds of pages of messy interview notes, threw out dozens of thank-you letters, and wiped down her computer screen. She stripped her bulletin board, and using four thumbtacks, she posted, directly in the center, a large, bright, and slightly warped watercolor of cheerful, idealized skyscrapers lined up on a wide city street. A yellow cab and traffic light were in the foreground, along with a cat wearing a conspicuous collar, loudly indicating that he or she belonged to someone. Written on the back of the picture, now out of sight, were the words "Here is a picture for your office. I hope you will look at it sometimes when you are at work. Yours truly, Claudia." Kate stepped back to get a better view.

In the early afternoon, when she saw she had nothing left to do, she walked out of her office, closed the door behind her, and locked it.

Pat was in Henry's office, unpacking a lunch he'd brought him. Maureen was right: June was so easy. There was time to do all kinds of frivolous and enjoyable things: Maureen had false eyelashes on, Kate had caught up on full seasons of *Scandal* and *Downton Abbey*, and Pat and Henry were having lunch together for the third time that week.

Pat had brought tabbouleh salad, kale salad, and chickpea salad. Looking thoroughly depressed, Henry was using a plastic fork to pick through the chickpeas and tomatoes to find the minuscule pieces of goat cheese. “Did you bring any potato salad?” he asked.

“Mayonnaise is not on your diet,” Pat said, “and kale is a power food. Try it.” He looked up and saw Kate standing in the doorway. “Look!” he exclaimed, getting up to hug her. “It’s your guardian angel, Henry.”

They’d finally met for the first time when Kate was in the hospital and so doped up on pain medication that she couldn’t quite get her eyelids to open. Pat had come into the room with Henry and whispered, “What a girl! I knew she was the right one. I said she would do you good, remember?”

“I remember,” Henry had answered. “Can you imagine how Nathan would have handled a situation like that?”

“By wetting his pants. And then hiding behind you while you got shot. To think she managed to talk those people down all on her own. I told you, I said psychology is a highly useful field to study, remember? I told you to hire her, didn’t I? Wasn’t I brilliant?”

“Yes, love, and I credit you entirely. But go ahead and say it again.”

“I told you so.”

Kate had been too sleepy to understand what they were talking about, and now she wasn’t sure if the conversation had even happened. Maybe she’d dreamt it. After that, Pat had visited her again in the hospital, being exceedingly kind and bringing her biographies of Hillary Clinton and Madeleine Albright, saying, “You Wellesley grads really are something, aren’t you? Is there anything you women can’t do?”

“Yeah, well, I’m nowhere near the same category as those two,” Kate had said with a laugh.

Pat looked at her with a serious expression. "That's because you're younger."

And now Pat offered Kate a fork and a paper plate. "Can you have some lunch with us?" he asked. "Very heart-healthy."

"I can't. I'm going out with Maureen," Kate said.

"Maureen agreed to go out with you?" Henry asked. "No kidding."

"Well, she doesn't know about it yet, but I'll talk her into it."

"I'm sure you will," Pat said. "Your powers of persuasion are nothing short of miraculous. Have you considered a career in law? I can imagine you would be a great litigator."

"Pat," Henry said.

"What?"

"I'd rather she not quit over the summer."

"I wasn't suggesting she quit over the summer. But she could think about it, study for the LSAT, see how she does."

"Actually," Kate said, "I was hoping to talk to you sometime about what you do."

"Really?" Pat asked. "Counseling? Outstanding! How about we have dinner one night during your break? When are you free?"

"I don't believe this," Henry said.

"Henry, you can't possibly think you'll be able to hang on to an ambitious woman with so much potential? She has bigger plans for her future."

"I need her here," Henry said.

"I'm staying," Kate promised. "It'll take a long time for me to live up to even half the compliments you've paid me this year."

"But you would make a good counselor," Pat said, and quickly turning to Henry, he added, "I mean down the road, in the future, eventually." He turned back to Kate and mouthed the words, "We'll talk."

"When I started here," Kate said, "I didn't think I'd make it through the year without getting fired."

"Firing you never crossed my mind," Henry said.

"Well, then," Kate said, "I guess I'll see you here next month."

"We'll be vacationing in the Scottish Highlands by the time you get back. I'll see you at the end of August."

"I'm taking Henry to Urquhart Castle," Pat said. "We'll hike the trails around the loch, keeping an eye out for Nessie."

"Castles and cryptids," Kate said. "It sounds perfect. What do I do while you're gone?"

"Just hold down the fort," Henry told her.

"It was a good year, wasn't it," Kate asked him, "under the circumstances?"

"Very good," he answered.

Kate wanted to say something important, words that would express all that Henry had done for her, but "Thank you for helping me get off the couch" was the best she could come up with.

"We'll hit the ground running in September," he reminded her, "so rest up."

She went down the hall to see Maureen. "I was thinking next year would be much easier," Maureen said, "since you almost know something about what you're doing, but now that we're moving the entire process online, you're basically a total beginner again."

"Want to go out for happy hour?"

"Don't take this the wrong way, but I'm so sick of you."

Kate made a face like her feelings were hurt.

"But if you really miss me," Maureen went on, "give me a call, and I'll try to make time for you."

"No, I meant now."

"No."

"Please? My treat."

"I have work to do."

"You do not."

"What do you know about it, newbie?"

"But it's my birthday."

"Lies."

"Just come with me, or do you want me out in some skanky bar, limping around, all shot up, drinking by myself?"

Maureen sighed heavily and picked up her purse, saying, "It is just sad the way you're milking this thing."

In the lobby, Albert was standing at his post by the front entrance, looking out at the street. Ever since the incident, he'd been on edge.

"I don't like it," he said, pointing. "That man out there, that man looks very suspicious to me." He had his other hand poised on the phone.

Kate looked out and saw Robert, handsome Robert, leaning against a mailbox, smoking a cigarette, waiting.

"I don't know," Maureen said. "He looks pretty good to me."

Kate thought through her options. Confront? Retreat? Ignore? Explain?

"Do me a favor, will you?" Kate asked Albert. "Can you deliver a message for me?"

Maureen made her mad face. "I thought you were buying me a drink."

"That's the guy who dumped me," Kate said, getting a piece of paper and a pen from the front desk.

"*Boring.* I told you: look forward, not back. What could you possibly have to say to him?"

"It's a little late," Kate said, "but I need to reject him."

"Well, do it fast."

With Maureen breathing down her neck, Kate wrote as quickly as she could.

Robert,

I got your email, and I appreciate your apology.

I'd like to apologize as well, starting with one small

admission: When I told you Zinedine Zidane was on my list of men I'd like to sleep with, I lied. He's not my type at all, which is not nice of me to say because, as you pointed out, you look a lot like him but with good hair. Also I don't even like soccer. The truth is I faked pretty much everything when we were together. It was terribly unfair and dishonest of me, not to mention exhausting, and I assure you I learned from my mistakes. My only explanation is that I desperately needed something to work out in my life, and you were a victim of that need. I deeply regret that I didn't have the presence of mind to accept that we were not right for each other and break up with you when I should have. I'm very sorry.

Vicki is an extraordinarily good fit for you (like a hook into an eye), so if you want my advice, you'll be careful, and you'll hold on to her, if you can. I think structure is exactly what a boy like you needs.

Honestly—no hard feelings. I wish you well.

Kate

July

On my wall there's a picture of me holding hands with George in Central Park. It's a candid and not a very flattering one; George's mouth is partly open in midsentence and my stomach is protruding in a way that my white linen dress clearly didn't appreciate, as it is pinched and puckered in all the wrong places. But look closely: Kate and Vicki are both there. I asked them to wear green that day, and, unsurprisingly, they chose dresses in wildly different shades, different fabrics, different styles. They don't even look like they're at the same party, but there they both are, one on the far left side of the frame and one way over on the right.

In the background, slightly out of focus, Robert poses accidentally, looking pleased, like he's lord and owner of the entire park. He's wearing a perfectly tailored suit with a paisley pocket square, holding a lit cigarette in one hand and a glass of champagne in the other. He watches Vicki carefully, as she dazzles three men who surround her. She is poised and stunning, although her high heels have sunk deep into the grass. On the other side of the picture (and this is my favorite part), there is Kate. She is barefoot, eating cake and feeding a piece to our dog, Carter, who licks her fingers. Beneath the A-line swing of her dress, one leg is lightly wrapped in gauze, and she smiles at Jonathan, who is blowing iridescent bubbles all around her head.

As far as wedding pictures go, it's a mess. The composition is cluttered and disjointed, everything is in motion, and I know that at one time this would have been a disappointment to me, a failure. I would have insisted on one of those pictures in which one's friends are arranged in a tidy row, everyone smiling politely with their arms around each other just so, a meaningless display in my case. What I have instead, what I now embrace, in spite of the obvious lack of symmetry and coherence, is an image of the people who enrich and complicate my life, just as they are and, somehow, miraculously, all within the frame.

*

About a year after that picture was taken, I was out with Carter, pushing Russell (as in Bertrand) in the stroller, on my way to Tompkins Square Park to meet Kate, who had made it smoothly through her second season in admissions. I chose a spot for us under the trees and settled in to wait for her. I put Russell on the picnic blanket, and as I began to unpack toys and snacks, I got a text from Robert:

I have a problem! Need you.

Can't eat, can't sleep.

I am a fool. *Merde.*

What have I done?

I was alarmed and texted back ?? *but he didn't respond.*

And right away an email came from Vicki. Robert, she said, was busted. He'd hooked up with some bimbo actress in London, and Vicki had the emails to prove it. It was over. Period. He was pathetic, had begged and pleaded, cried even, on his knees, but she wasn't having it. She didn't tolerate such things, she reminded me, and she had told him so a hundred times. Her email ended with "I admit that I'm beyond upset, naturally, but unlike some people, I will be perfectly fine. I refuse to let him break me down, so don't expect to find me in a puddle on my couch. But in case you don't know this already, your cousin is an asshole. Ciao."

I was sorry, I really was, but I realized I didn't feel that bad. Or even guilty.

"Robert's an idiot," I told Russell, who kicked his legs and squealed. Carter rolled around in the grass next to me.

I answered Vicki: "That's terrible. Let's have drinks tomorrow night." Nothing more. She had known all along what she was getting into, and she wouldn't want my sympathy anyway. But she would need to vent, and as her friend, I would be there for her.

I went back to Robert's pitiful text and answered him: I'll call you tomorrow, but brace yourself—I won't go easy on you. I figure you deserve some heartache.

I hit send and looked up to see Kate walking across the park, bouncing actually, holding on to her backpack straps with both hands.

"What a day!" she said, dropping down onto the blanket and kicking off her sandals. "What a spectacular day."

"Yes, it is," I agreed.

Happiness is not a zero-sum game. It's the only case in which the resources are limitless, and in which the rich can get richer at no expense to anyone else. That day in the park, I found it remarkably easy to own my happiness and celebrate Kate's as well.

It's a strange thing, though, how rare, maybe impossible, it is to have everyone you care about thriving at the same time. For a short spell, life seems certain and stable, until something shifts and redistributes, randomly, unpredictably, and when you look around at the new landscape, you see that it's someone else's turn now. You redirect your attention to focus on the friend in need. You hope—you know—they will do the same for you, when your turn comes.

Acknowledgments

Thank you so much to Emily Bestler at Emily Bestler Books. I truly appreciate her enthusiasm, humor, kindness, and editorial smarts. Thanks also to Stephanie Mendoza, Lara Jones, Albert Tang, Lynn Buckley, Megan Reid, and the whole team at Atria/Simon & Schuster.

I am extremely grateful to my agent Linda Chester for taking me on, when all I had was a quirky manuscript about an old Texan couple, and for encouraging me to work on this book first. And to Anika Streitfeld, for being patient, thoughtful, funny, and insightful. Working with these two is an absolute pleasure.

For their friendship, generosity, and support, thank you to Hilton Als, April Benasich, and James Melcher.

Many wonderful people were kind and critical early readers: my amazing family, David Poeppel, Wendy O'Sullivan, Laurie Mitchell, and Jere Mitchell, and my stalwart friends, Amy White, Candy Moss, Jan Testori-Markman, Leslie Carr, Gregory Greenleaf, Karina Schultz, Ana Blohm, Hilton Als, and George Kryder. Also big thanks to my nieces, Sophie and Maddie Woods, and Megan O'Sullivan, for embracing my main character.

Thank you to Amy Shearn, for getting my writing off the ground. And thanks to Patricia Bosworth and the Playwrights/

Directors Unit at The Actors Studio and to the cast of the play that was the origin of this book.

I am so appreciative for the expertise, levity, concrete help, therapy, alcoholic beverages, friendship, inspiration, and/or moral support provided by the following fabulous people: Anna Salajegheh, Felice Kaufmann, Emily Middleton, David Harman, Donna James, Diane Meier, Frank Delaney, Dacel Casey, Zuzanna Szadkowski, Albert Aeed, Lolly Winston, Stephen McCauley, George Baier IV, Max Fenton, Sabrina Khan, Theo Theoharis, Brent Woods, Mitchell Moss, Peter Mitchell, Jenna Drudi, Ben Binstock, Pam Clarke, John Kim, Honore Comfort, Amy Weinberg, Norbert Hornstein, and the members of the Brooklyn Writers' Salon. Thanks also to my fun and loving German and Venezuelan family-members-in-law, especially my *Schwägerinnen* Julie Bruhn and Lili D'Huc.

As for Carmen Davis, Kristin Harman, Karyn Delay, Dan Feigin, and Maria Allwin—I could not have written this book without their friendship and truly outrageous humor.

Most importantly, love and thanks to the men in my life: David, Alex, Andrew, and Luke Poeppel.